I0616736

The
Obsidian
Serpent

Also by J.T. Fleming

Tracks of a Pigeon-toed Horse

The Obsidian Serpent

Mouriel
{Coming soon}

REVIEWS FOR

J.T. FLEMING'S
Tracks of a Pigeon-toed Horse & The Obsidian Serpent

Unique in its combination of western history from a still little known but vast area called the Utah Territory, and a culture known then as the "Mormons." There is much to learn about this people and these times. This was a wild west still not fully explored on the written page, and few western writers have the background and ability to do this. Fleming writes his characters off the page and into your heart....

With just a touch of mysticism, great descriptions of these lands and the people on them, Fleming combines all this to create one very good story after another. Anyone who loves westerns will really appreciate these books, and it is refreshing to have women characters just as interesting as the men....

Western fans will love this true balance of dialogue, descriptive prose and action. The historical information is skillfully woven into these stories which are filled with humor, sudden fast paced action scenes and a clear love of nature and the out-of-doors. I highly recommend these books and those yet to be written....

Author LINDA DUNNING
(Ghost Lights; Lost Landscapes; Restless Spirits; Specters in Doorways)

I bought this on a chance—one of those 'pick-it-out as you look'. It pulled me in and kept me up late into the night reading. Kept the suspense until the end. A great mystery in the main plot and a secondary plot that had me buying his second book before I finished the first!
cinderpf; Utah

Being an avid reader of all types of books, from J.K. Rowling, to James Patterson, and everything in-between, I began this book with high hopes of many evenings of entertainment. I was not disappointed. Mr. Fleming's knowledge of the Utah area I grew up in was evident, and it was obvious he had done his homework.

This book covers the very controversial area of Mormonism in the 1800's, and examines the pro's and con's of plural marriage, and a people who were not saints, but very much wanted to be.

I was impressed with the way I was pulled into the story, from page one. I give this a definite thumbs up, and also recommend "The Obsidian Serpent" which continues the story of Collin Mitchell and makes you want for more.
nana211 Oregon

J.T. Fleming

The Obsidian Serpent

BY
J. T. Fleming

Library of Congress #TXu001701205 / 2010-09-20

ISBN: 978-0-9832461-1-4   (PBK)
ISBN: 978-0-9832461-5-2   (epub)
ISBN: 978-0-9832461-3-8   (mobi)

This novel is a work of fiction. Names, characters, places, and incidents are the product of the author's imagination or are used fictitiously. Any resemblance to actual events, locales, organizations or their doctrines, or persons, living or dead, is entirely coincidental and beyond the intent of either the author or publisher.

FORTRESS PUBLISHING, LLC
www.fortresspublishing.net

*Dedicated to my wife, Gail,
proofreader, critic, typist, and
best friend.*

With special thanks to all those who took the time to read and comment on this project while it was in progress.

The Obsidian Serpent

Siege
Tenochtitlan — August 1521

Smoke and flame exploded from the muzzle of the weapon, and the stone face of the Hall of Warriors erupted in a hail of shattered rock. A second blast echoed across the lake, and the altar atop the temple of Huitzilopochtli burst into a thousand fragments of splintered stone.

Tlacmatzin, first captain of the triple alliance armies, stood in silence beside Cuauhtémoc, Lord of Tenochtitlan and the Azteca Empire since the fall of Motecuhzoma, and watched stoically as the next ball from the Spanish cannons smashed the doorway of the hall of warriors into a pile of rubble. Tlacmatzin raised his war axe in signal as the Spanish and their allies rushed the barricades on the southern causeway leading into the royal Aztec city. Three-thousand obsidian-tipped arrows pierced the darkening sky, falling like a torrent of rain on the attacking conquistadores—a torrent shed like water from a duck on the steel armor of the Spanish.

For a moment, the savage assault of the Spanish seemed to slow, then Tlacmatzin cursed as Pedro Moreno's artillery found its range, and the first barricade erupted in a fountain of soil, rock and dismembered warriors. The Spanish renewed their attack, and the Spanish horsemen plowed their mounts through the dazed and wounded warriors beyond the barricade.

Tlacmatzin signaled again and watched as two-hundred warriors charged from the narrow causeway leading to

Coyoacan and speared into the Spanish flank. For an instant, hope surged in his heart as the Spanish and their horses recoiled from the savage onslaught. But hope died as Moreno's cannon thundered again, clearing the eastern causeway with a barrage of grapeshot.

Tlacmatzin glared to the south as the Spanish cannons smashed the barricades and shredded the first wave of canoes and a hundred Jaguar warriors in a horizontal swarm of lead the Spanish cannon-men called *uva pelotas*. Under his breath, Tlacmatzin cursed Pedro Moreno again and realized that he was witnessing the destruction of the alliance and the fall of the empire. Suddenly, he felt a strange sense of kinship to the advancing Spanish conquistadores. They were not as different as he had first imagined, and suddenly, he knew that Cuauhtémoc was wrong.

The Spanish cared for more than gold and silver. Perhaps it was a driving force behind their actions, but it was not the only thing that drove the Spanish-men across the great sea to rally the enemies of the alliance and wage the desolating battle that would certainly destroy the empire. No.... The Spanish wanted more than gold. The Spanish wanted land. They wanted power. They wanted an empire and tribute in gold and silver. The Conquistadores might worship the god who hung from the cross, but they followed and made sacrifice to Huitzilopochtli, the god of war.

As the Spanish flooded past the barricade, the drums of Huitzilopochtli began a rhythmic thunder. The conches and horns of the temples sounded, and the trumpets of the warriors rang out in answer. The warriors on the causeway began to chant.

Tlacmatzin turned toward the Tlatoani and lowered his eyes. "They begin the chant of death," he declared loudly over the thunder of the drums and the powerful roar of the warriors.

"True warriors," Cuauhtémoc answered. "They know we cannot win, yet they will fight Cortez and his soldiers until we are overrun."

Tlacmatzin frowned and looked down the causeway toward the flaming muzzles of the Spanish artillery. "I should have killed Pedro Moreno when I had the chance," he growled, realizing that his plan to dispose of Cuauhtémoc and proclaim himself Tlatoani of the city had never been realistic.

"Better to have stolen their cannon and the secret of their black powder," Cuauhtémoc snarled.

"If they break the fourth barricade, the city is lost," Tlacmatzin concluded unhappily.

"And they gain nothing," Cuauhtémoc replied. "The city is lost anyway. After ninety-three days of siege, the city is a crypt filled with the dead and dying. And the treasury is gone where they will never find it."

"The treasury is gone?"

"Gone before the siege began. I sent everything north, to be hidden in the land of Atzlan."

Tlacmatzin felt a sudden flare of hope. "All?"

"All but the treasure of Axayacatl, my father's uncle."

Tlacmatzin frowned. "Impossible," he muttered. "The treasury of the alliance must be a hundred times as great as Axayacatl's horde."

Cuauhtémoc glared at the Jaguar. "Fool!" he snapped. "Only part could be rescued. Much of it is hidden within the city. The Spanish care for nothing except gold and silver, but I think they will be convinced that they have it all. Truly, they will get little of either.

"I sent Qetzalcatl with five-hundred warriors and nearly two-thousand llamas laden with the treasury of the alliance. Qetzalcatl will hide the treasury and map the locations in such a way that the Spanish will never find it. If we ever rid ourselves of Cortez and his soldiers, we can recover the treasury then."

Tlacmatzin lowered his eyes. "Yes, Tlatoani," he muttered, letting his thoughts pursue the implications of Cuauhtémoc's words. Cuauhtémoc might be young, but the cousin of Motecuhzoma was no fool or the council would never have elected him Tlatoani of Tenochtitlan.

The drums of Huitzilopochtli filled the darkening sky with a thunder-like cadence, punctuated by the roar of Spanish cannon. Tlacmatzin smiled suddenly, imitating the bare-toothed smiles he had seen on the faces of the Spanish when Motecuhzoma had first allowed them within the city.

"There will be no escape," he observed calmly. "Cortez has placed warriors at the head of every causeway."

Cuauhtémoc stared in disbelief as the fourth barricaded ruptured and the Spanish horsemen poured through the breech in a column four horses wide. Cuauhtémoc gaped at the rupture in the barricade. "Take fifty Jaguar warriors and reinforce the Eagle warriors defending the southern entrances to the temple plaza," he commanded suddenly. "I will withdraw to Tlatelolco and organize our defenses there. If you cannot hold back the Spanish, then delay them as long as possible then fall back to the temple plaza at Tlatelolco. If we fail to hold Tlatelolco, we will take canoes through the canals and into the lake. In the darkness we can cross

Netzahulcoyotl's dike and reach Tetzcoco and reinforcements."

Tlacmatzin's eyes narrowed momentarily. "As you will, Tlatoani," he responded mechanically, glancing to the south where the Spanish armor and the steel blades of their halberds reflected the last red light of Tonatiuh as he fled beyond the mountains to the west.

There would be canoes waiting at the canals near the ritual plaza at Tlatelolco, but there would never be enough. Cuauhtemoc was condemning them all to death, for the Spanish did not fight as the Aztec or even as the Maya farther to the east. The Spanish seemed to have no concept of a warrior's honor and the face to face struggle that brought vanquishment and death to the conquered and to the conqueror, power and prestige. Instead, the Spanish charged the loosely formed lines of Aztec warriors, battering the opposing forces with armored horses and following up with spearmen packed together like the pods of a cactus bristling with twelve-foot spears.

Without another word, Tlacmatzin descended the steps of the pyramid and made his way across the temple plaza, toward the southern gates. He moved swiftly, wending his way past several raised platforms to the center of the plaza. At the rack of skulls, he paused for an instant and searched the open plaza for signs of movement. Nothing moved. All was still in the plaza, save for the constant din outside the plaza walls. The fighting was still confined to the long causeway leading into the city from the Southern shores of the lake.

Deliberately, his movements reeking of disdain, Tlacmatzin threw his shield and the obsidian edged war-club to the ground and snatched a carefully rolled bundle from atop the fifth row of pierced skulls. His hands trembled slightly in anticipation as he laid the bundle on the pavement and sliced the binding cords. Quietly, he unrolled the woven blanket until its contents gleamed red with reflections of the fading sunlight.

"You promised me a cartload of gold," a harsh voice demanded from the shadows beyond the eastern edge of the rack. "I see no cart, and I see no gold."

Tlacmatzin snatched the Spanish sword and dagger from the blanket and sprang to his feet, facing the shadowy form of the armored conquistador.

"The gold, or you get nothing," the man hissed.

Tlacmatzin struggled to find the Spanish words. "Por mé villa," he responded with difficulty.

"Your villa?" growled the Spaniard. "You were to have the cart here, with three slaves to pull it to a place of safety. Nothing was said of your villa!"

Tlacmatzin watched the face of the angry Spaniard. The words meant nothing, but the anger was plain to see and easily translated to any language without the need of words. Surreptitiously, Tlacmatzin flexed his wrist, testing the unfamiliar balance and the weight of the Spanish saber. He had expected an unwieldy monstrosity, but the sword was pleasantly light and the balance distinctly superior to that of the heavy war club.

"Oro por mé villa," he insisted quietly.

The Spaniard hissed and threw his helm against the rack where it shattered a grinning trophy and wedged itself between the railings. For an instant, the soldier stared at the rack and its newest trophy. With a strangled cry the Spaniard yanked his sword free of its scabbard and lunged, thrusting the point of his sword at Tlacmatzin's chest.

Silently, Tlacmatzin shifted his weight and twisted his upper body. He felt the sharp kiss of steel as the blade's edge sliced the Jaguar pelt, leaving a bloody line across his chest. Instantly, he struck. The steel blade that had dangled so lightly in his grip scythed upward so swiftly that the Spaniard had no time to recover from his lunge. The man's eyes widened in disbelief as his hand leaped from his extended arm and fell to the pavement with the clatter of steel against stone. In terror, the Spaniard scrambled forward, reaching for his lost weapon. Remorselessly, Tlacmatzin struck again, removing the outstretched hand. The Spaniard screamed and dropped to his knees, moaning in the agony of his loss. Callously, Tlacmatzin stepped upon the severed hand and pried the officer's finely crafted saber from the dead fingers.

"There is no time," he said quietly, "or I would roast you slowly and suck the marrow from your bones. I am partial to the taste of dog."

Then with the swiftness of a Jaguar warrior, he struck the Spaniard's head from his shoulders.

Obsidian Serpent

Wasatch Mountains — May 1522

Qetzalcatl tossed a small piece of wood on the campfire and let his eyes rove the small valley where smoke from more than a hundred fires drifted into the cloudless blue of the morning sky.

We must leave, he thought.

The camps were low on food, and there was little or no game within a day's walk of the valley. With the treasury hidden among the mountains at last, the llamas had not lasted more than a few weeks. Now the men were hungry and swiftly growing bitter over the forced march and the prolonged encampment amid a wilderness of rugged mountains and towering trees as thick as any jungle in their homeland.

"The hunters have not returned," Itzcoatl said suddenly from across the fire. "They should have returned yesterday."

Qetzalcatl looked across the fire at the old man who had been his closest friend since his childhood in the chinampa farmlands south of Tenochtitlan.

"Something has happened or they would have returned by now," Itzcoatl insisted quietly.

Qetzalcatl frowned, but nodded in agreement. "I sent ten men to search for any signs of the hunting parties," he admitted. "They left at daylight with orders to return by midday."

Itzcoatl frowned unhappily. "I fear they will find nothing," he muttered. "The hunters have probably deserted."

"Xoyocoyotin was with them," Qetzalcatl advised.

"Your brother would never desert," Itzcoatl admitted, "but there were those with him who would cut his throat in an instant if he tried to prevent them from leaving these mountains. You know as well as I do that there are rebels at every campfire, and they are deserting faster than you can count them. Soon you and I will be the only ones left, and we will be eating the bark off of the trees."

"What are you suggesting?" Qetzalcatl asked cautiously.

"The same thing you have been thinking. We cannot stay here another day. The llama meat is gone. We have hidden the treasury, and there is no reason to stay here any longer. Let us return home before these mountains kill us all."

Qetzalcatl took up his spear and stood. He was considered tall among his people and perhaps the strongest of the Eagle warriors. Normally, his men would have obeyed his every command, and in battle they would have willingly suffered hunger and even death to overcome the enemy. But this was a different place. A different feeling seemed to permeate the very air they breathed, and the men were filled with restlessness. Not the restlessness that comes before battle—that restlessness he knew well—this was something other, like an overwhelming immensity that enveloped each man with an almost unbearable solitude.

"You are right," he admitted finally. "Send word to break the camp. We will march when Tonatiuh is at his highest point."

Itzcoatl smiled. "Better to die marching home with war axe in hand rather than starve at the fire like a crippled old woman."

* * *

Qetzalcatl hefted the spear in his right hand and took a tighter grasp on his shield.

"Something stirs," he muttered, as an ominous silence settled on the long line of warriors strung out on a narrow trail snaking its way along the bottom of a flat river valley. On either side, ragged cliffs of red sandstone rose steeply, blocking all but a narrow strip of the sky above.

Ahead, someone signaled and Itzcoatl ran nearly five hundred paces to bring the message from the front ranks of the warriors. "One of the scouts is dead," he panted, his old man's chest heaving to catch his breath.

"Who?"

"Tizoc—of the Wolves."

Qetzalcatl shook his head in disbelief. The Wolf warriors were little known among the people, but their abilities were well known and respected among all the warrior clans.

"How was it done?" he asked. "One of the huge creatures covered with fur?"

"No animal," Itzcoatl replied. "It had all the signs of a single combat with a Jaguar."

"Jaguar!" Qetzalcatl hissed. "One of ours?"

Itzcoatl shook his head. "Only two of ours are missing with the hunting parties. The victor's mark is familiar."

Qetzalcatl looked quickly to the south where the head of the column waited and watched the surrounding terrain for signs of the enemy. "We've been followed," he growled.

"It would seem so," Itzcoatl agreed.

Qetzalcatl smiled at the old man. "You are a strange old man Obsidian Serpent. You were a strange old man when I was a boy. I never understood how you could know so much about people you have never met. I suppose that even now you know the enemy who has followed us from Tenochtitlan and challenges us to battle."

Obsidian Serpent looked into the eyes of the boy who had grown into a formidable Eagle Warrior. "Tlacmatzin, of the Jaguars," he answered quietly.

The battle erupted even as Itzcoatl spoke the name of the Jaguar revered by half the alliance and hated by the rest. Itzcoatl turned, hefting the obsidian edged war club salvaged from the dead Tizoc's possessions. Qetzalcatl reached out and grabbed the old man's arm before he could move toward the battle. "You're not fighting today, friend."

"I'm fit enough, and you will need every warrior today. Tlacmatzin would not come to battle if he did not have a large enough force to win easily, and if he intends to fight here and now, I suspect he intends to take no prisoners."

"You are not a warrior, old man. You do not even follow the gods of the people. Your god speaks inside your head, and the things you tell me are beyond belief. If you behaved as the Spanish, I would think you followed their Christian god."

"None of us will survive if we do not isolate Tlacmatzin and butcher him in single combat." Itzcoatl hissed. "You cannot afford to let anyone stand idle in this."

Qetzalcatl frowned and shook his head. He handed the old man a small, yet intricately carved wooden box. "You cannot stay. I want you to go back to the stone staircase and guard the part of the treasury we left hidden in the caves. If Tlacmatzin defeats us here, he will be able to discover every cache we have made. I cannot allow that to happen. Those caves are well situated; they cannot be forced by numbers, and you alone could defend them for months. Tlacmatzin will not go farther as long as you are there."

The old man opened the small box and removed the dark serpentine shape from within.

"Itzcoatl," he whispered, as he turned the multifaceted obsidian serpent upon the palm of his hand.

"Your namesake," hissed the Eagle warrior. "It took nearly a year to get it right. Now go while I kill this Jaguar."

In a moment, Qetzalcatl was gone in a headlong rush down the trail and into the battle among the tangled willows of the river bottoms. For a moment, Itzcoatl studied the fine craftsmanship of the little serpent. Finally, he smiled and replaced the little god within its box and hid them both at the base of a nearby aspen.

"That boy never listens to a word I say," he muttered in a language foreign to the alliance. "He'll get himself killed; then I'll collect the Jaguar… just like the voice says.…"

* * *

They were dead. They were all dead. Itzcoatl could feel the silence of the mountains like an oppressive weight. Somewhere in the brush near the river, the Jaguar had killed the last of Qetzalcatl's warriors. Spattered with the blood of his victims, the Jaguar stalked the last of his prey through the undergrowth at the river's edge. The Jaguar was near—near enough for the old man to hear the soft pad of the Jaguar's feet as the warrior slipped almost silently through the tangle of brush near the river. The others were somewhere close by, but none were near enough to challenge except the Jaguar leader who even now stalked less than twenty paces from his place of concealment.

Itzcoatl waited patiently and quietly. He knew there was no point in running or in concealing himself indefinitely. Tlacmatzin would not give up. Sooner or later, the Jaguar and his followers would track him down, and it would be necessary to kill them all. His only hope was to take them one by one and give them no chance to combine their efforts against him.

Silently, Itzcoatl slipped away from the Jaguar, moving swiftly along a narrow game trail to a position a hundred paces farther up-river—a position he knew would bring the Jaguar to him, without alerting the others. When the Jaguar stepped into the small clearing, Itzcoatl raised his war-club in greeting.

For the first time since he had become a warrior of the Jaguar clan, Tlacmatzin felt a subtle stab of unreasoning terror. War-club in hand, the old man called Itzcoatl stood waiting, blocking the trail. The old man stood defiantly, as though he would prevent the passage of twenty Jaguars—an old man with an obsidian mask thrust back from his face. He knew the old man—an old man whose mind was crippled—an old man who had never been accepted by any warrior society. The old man had followed along with the Eagles, kept as nothing more than Qetzalcatl's pet and barely tolerated by the Eagle society.

Tlacmatzin frowned and raised the steel point of the Spanish saber to the old man's throat. "Stand aside old man. I would hate to waste the time killing you."

The old man stepped back from the deadly point. "I've been waiting for you," he said quietly.

"Waiting for your death?" Tlacmatzin hissed.

"That will come too," admitted the old man.

"Sooner than you expect," Tlacmatzin growled. "What society are you old man? You have no honors...no quetzal feathers. You are clanless, worse than a dog to be slaughtered without honor!"

Suddenly, the Jaguar rushed forward and slashed at the old man's throat. The old man arched backward, twisting away as the razor like tip of the Spanish blade ripped the air, slicing a hank of hair from the back of his head. Tlacmatzin let the momentum of his rush carry him beyond the sweep of the old man's war axe and waited for the weight of the heavy weapon to drag the would-be Eagle into an unbalanced position. When the old man had twisted beyond recovery, the Jaguar pounced, driving the steel of the Spanish blade deep into the old man's unprotected thigh. A second thrust pierced the old man high in one shoulder. Tlacmatzin sneered at the old man and prepared for the kill.

"I will not even offer your heart to the god, old man. You make a pitiful sacrifice."

Itzcoatl smiled and drew the obsidian mask downward to cover his features.

Tlacmatzin fought the sudden fear that clutched at his belly. The strange old man still stood his ground, and the fire hardened war axe deflected the stroke that should have severed the old man's head. Visions of a new empire blurred.

"Death comes for you now, old man!"

"I *am* death," hissed the jet-black face of the Obsidian Serpent.

Conquistadores

Wasatch Mountains — September 1722

The white horse screamed in pain. The animal shook its head violently and struggled to free its mangled forelegs from the rockslide. Antonio de Guevara scrambled out of the saddle, snatching musket, sword, and saddle bags as he ran for safety among the trees on the lower trail. The horse screamed one last time then disappeared beneath a tumble of boulders as the rockslide shifted again. Guevara watched from the protection of the trees as small rocks from the crumbling mountainside flowed like water until six-hundred paces of the trail simply vanished beneath an alluvial fan of shattered stone.

I will die now.

The thought came as a swift and certain knowledge that his predicament was now desperate, if not hopeless. Unhappily, he dropped his gear within the sparse copse of stunted pines, dug his journal from the saddlebags and carefully opened the small wooden box containing his writing tools. Silently, he touched a shaky pen to the parchment.

The Shinob is coming. The expedicion has failed. Salazar is dead. I heard his screams in the night, and I did nothing. I would have run, but there is nowhere to run in the Sierra de los Yutah's. The Yutahs hate the conquistadores, and though I might escape the Yutahs, it is two-hundred leagues to Santa Fe, and I will never escape the Shinob and the curse that is on the gold of these mountains.

From here, I can see the icy waters of the lake that lies at the foot of the bald mountain and the camp of the conquistadores near the northern shore. For more than a month, the terror that stalks the dark places of these mountains has taken my companeros and torn them like parchment. Now I am alone, and the mines are lost.

I searched the camp for Salazar's mapa, but I could not find it. Without it, the mines cannot be found. The caverna de los plata arboles lies south of the Rio de Timpanogos and west of the bald mountain. Look for the markers at the puerta del cañón de los serpiente de piedra. The treasure is there. For myself...I would not touch the gold even though I had the mapa. It is death.

Something moves within the bloody remains of the camp. It moves swiftly and disappears within the shadows of the forest. I know what it is, for the Yutah slaves warned us that we had angered the god, Towats, when we took the gold from the sacred mountains. We did not believe.

The slaves escaped, and one by one, the Shinob took my companeros. Those of us who survived hunted it, thinking it some animal of the forest. But this demon is no animal. Now I am alone, and the Shinob comes.

The Obsidian Serpent

CHAPTER 1

Utah Territory
Wasatch Mountains — 22 September, 1868

Collin Mitchell slapped a four-inch long ironclad from his pant leg and watched as the big grasshopper tumbled wildly for a moment then snapped its wings open and clattered off into the brush. The insect's twin rumbled past his ear, and Mitchell felt a sudden foreboding. He reined the dun gelding to a halt, spinning the animal one-hundred and eighty degrees. The dark cloud filling the western sky was nearly upon them.

"Ironclads!" He bellowed.

Sarah Mitchell started from the uneasy dream of Aztecs and the Spanish siege of Tenochtitlan, yanked hard on the reins, and dragged the team to a halt. Before she could move, her motley-colored dog leaped from the wagon's seat and pounced on the nearest insect. Quickly, she locked down the brake and began closing-up the canvas at the front of the wagon.

Mitchell slid from the saddle, dropped a loop over the dun's head and tied the end of the rope to the rear wheel of the wagon. "Help me get the tarps out!"

At Mitchell's yell, Daniel Pratt spun his own mount and raced back to the wagon, arriving just as Mitchell dumped the rolled canvas from the bed of the wagon. "Throw one over the team and tie it off somehow," he told the kid. "That horde will be on top of us in no time."

The Pratt kid dragged one tarp to the front of the wagon and fought the canvas until Mitchell grabbed one corner and helped drag it forward, covering the team. The team shifted uneasily at the sudden change in their situation. The four saddle horses were even less amenable and struggled in the confinement of the canvas, but Mitchell ignored their stamping feet, tossed the dog into the wagon, and climbed in behind the Pratt kid.

Inside the wagon, Sarah and Susan Mitchell had barely snugged down the last of the ties when the heavy insects began pelting the wagon like a living hail storm. The sound grew to a continuous roar as insects by the thousands hammered the canvas.

In the dimness, Mitchell watched both women closely. Neither seemed overly concerned as the insects pounded against the canopy. "Tell me about that letter again," he suggested, hoping to divert their attention from the plague hammering the canvas walls.

"Lynne Campbell wrote it," Sarah said, raising her voice over the sound of the insects. "She heard how you found Melinda Tolson."

"That was only two weeks ago," Mitchell objected. "How did she hear about that, way up in Heber City?"

"Lynne's father was in Ogden the same time we were," Susan replied. "He told everyone in town when he got home last week."

Sarah, the older of the two sisters, brushed at her hair with one hand. Again, Mitchell noted how alike the two women were. Had it not been for the difference in age, the sisters might easily be taken for twins.

"Lynne sent the letter as soon she could," Sarah added. "She wants you to find her missing fiancé."

"Probably got cold feet and run off," the Pratt kid suggested. In the dimness, his close-cropped hair stood like a tangled crop of weeds on top of his head.

Susan frowned and shook her head. "Lynne doesn't believe he would do that," she argued. "They've known each other for a long time and they've made some definite plans. She says that's why Aaron was going down to Salt Lake. He was going to pick up a stove and a few other things for the house he was building."

"How long ago did he disappear?" Mitchell asked.

"A little over a year ago," she answered. "Lynne says she just fell into a routine of watching and waiting for him to come back. Weeks passed, and she started to panic. Finally, she went to the county sheriff. But winter hit the town hard and no one could get through to Provo or Salt Lake until spring. The sheriff finally told her there just wasn't anything he could do."

"Then some boys found a human skull," Sarah chimed in. "That got her wound up all over again. And when the sheriff told her it was just an old Indian skull, she decided to have you find Aaron so she can get on with her life."

Mitchell frowned. "A year is a long time," he muttered. "He could be anywhere, if he's even alive."

With a rolled up newspaper, Susan knocked an ironclad senseless and shoved the stunned insect under the edge of the canvas wall. "Lynne doesn't expect a miracle," she argued. "She decided months ago that their relationship was over. She just wants to know what happened."

Sarah adjusted the wick of the kerosene lamp and leaned back against a stack of folded blankets. "Lynne says the Stokes family has tried to find their son, but the family has a farm to take care of, and they've only been able to spend a few days searching since spring. She says they're frustrated and unhappy with the sheriff."

Susan leaned back against the rolled up tent, rubbing the dog's black and gray speckled ears. "The sheriff isn't happy either," she added. "He told Lynne the boy got cold feet. Just like Daniel said."

"It ain't that hard to believe," Daniel muttered defensively.

"But he never came back for his belongings," Sarah concluded quietly, "and he left a small bag of gold with Lynne."

Mitchell looked up, and the smile left his face. "Gold?"

"Just a small bag of ore," Sarah said quietly. "Wire gold mixed with quartz."

"Gold's like stink on a polecat," Mitchell growled. "Find some, and folks can smell it for miles. Someone's probably killed him for it."

"That may be," Sarah acknowledged grimly. "If it's true, Lynne wants to know that too."

Mitchell watched the two women quietly, wondering if they truly expected him to find the girl's missing fiancé. Sometimes, their confidence in his abilities seemed too far-fetched to believe. Still, their trust and confidence gave him a sense of satisfaction he'd never had before he met them, and the thought of disappointing them was a bitter pill he had no intention of swallowing. "All we can do is try," he said, watching both of them smile as they anticipated the next few weeks.

"Mama says she's had a wonderful time with the children," Sarah said suddenly, as though anticipating his thoughts. "She's glad to have them for another couple of weeks."

Mitchell shook his head. "I don't know how your mother can stand it," he confided. "Every time I'm around them, they're like a bunch of wild Indians."

Susan smiled. "They just don't see you enough," she observed. "When you're home, they get excited."

Sarah smiled and leaned forward, pointing a finger at Mitchell's chest. "*You* incite them," she admonished. "I've seen you do it."

Mitchell smiled disarmingly. "Not me," he protested dryly. "I'm a strict disciplinarian."

"Hah!" Sarah squawked. "More like a big kid looking for someone to play with."

"I'm an old man; I don't know how to play."

"I'd forgotten that," Sarah responded sweetly. "I was just remembering how the crippled old lion attacked the safari hunters and gummed them to death in our living room just two weeks ago."

"A horrible scene," Mitchell admitted.

Sarah smiled. "A terrible carnage," she conceded. "I'm worried the creature might attack while I sleep."

"And gum you to death," Mitchell responded.

Sarah shook her head. "Only into submission."

The Pratt kid groaned, and looked at the ceiling. "I'm too young to hear this kind of talk," he muttered. "Besides, I think the hoppers have gone to ground."

Mitchell removed his hat and swiped a sleeve across his forehead. "Guess we'd better move on, before they have time to eat the paint off the wagon," he suggested.

"I seen 'em do it!" The Pratt kid responded. "Stripped the paint right off the house... even ate the bark off the trees."

An hour later, the invading plague of ironclads had nearly disappeared. The Provo River veered northward, away from the road leading to Heber City and the center of the mountain valley. Mitchell turned in the saddle and pointed south. "The hoppers must have turned south, toward Wallsburg," he reported.

Susan made a face. "Thank goodness! I hate the things."

"How much farther to Heber City?" Sarah asked.

"Another ten miles," Mitchell answered. "We'll be there by noon. That should give us time to talk with your friend and find a place to set up camp."

Sarah shaded her eyes with one hand and looked east, across the valley. "It's been a long summer," she acknowledged. "I hope the weather holds. I wouldn't want to be caught in an early snow storm."

"We might not see snow until late October or November," Mitchell reasoned. "Even then, the first snow might be kind of light."

"That's very reassuring," Sarah responded congenially, "but Mother Nature is not always predictable."

"I promise; we'll head for Provo at the first sign of snow," Mitchell offered.

Sarah watched as her husband reined the dun to the south in a long, sweeping ride that left no part of their flank unchecked. She loved the mountains and deserts of the Utah Territory and hated to admit that there were still places that could be dangerous, places that held their share of people who delighted in making trouble. But she knew that Mitchell held no illusions of any paradise on earth. For Mitchell, the mountains could be a beautiful place, but they could easily love you one minute and kill you the next.

She watched as Mitchell cut the dun through a thin stand of pines and wondered at the strange turn their lives had taken in the past year. They'd gone from a poorly paid job with the county sheriff and a hand to mouth existence in a rented home in the avenues of Salt Lake City to unemployment and wealth beyond her wildest dreams. Their bank account had soared from nothing to well over fifty-thousand dollars in a matter of weeks as Collin's half-ownership in a Colorado Silver mine had suddenly gone bonanza. Now, they had more money than they needed and a ten-percent tithe to the church had barely put a dent in the account.

"Seems like Collin's paying a lot of attention to those pines," Susan observed, interrupting Sarah's thoughts.

Sarah peered toward the pines where Mitchell had dismounted to search the trees on foot. "Something has his interest," she answered, watching her tall husband hitch up his trousers and snug down the gunbelt carrying two flute-cylindered Navy Colts.

"That's not a good sign," Susan muttered. "He never cinches that gunbelt like that unless he expects trouble."

Sarah snapped the reins, urging the team to a faster pace. "Hand up that scattergun. Just in case...."

Susan handed the shotgun forward and took up a position near the tailgate of the wagon. "Daniel's over near the river," she called out. "He's headed this way now." She turned her attention back to Mitchell and watched as her husband climbed into the saddle and rode back to the wagon. Carefully, she watched the trees beyond him for signs of trouble. For a moment, it looked as though Collin was headed toward the front of the wagon, but his pace slowed and eventually, he brought his horse to the rear of the wagon. He leaned out and took Susan by the hand.

"There's a dead horse in those trees," he explained. "I saw a rider, three or four-hundred yards out, back in the quakies; seems like he's keeping pace with us."

Susan gave Mitchell's hand a squeeze, and with a sigh, settled back against a rolled-up canvas. She was grateful that Collin had spoken with her first. In his own way, it was an attempt to show her that while, technically, she was the second and junior wife in their plural marriage; he had no intention of treating her as anything but an equal in every respect. He had told her as much on several occasions, but every now and then he did something very deliberate to prove it. Often, it was some seemingly insignificant act, but more often than not, it was unplanned and from the heart.

Silently, she watched him ride toward the Pratt kid, and she thanked God that their marriage worked as well as it did. There had always been a kind of grim competition between Sarah and Susan Flitton. That competitive nature was still alive and well in both of them, but when it came to their relationship with Collin Mitchell, the two women had made and kept an agreement that neither would ever attempt to undermine the other's place in Mitchell's heart. It didn't stop the occasional urge to give one another a good hair pulling, but it *had* helped them avoid confrontations that could have made them both the focus of Mitchell's ire.

Susan forced her thoughts back to the present and Collin's message. "Collin says someone is pacing us and keeping just out of sight!" She called out.

"Does he want us to stop, or keep moving?" Sarah asked.

Susan shrugged. "He didn't say, but *I'd* rather keep moving. We're only a few miles from town, and I don't like being watched."

From the corner of her eye, Sarah glimpsed movement among the trees far to the southern edge of the valley. For a moment, the movement seemed shadowy and indistinct within the thickness of the aspen. But as she watched, the shadows moved eastward, and one by one, twenty-five mounted figures crossed a small sunlit clearing. For an instant, sunlight glittered on the polished steel of helms and breastplates. Then the riders were gone, dissolving amid the deep shadows of the forest. Sarah shivered involuntarily and felt the hair rise on the back of her neck. Nervously, she rubbed at the goose bumps on her arms.

Susan moved forward suddenly, taking the seat beside her sister. "What's wrong?" She asked quietly.

"Conquistadors," Sarah whispered, pointing toward the trees.

"You're seeing things," Susan responded. "They don't exist anymore, do they?"

Sarah shook her head. "Not real... shadows... like ghosts in the trees," she murmured quietly.

Mitchell dismounted in the thick aspens nearly half a mile south of the road and the wagon rolling steadily north toward Heber City. In the distance, both women were clearly visible on the wagon's bench seat, and Daniel Pratt rode a hundred-yard perimeter around the wagon with his brand-new Winchester *Yellow Boy* out and ready for trouble. Not that Mitchell really expected any trouble, but it didn't hurt to be ready, just in case. Sarah wasn't a woman to jump at shadows, and she certainly had never shown signs of a superstitious nature. But something had rattled her, something she had been almost reluctant to have him investigate.

Slowly, he turned his attention back to the forest and the sounds and smells that permeated the shadowy landscape. Here, the aspen grew thick, and their trembling leaves clattered softly with every breath of wind that buffeted the yellow canopy and threatened to send them all tumbling to ground already matted with fallen leaves. The noisy squawk of a magpie lent an eerie familiarity and peacefulness to the place as two fractious squirrels chased one another around the rotting trunk of a fallen pine, and a tiny lizard raced for cover beneath a small clump of sagebrush.

Like a perfume drifting with the passage of a fine woman, the scent of pines came faintly on the breeze. Here, the pines were sparse, and the aspen covered the mountainside like a blanket. Cautiously, Mitchell let his eyes search the trees for furtive movement, while his ears strained for the sounds of human presence. But the forest lay quiet about him, placid and benevolent for the moment, yet pulsing with a primal yet dispassionate malevolence.

Quietly, Mitchell fished around in a shirt pocket and extracted a lint-covered piece of jerky. Deliberately, he cut a *plug* from the ragged-looking strand of meat and pitched it across the small clearing. With an explosion, Sarah's motley-colored dog burst from the cover of the tall grass and snatched the tidbit from the air.

"Thought I couldn't see you hiding in that grass, didn't you?"

The Lady-dog barked once in answer, planted her rear on the rocky soil and watched intently as Mitchell cut a chunk of jerky for himself. "That's all for now," he told the animal. "You're a greedy little pig, and this is the last piece of the good stuff. That other batch is a little too gamy for my taste."

With the prospect of a meal disappearing into Mitchell's shirt pocket, the multicolored dog dipped her head and began licking a hind paw. Mitchell shook his head at the animal's sudden and complete dismissal of its primary food source and turned his attention back to the clearing.

He let his eyes probe the depths of the forest on all sides, searching every opening, prying into every space between the trees, watching for the tell-tale signs of Ute renegades looking for trouble. Antonga Black Hawk may have made peace with Brother Brigham and other Mormons in the territory, but years of raiding, fighting, and killing had left both Mormon and Ute on edge, and some were still ready to fight at the least provocation.

After a year of fighting and chasing Black Hawk and his raiders through the mountains of Central Utah, Mitchell had lost all desire to fight the Utes and now realized just how damaging Mormon settlements had been to the Utes and other natives in the territory.

Now, he felt a strong sense of wariness and the uneasy pressure of eyes watching from deep within the shadows of the surrounding trees. For a moment, his eyes searched the trees again, only to freeze on the shadowy figure of a man on horseback, a man still as a monument cut from stone, yet as insubstantial as smoke from a smoldering fire. Mitchell shifted uneasily, losing focus on the distant watcher. When his eyes returned to that place among the trees, the shadowy figure was gone, as though it had never been.

Mitchell felt the hair prickle on the back of his neck, as his focus swept closer, resting finally on the dead and rotting remains of an ancient pine. The huge bole of the trunk tipped crazily to the west where the upper portion of the trunk and the stubs of shattered, needle-bare branches lay finely wedged amid the clutching arms of a small yet thick stand of newer growth. The bole of the old tree was easily twice the span of a man's arms, and the ancient roots, now jutting from the ground in a tangled mass, were easily as tall as a man on horseback.

Yet it was not the tree itself that captured his attention, rather it was a weathered chunk of sun bleached bone; a small disc pinned to the ancient trunk with a short shafted quarrel, like a small plate nailed to a fence post in some farmer's field, and beside it—intricately and deeply carved into the rotting trunk—a long, curling stem and a multi-petaled flower.

"What the hell...."

Curious, Mitchell dragged at the reins and led the dun closer to the tilted hulk of the ancient pine. Leaning closer, he studied the whitened bone and the short-shafted bolt pinning it to the rotting tree. Carefully, he reached out, rubbing his thumb across the nocked end of the shaft. "That's not a Ute arrow," he advised the dog, who was now rooting happily at the base of the tree.

For a moment, Mitchell stood quietly, contemplating the bony plate and the force it would take to drive the short-shafted arrow through the bone and into the pine. Carefully, he shifted the dished-out bone, noting the roughness of the inside surface and the marks of time marring the rounded outer surface of the plate. He touched a finger to the ragged edge of the roughly circular plate.

Mitchell frowned and looked down at the rooting dog. "You better not chew on anything you dig up around here," he muttered. "This thing is the back of somebody's skull, and I don't want you gnawing on some dead feller's leg bone."

The long-haired dog looked up for a moment, twitched her ears, and resumed her mad clawing at the humus lying at the base of the tree.

Irritated, Mitchell reached out with a boot and gave the animal's hind quarter a shove. "I told you to stop digging. Now, drop that!"

The dog scrambled backward and turned to run, but Mitchell snagged her by the tail and dragged the growling animal to a standstill.

"Spit it out!"

Hand-over-hand, he worked his way forward, grabbing hair and hide until he had the animal by the scruff. "Now drop it!"

He pried at the animal's jaws until finally; the uncooperative beast dropped its treasure, flopped heavily to the ground, and lay there panting and grinning.

Mitchell stooped and retrieved the bone before the motley colored animal could snatch it again and run. "Rotten mutt! I told you not to chew on those bones!"

Quietly, Mitchell dropped the mandible and its yellowed teeth back into the lady-dog's shallow pit.

"No!" He commanded, as the animal sprang to its feet, ready to pounce on the suddenly relinquished prize. "I'll kick your tail if you start digging in there again!"

The lady-dog barked once and gave voice to a guttural combination of a growling, whining complaint. Then suddenly the dog flopped heavily on her belly, laid her head on her paws, and watched curiously as the tail-kicking and dangerously dominant male snapped the quarrel shaft and dropped the bony plate into the hole.

Mitchell frowned as he kicked dirt and leaves into the hole, uncovering the remains of a rust cankered helm of a Spanish conquistador. For a moment, he stared quietly at the rusted metal. "Now don't that beat all," he grumbled dryly.

Sarah reined the team to a halt on the dusty main street of Heber City and shifted uncomfortably on the hard planks of the wagon's seat. "I vote we sell the wagon and buy a couple of mules to haul this junk," she groaned. "My tailbone is killing me."

Susan smiled and climbed slowly over the tailgate. She shook out her skirts and brushed at the clinging red dust of the trail. Quietly, she surveyed the dusty street and the small town that was hardly a decade old. "I told you to put a couple of horse blankets on that bench. An old woman of thirty needs a little something to protect those old bones."

"Right now, I wish I had listened to you."

Susan helped brush the dust from her sister's skirt. "Just walk around a bit and work out the kinks," she advised.

"Cold water," Sarah declared grimly. "That's what I want right now."

Mitchell reined in the dun and dismounted between the two women. "I ain't sure, but that looks like a pump and a watering trough under them trees across the road," he said, pointing toward a shade covered yard and a small white-washed farmhouse. "I don't suppose them folks would object if the two of you had a drink from their well."

Sarah shaded her eyes with a hand and looked longingly at the shade and the pump. "Ain't, ain't a word, Collin," she corrected absently, knowing that his grammatical lapses were mostly the product of intent rather than a lack of vocabulary or linguistic skill. In fact, she often suspected that Mitchell's down-home *Mormon* dialect was a deliberate means of putting people at ease. She had asked Susan about it once, and her sister had simply smiled and offered two words—'Damn right.' After that, Sarah had let up a bit, but her own habits were hard to break, and Collin seemed to take the occasional editing of his grammar with good humor.

Quietly, Mitchell removed his hat and wiped a sleeve across his forehead. "Why don't the two of you wander over to that shady little place and meet the folks that live there. Maybe they can give you directions to the Campbell place. "While you're doing that, I'll see if I can find the Sheriff and get a look at that skull."

"What about the team?" Susan asked.

"Mr. Pratt can find some water and shade for the animals," Mitchell suggested." We can all meet at the dry goods store in an hour or two."

Thirty minutes later, Mitchell emerged from the local shaving parlor, slapped his hat on his head, and rubbed at a face scraped raw by a razor that hadn't been sharp since the day old man Jennings had taken it new from the box.

"Feelin' like a skinned rat about now, ain't ya?"

Mitchell looked toward the sound of the voice and the white-haired old man sprawled in a rickety chair, ten feet down the boardwalk in front of the dry goods store.

The old man raised a hand to the stubble on his own chin. "Two… maybe three times a year, I get lazy and go in there and let Jennings scrape the hide off me with that blunt-edged tater peeler he calls a razor, then I run back over here, check for open wounds, and slap on some liniment to ease the fire.

"Old Jennings never could keep that razor sharp an' I swear he could teach them fellers of the Inquisition a thing or three about skinnin' a feller alive."

"I reckon that's what he done to me," Mitchell admitted grimly. "See any open wounds or blood?"

"Nary a drop. But that don't mean nothing. Old Ben Stokes never even started bleedin' 'til three days after Jennings done his torture. He dang near to bled to death before his wife and kids could get him bandaged up. An' that's the truth."

"Sounds kind of grim." Mitchell acknowledged. "I suppose Stokes survived, but was scarred for life," he added.

The old man shook his head and rose from his chair. "Not so you'd notice. But then Stokes was always an ugly fellow anyways."

Mitchell arched his back and felt the popping of vertebrae as he tensed the muscles between his shoulder blades.

The old man waved a hand at the rickety chair. "Grab a seat, and I'll fetch a bit of that liniment for you. It's good stuff."

The old man was gone in an instant. Mitchell dropped into the chair and slouched back in imitation of its previous occupant. Thoughtfully, he watched as wispy tendrils of clouds streamed across the sky, and a cool breeze whipped the tree tops, hissing through the tall poplars and rattling the dry, yellow leaves of the aspen. He took a deep breath and let the quiet, peacefulness of the place seep into his bones while his thoughts sailed amid the drifting clouds.

Suddenly, he realized that his life was at a turning point, and the plans he had been making for the past few weeks would reach farther into the future than he had ever realized.

"Must be some deep thinkin' you're doin.'"

Mitchell started, realizing that the old man had dragged up a second chair and was now seated beside him. "Just wondering if the plans I've been making are right for my family," he confided.

"Can't help you none with that," the old man responded. "Made a big enough mess of my own life, often as not."

"Lived here long?" Mitchell asked casually as he took the proffered liniment and rubbed the soothing liquid onto his burning face

"Five or six years," the old man responded. "Got here after the fort was built, and folks was just startin' to build up the town. Name's Murphy," he said, holding out a hand. "Louis Murphy."

Mitchell shook the old man's hand, offered his own name, and tipped his head toward the buildings running north along the boardwalk. "Don't see no Fort," he told the old man.

"Wasn't much of a fort," Murphy admitted. "Mostly just some log homes lined up real close together, all formin' a big square with all the houses facin' the center of the square. Kinda used the back walls of them houses as the walls of the fort. Never had much trouble with the Utes up here, 'cept when old Black Hawk was raidin'. Folks got all wound up then, but we never had any real trouble."

Mitchell removed his hat, letting the cool breeze tug at his hair. "I heard a couple of boys found some fellow's skull up here a few weeks ago?" He suggested thoughtfully.

"Ah… So you're the fellow the Campbell girl asked to come and look for the Stokes boy." Murphy accused. "I wondered if you'd show up at all—what with the way she bragged you up as a big time detective, like them Pinkertons back east, I figured you'd want a big fee, an' the Campbells got no more money than anybody else around here. I figured you just wouldn't show up at all."

"We never talked about any fee," Mitchell admitted.

Murphy shook his head. "Don't be countin' on any," he advised. "Them folks is dirt poor. But don't you be lettin' on that I said anything about it. Ain't none of my business anyway."

Mitchell smiled. "I know," he offered, "Mormon Creed."

"Damn right," Murphy agreed. "Mormon Creed—*mind your own business*. But the Campbells are good folks, and I don't want 'em embarrassed or impoverished 'cause you come up here askin' for money they ain't got!"

"I don't expect I'll be doin' any of that," Mitchell replied congenially.

"Just better not," Murphy grumbled under his breath.

"What's that?"

"Nothin'. Just clearin' my throat. Kinda dry out here, what with the wind an' all."

"What about the skull," Mitchell prompted patiently.

"Don't know much about that," Murphy responded. "All I heard was Bruce Taggart and a couple of other boys was out near the Stokes' farm a lookin' for rabbits and they found an old skull amongst some rocks. They told the sheriff, an' he sent

Jared Turner out there to collect the thing an' look around a bit. Never found anything else as far as I know."

Mitchell leaned forward, resting his elbows on his knees and fiddling with his hat. "Near the Stokes' place?"

"That's right. An' that's what got the Campbell girl all riled up. She's just certain it's Aaron Stokes, and he's been killed."

Mitchell pondered his hat band for a moment. "You think the sheriff will mind if I look around a bit?"

Murphy shrugged. "Don't see why he would," he concluded. Hamilton ain't a bad sort, most times. Ain't much he can do about it anyways, it's a free country."

Mitchell looked up and leaned back, popping a few more vertebrae and slapped his hat on his head. "Some folks get a mite ornery when strangers start poking their noses into local affairs," he suggested.

Murphy shook his head. "John Hamilton ain't the kind to get his nose outa joint over somethin' like that. Fact is, he'd probably be glad to have you look things over; might keep that Campbell girl outa his hair."

"That's good to know," Mitchell responded.

"Jared Turner ain't so neighborly," Murphy added casually. "He's the deputy, and he can be a mite testy sometimes."

"Guess I'd better talk to Hamilton," Mitchell conceded.

Murphy shook his head." "Not this week," he predicted. "Hamilton's out with the militia. Probably won't be back for at least four or five days."

CHAPTER 2

22 September

"What is he up to now?" Lynne Campbell demanded as she watched the Pratt kid dodge into another shop on the Main Street boardwalk.

"I haven't the foggiest idea," Susan responded. "I'm sure Collin told him to keep an eye on us and make sure we didn't run into any trouble."

"And this is his way of discreet observation?"

"I'm sure he's up to something else," Susan replied. "He's a bit of an inventor, and you never know what he's tinkering with."

"What does he invent?"

Susan thought for a moment then grinned from ear to ear. "His last invention was a fan for the wagon… to give us a nice breeze during the heat of the day. Not the kind with blades— something like a small flag attached to an overhead shaft— which he wired to one bow of the wagon's top. That was attached to a lever and some kind of eccentric strapped to the spokes of the front wheel."

"Did it work?"

"Oh, it worked just fine. Collin took a good look at it and got that prankish grin on his face and said, 'Sarah, why don't you give the team a little run just to stretch them out.'

"So Sarah slapped the reins. The team took off, and the fan went berserk. Next thing I know, Sarah is hollering *Whoa! Whoa!* And the fan is slapping her backside to-beat-the-band— and I'm lying in the back with my skirts blowing everywhere and laughing myself silly!"

Lynne grinned and glanced toward the shop where the Pratt kid had disappeared. "You're joking!"

"Honest! Daniel unhooked it when the wagon stopped, because Sarah refused to drive with an *implement of the inquisition* at her back."

Lynne smiled tolerantly. "The two of them must be impossible!"

"Goodness; you'd think they lived for the chance to pull some kind of prank on one another, and Sarah and I always get caught in the middle!"

Lynne grabbed Susan by the arm and turned her to face the street. "Hush… Here he comes."

"What are you two grinning about?" The Pratt kid demanded when he caught up with the two women.

Lynne smiled at the Pratt kid. "Susan has just been telling me a funny story," she said happily.

"So tell *me*… I like funny stories."

"Good heavens, no!" Lynne groaned. "It's a woman thing… not fit for the sensitive ears of a young boy."

"Boy! You ain't no older than I am!"

"Perhaps… But age has nothing to do with maturity."

"I'm as mature as anybody else. Maturer even."

"We'll see," Lynne responded sweetly. "What are you shopping for?"

"Stuff."

"Just any kind of stuff, or special stuff?" The girl prompted.

"Kind of special. I may not be able to find what I need."

"And what do you intend to do with this special stuff?" The girl asked disarmingly.

The Pratt kid's face broke into a smile. "Can't tell you," he declared. "It's man stuff and not fit for your pretty little ears."

Susan waved a hand toward the northern end of Main Street. "Daniel, we're only walking around town. You needn't dog our heels every step of the way."

The kid's face took on a stern look, and his voice took on a deeper, affected tone. "Beggin' your pardon ma'am, but his lordship will be kickin' my butt, if I let you out of my sight for one instant." The face changed, and the kid smiled indulgently. "It's another man thing, you know… the butt kicking, I mean."

"Sounds cruel," Lynne suggested casually.

"Oh, Miss! You don't know the half of it… the beatings, the humiliation," the kid whined. "He starves me horrible like and leaves me tied to the wagon at night so I can't run away. You'd think the war hadn't never been fought the way he treats me, Miss. And there ain't no hope of ever bein' free… unless *you* was to *buy* me and set me free.…"

For a moment, the girl looked at Susan with shock filling her eyes. "He can't be telling the truth, can he?"

Susan's face turned hard, and she stared at the kid with eyes like green ice. "You'll get whipped for sure now," she hissed.

"Please don't tell him, ma'am!"

"If you think *I* want to be whipped for protecting you, you are quite mistaken."

"Aw… please, ma'am."

"Stop sniveling. It's time you learned to take your punishment like a grown man."

"Susan.…" The girl's protest sounded strained.

The kid turned to the girl, tears suddenly in his eyes. "Please, Miss.... He nearly shot me a couple of weeks ago... had his pistol pointed right between my eyes, and he threatens to hang me most every day."

"Oh, stop it," Susan commanded suddenly. "I promise not to tell."

Lynne frowned, suddenly comprehending. "You're terrible," she scolded, "pulling my leg like that!"

The Pratt kid took off his hat and wiped his forehead with a sleeve. "Aw heck, a little leg pullin' ain't bad—long as you don't go too far. Besides, he would have shot me for certain, if Mort hadn't stopped him. And he threatened to hang me just the other day."

"So, just what is Brother Pratt's situation?" The girl demanded.

"Brother Pratt is the foreman of our non-existent cattle ranch," Susan explained.

"Nonexistent? I don't understand."

"I'm foreman, but we ain't got a ranch yet," the kid explained.

"Oh."

"We've been looking for land," Susan added, "but things have been rather busy the last few weeks. We met Brother Pratt while we were in Ogden just three weeks ago. He had taken a job with some men he didn't know and was an unsuspecting participant when they kidnapped me and took me to Corinne. Brother Pratt helped me escape, but Collin nearly shot him before we knew that Daniel was not really part of the gang."

The girl frowned. "I shouldn't have asked you to come up here and waste your time," she said quietly.

"It's not a waste of our time," Susan assured. "Sarah and I love puzzles, and Collin seems to have a talent for discovering the answers to problems like this. Mort says God has a calling for Collin and he's sort of 'prodding him toward it every now and then'...whatever that means."

"Now that's one scary old goat," the Pratt kid muttered.

"Mort is not scary," Susan countered.

"Well, he scares *me*."

"It's your guilty conscience," Susan suggested.

"It's been an awkward year for me," the Campbell girl confided quietly. "I haven't felt as though I could talk about it with anyone... not even my mother."

Susan turned to the Pratt kid and waved him backward. "Take a minute and look for your stuff, Daniel. Lynne and I will walk slowly so you can make sure we're not getting into trouble."

"You're sure?" I wouldn't want another whippin'."

"Stop joking and go find you stuff."

"Yes Ma'am."

Susan waited until the Pratt kid had disappeared into a nearby shop, before turning back to the girl.

"He seems like a nice young man," Lynne said thoughtfully.

"He's almost eighteen, and he's a very nice young man," Susan responded.

"I thought Aaron was a nice boy," the girl said suddenly. "We were engaged nearly a month when all the gossip started about Jean Kelson being pregnant. The rumor was all over town, and Brother Kelson was in a rage. It wasn't long before rumor had Aaron as the father.

"He told me it wasn't true, but I had been having second thoughts anyway. It gave me an excuse to break off the engagement."

"You didn't believe him?"

"By then, I didn't care if he was telling the truth or not. I was scared silly and didn't want to be married to anyone."

"Probably just the jitters," Susan suggested thoughtfully.

"I don't think so... It's hard to describe how I felt at the time. Papa was so upset by the rumors about Aaron he told me he wouldn't allow the marriage.

"I had already broken the engagement by then, but Papa made me so angry that I argued with him and told him I was old enough to make my own decisions and to stop trying to ruin my life."

"You never told him you had broken the engagement?"

The girl looked at the ground and shook her head sheepishly. "No. I just let things rest and tried to ignore what people were saying."

"Then Aaron disappeared."

"Aaron and his cousin, Nathan."

"His cousin?"

"Nathan Larkin. They did everything together."

"You didn't say anything about Nathan in your letter."

"I should have, but I didn't want to complicate things any more than they already were."

"How does Nathan complicate things?"

"Nathan and Aaron were always off somewhere hunting or fishing—whenever they got a chance. At least that's what everyone thought.

"Nathan came to me a few days before they left for Salt Lake. He told me what they were really doing and made me swear to keep it a secret. He left some things with me and told me to be careful not to talk to anyone about it. Then he told me they had found an old journal and a map to an old Spanish mine."

"You mentioned gold in your letter," Susan prompted.

"I don't think they found the mine, but Nathan gave me a small bag of gold and told me he thought they were very close. He also told me someone had torn up his father's house. He thought they were looking for the map.

"They left for Salt Lake a few days later, and that was the last I heard from either of them."

"Did he say who had torn up the house?"

"No… And I've been very careful not to mention the things he left with me to anyone."

"What did he leave with you?"

The girl glanced around nervously before answering. "A little bag of gold flakes and a map," she said quietly.

Jared Turner was a dark haired young man with a heavy beard and a bearing that showed no estrangement to hard physical labor. Like nearly every man in the valley, Turner had a farm with animals that needed feeding and crops that needed tending. Much of that labor was done in the early hours before sunrise, or late in the day, before the sun went down, leaving Turner an honest, yet tired and often cantankerous man.

When he shook the man's hand, Mitchell could see the tiredness in the deputy's face, and knew instantly what fueled the irritable disposition. "Louis Murphy says you're the deputy in charge while the sheriff is out with the militia."

Turner gave a half-smile. "Lucky me," he observer dryly.

"Rough day?" Mitchell asked.

"Rough year. I'm hoping next year goes better." The deputy stepped back and sat on the edge of the sheriff's desk. "I got a farm about five miles south west of here, what's left of one anyway. My boy just rode in to tell me that a swarm of grasshoppers came in after I left this morning and pretty much ate up everything—except the house and the cows. We ain't sure about the chickens. A couple of 'em are still missing."

Mitchell smiled. "I seen them ironclads eat green paint," he offered.

"Probably ate the chickens," Turner muttered unhappily. "Hope they choke on the feathers. Only thing worse is the damn jackrabbits."

"Plenty of them down in the valley too," Mitchell offered. "They seem even worse the farther south you go."

Turner shrugged. "Don't know about that," he answered bleakly. "All I know is the jacks eat plenty, and the grasshoppers ate my chickens."

Mitchell looked out the window and shook his head. "I've seen 'em eat the clothes right off the wash line, but I ain't seen 'em eat chickens yet."

"Maybe them chickens ate the hoppers and are headed for the Great Salt Lake to throw 'em up, like the gulls did twenty years ago," Turner suggested. "Might have my own miracle of the chickens here.... Don't tell the Bishop I said that. He ain't partial to pokin' fun about things like that."

Mitchell smiled. "Reckon you won't see your chickens for a couple of weeks," he observed casually.

"How's that?"

"It's a long walk to the lake, and them birds don't fly too good—especially when they're stuffed full of grasshoppers."

Turner barked out a laugh. "Reckon they're gone for good then. Once they get down to the lake they'll start loafin' around on the beach and get too fat and lazy to climb back up the mountain."

"Reckon you're well rid of 'em if they ain't got more loyalty than that," Mitchell advised grimly.

"Reckon I'll be pickier about where I get my eggs in the future," Turner agreed.

The room was silent for a moment as each man waited awkwardly for the other to speak.

"I suppose you're the fellow the Campbell girl sent for," Turner announced suddenly.

"I am," Mitchell agreed. "I came over to take a look at the skull she wrote about."

"The sheriff tried to talk some sense into her, but she got all fired up, thinkin' it's her fiancé—the Stokes kid. She wouldn't listen though, just kept howlin' about how Stokes has been missin' for a year and we still ain't found him."

"You don't think a year is a long time for a man to stay away from his family and everything he knows?"

"Of course I do." Turner snapped defensively. "A year is *way* too long in my book. But the mail ain't that slow. He could have written a letter and let someone know he was doin' alright."

"But you don't think he's doing *alright*, do you?"

Turner shook his head. "I think the boy's dead and gone. The Campbell girl would be better off if she put it all behind her and moved on with her life."

"Maybe so," Mitchell conceded, "but I don't think it's that easy to give up on someone you love. You wouldn't give up if it was your wife or one of your kids, would you?"

"You know I wouldn't," Turner muttered grimly. "I just don't see any way to prove who that fellow was. That skull could be a thousand years old or just some old trapper that dropped dead before the gulls ate the crickets."

"Why don't you let me take a look at it," Mitchell suggested. "I've got a friend who's a doctor, down in the valley. I had a talk with him before we came up here. He gave me a few pointers on what to look for."

"Look all you want. I'll bring it out."

Turner disappeared into a back room and for a few moments, the only sound in the small office was a muffled thumping from the back room. "The place is a rat's nest," Turner growled when he returned. "There's stuff in there that should have been thrown out years ago."

The deputy dropped a battered old hat box on the sheriff's desk and flopped in the nearest chair like a lanky rag doll. Carefully, Mitchell opened the box and removed the sun bleached cranium and the detached mandible.

"Looks pretty much complete," Mitchell suggested casually. "The teeth are all in place, even though the lower jaw has come loose."

Turner scrunched lower in his chair and tipped his head back, starring at the ceiling. "Don't know about that," he responded. "It was settin' on the ground pretty as you please when I got there. Them boys was plenty curious about it, but they hadn't got up the nerve to mess with it. The jaw bones come loose when I picked it up."

"No harm done," Mitchell acknowledged as he rolled the cranium on its top and peered at the upper teeth. Unsurprised, he noted the flattened inner face of the incisors and the barely erupting surfaces of the wisdom teeth. Almost reluctantly, he picked up the cranium and rolled it over in his hands. For a moment, he let the odd, waxy feel of the bone impress itself on his fingertips.

"Gave me the willies, pickin' that thing up," Turner muttered.

"Only touched one myself, before now," Mitchell admitted quietly.

He rotated the cranium, noting the smooth surface, the sutures joining the plates, and a starburst of fine cracks radiating from a point near the joining of the left zygomatic to the bridge-like zygomatic process.

"See anything interesting?" Turner asked suddenly.

"Some," Mitchell responded. "Take a look at these cracks."

"Okay, it's cracked," the deputy muttered when Mitchell pointed out the hair-like lines. "What's it mean?"

"It means something hit this fellow and cracked his left cheekbone, not long before he died," Mitchell explained.

"Could be a woman," Turner objected, "and them boys could have thrown a rock and busted that cheekbone."

"Could be a woman," Mitchell admitted. "But Doc says women are smaller and more petite. He says men are thick skulled and have big heavy brow ridges 'supra orbital tori' he calls 'em.

"As far as the rock throwin'… The surface of the bone ain't chipped. If those kids had hit it with a rock, it would have knocked chips all over. The cracks ain't healed, which means this fellow didn't live long enough for 'em to heal."

"That's it?" Turner asked.

"There are a few other things, "Mitchell admitted. "Doc White knew I was looking for a boy about eighteen years old, so he gave me a list of things to look for and some drawings.

"Take a look at these separations between the plates of the skull... Doc White says the plates fuse together and the separations disappear as a person gets older—but when folks are younger than about twenty-five or thirty years old, the plates are still pretty much separate, like these."

"So you got a man under thirty with a busted cheekbone," Turner surmised.

Mitchell nodded. "Younger than twenty, maybe...the wisdom teeth are barely coming in," he replied. "A white man—maybe black," he added, "but not an Indian. And he ain't been dead very long."

Turner peered closely at the skull. "How the hell do you know that?" he squawked.

"The teeth and the smell," Mitchell replied. "Up close, it still smells rank, a little sweetish like rotten meat. And the front teeth are flat on the inside surface. A dentist, up in Ogden, told me that the few Indians he's looked at had front teeth that looked like little shovels—all scooped out on the back side."

Turner shook his head as Mitchell rolled the cranium over, exposing the inner surfaces of the teeth. "I'll be damned," he muttered thoughtfully.

"Maybe it is the Stokes kid."

"And maybe it ain't," Mitchell responded.

"I learned a new word the other day," Turner announced. "Vacillation.... And you're doin' it...vacillatin'. Either it's the Stokes kid, or it ain't. You can't have it both ways."

Mitchell set the cranium back on the desk and picked up his hat. "Hell, I ain't no expert. Up until a few weeks ago I was chasing Utes with the Legion. Before that, I was locking up drunks or tracking down chicken thieves. Everything I told you about that chunk of bone I learned in the last week, and if

I didn't have the notes and drawings Doc White gave me, I wouldn't know that much."

For a moment, Turner looked surprised then he shrugged and loaded the bones back into the hat box. When he finally spoke, his tone was casual and friendly. "By tomorrow, I won't remember half of what you said about sutures and such. So, I reckon you'll be the expert, like it or not."

Mitchell frowned, lowering his brow to a habitual glare that Susan claimed had unnerved full grown men and terrified little children.

"Sheriff Hamilton is convinced that skull belongs to some old Ute, what with all the trouble we've had with them lately," Turner offered.

"I thought you folks got off pretty easy," Mitchell suggested.

"We did," Turner admitted. "When Black Hawk first started raiding down in the valley, Captain Wall took out twenty-four mounted militia and had a talk with Chief Tabiona. Things were kind of touchy at first go, but we finally come to terms, and Chief Tabby agreed to keep the peace and not get involved with Black Hawk's raids. We've been pretty well off except for a few folks out on the edges of the valley. Folks like the Stokes bunch from over at Center Creek, had to pack up and move in closer to town 'til Black Hawk and his friends settled down a bit."

Mitchell frowned, remembering how folks in the Central part of the territory had been torn by the change in their relations with the Utes. True, the change had been gradual enough, but most Mormons in the Valley had been taken by surprise when a gathering tension between the two cultures had suddenly flared into violence.

"The sheriff can believe what he wants," Mitchell replied thoughtfully. "He might be right," he added.

At the front door of the office, Mitchell glanced upward at the afternoon sky. The sun was past its zenith, yet still high over head. "Do you have time to ride out and show me where those boys found that thing?" he asked, nodding toward the box.

Turner took out his pocket watch and noted the time. "It's a little after noon," he observed. "Meet me here in half-an-hour, and we'll ride out there. You can look around all you want."

"Make it an hour," Mitchell suggested. "That'll give me time to gather up my womenfolk and our wagon."

"You planning on settin' up camp out there or stayin' in town somewhere?"

Mitchell shrugged. "I'm not sure. I'm a little green at this business of tracking down missing folks. Mostly, I'm just feeling my way around and hoping to stir things up a bit and see what happens.

"Won't take much to stir up that Campbell girl," Turner muttered unhappily. "That one's got a burr under her saddle for certain."

Mitchell grinned at the deputy's obvious discomfort. "I'll have a talk with her," he offered. "Maybe she'll give you some peace, if she can hound me, instead of you."

Turner sucked in a chest full of air and sighed deeply. "You don't know what a relief that'd be," he admitted gratefully.

CHAPTER 3

22 September

*H*alf a block from the Sheriff's office, Mitchell paused to inspect a small sign jammed into one frame of a multi-paned window at the dry goods store.

"They wanted skinny little fellers with no kinfolk," declared a voice near Mitchell's left shoulder. "They went belly up after the telegraph came though."

Mitchell's heart jumped at the unexpected presence. "Dangit, Mort, you're gonna give me a heart failure sneaking around like that!"

"Sorry, boy. I mistook you for that Collin Mitchell fellow. You know—the Mormon gunman with nerves of steel."

"And a heart of mush 'cause some old fart keeps scarin' the hell outa me!" Mitchell squawked loudly.

"You oughta be tougher than an old boot by now, boy."

Mitchell shrugged and looked closely at the old man. "Two weeks ago, you were headed for Paris, France. What changed your mind?"

"Nothin'. Been there and back."

Mitchell frowned and shook his head, knowing the old man heard voices and believed himself to be the *angel of death*. "Reckon that's a mighty fast trip for a fellow that's older than dirt. A Nephite could have done it on foot in a week. That pigeon-toed horse must have slowed you down some."

The old man scowled and waggled a finger under Mitchell's nose. "Sassy pup. You got no respect for your elders. One day you'll get your comeuppance. You'll see this calling ain't no cakewalk."

"What calling might that be, Mort?"

"You know what calling."

"Like a church calling, you mean?"

"Sorta."

"Like the Bishop callin' you to be a Sunday school teacher?"

"Sorta."

"Sorta what?"

"A calling, like one of them priesthood callings."

"I didn't know you was a Mormon, Mort."

"Sorta."

"You been hearin' that voice again, ain't ya?"

The old man scowled and glared at Mitchell. "Some friend you turned out to be. You think I'm some kinda lunatic, don't ya? I'll bet Sarah and Susan don't think so poorly of me."

"I don't think poorly of you, Mort. I just figured if I ever was to see an angel, he'd be all bright and glorious."

"An' I ain't?"

"Well…."

"You expectin' wings and a golden halo?"

"No. But I wasn't expectin' a buffalo coat an' worn out moccasins, and when you decide to visit the bath house, I'll pay."

"Listen here Danite; I bathe regular, just like everyone else."

Mitchell shook his head and opened the door of the dry goods store. "Then it's that coat, and it's over ripe. Why don't you throw it in a hole somewhere, and I'll buy you a new one."

The old man sniffed at his shirt. "You couldn't smell that coat no how. I got it tied to my saddle."

"We must be down wind."

The old man looked doubtful then shrugged. "Okay," he muttered. "You got plenty of money. I'll let you foot the bill for a new outfit."

Inside the store, sunlight poured through the windows, illuminating shelves loaded with bottles, tables stacked with cloth, and racks crammed with clothing. Behind the main counter, a blond haired woman turned at the sound of the bell above the door and smiled.

"Good morning," she greeted.

"Morning," Mitchell responded.

"Howdy, Sister Murphy," Mort called happily.

"How can I help you fellows?" The woman responded.

"I need some new duds," the old man announced.

"And supplies," Mitchell added.

"Well, you're plenty old enough to pick out your own clothing, so I'll help your handsome young friend."

"He ain't all that handsome, an' I ain't all that old," Mort complained.

Mitchell leaned over the counter, beckoning the woman closer. "He's older than dirt," he whispered congenially. "Wrinkled like a dress that's been stuffed in the laundry pile too long. Hides it with all them whiskers."

"You whisperin' meanness behind my back, Mitchell?"

"Not a word," Mitchell lied. "Just giving Sister Murphy a list of supplies."

"Since you're feelin' so generous, why don't you buy some nice thick beef steaks and invite an old man to dinner?"

"For a resurrected fellow, you seem to be eatin' all the time," Mitchell muttered.

"Ain't hunger in the usual manner," the old man confided, "just an enjoyment of the taste of food."

Mitchell smiled and shook his head. "Can you add six or eight thick steaks to that list, Sister Murphy?"

Mitchell watched as the woman smiled and took up a pencil, adding the request to the list.

"I think we've got what you need, Bother Mitchell. There was a fellow in town just yesterday with a hind quarter he wanted to trade. Kelson turned him away, but my husband took it on trade for flour and a side of bacon."

"Kelson?"

"The fellow who owns the store two blocks south. There are others in town, but Kelson's place is the one that gives the most trouble for the rest of us. Louis says Kelson's got money backing him from somewhere."

Mitchell nodded, almost instinctively understanding, how a small operation like Murphy's store could find it difficult to compete with a better funded operation. "You seem to have everything I might need," he confided. "Besides, I'm a creature of habit. Now that I've been here, I'll just keep coming back."

"Like a bad penny," the old man advised from a far corner of the store. "Draws trouble like flies," he warned.

"I ain't that bad," Mitchell squawked defensively.

The old man shrugged and pulled a gray cotton shirt from a neatly folded stack.

"Reckon not," he admitted, "or I wouldn't be here."

"Why are you here?" Mitchell demanded.

"Same as you, Danite. I'm magnifyin' my calling."

"I ain't no Danite, Mitchell growled, noting Sister Murphy's tight lipped frown at a word that seemed destined to cling to the church like a bloodthirsty leach.

The old man crossed the wooden floor and tossed a pile of new clothing on the counter then leaned forward and winked at the scandalized woman.

"Don't worry, ma'am. I just say that stuff 'cause I know it'll get his goat."

For a moment, Mitchell stared at the old man, contemplating Mort's seemingly sudden knowledge of Mormon theology and the concept of callings and their magnification.

"Mitchell thinks I'm the *angel of death*, the old man continued, as he tossed a new pair of boots on the counter beside the clothing. "But somehow he's got it into his head that the angel of death is some kind of demon, dropped in from outer darkness, instead of some wise old fellow with a calling and a purpose. Seems like a narrow minded paradigm, don't you think?"

"I suppose so…"

Mitchell frowned and shook his head. "I may be narrow minded, but I ain't no paradigm."

The old man scowled. "A paradigm is the way you see the world, Mitchell… the set of rules you think makes everything run like a well made watch… your world view. And yours is a bit narrow. That's why I'm here—to help you shift that big boulder of a paradigm just a smidgeon, so you can get a little better view of the way things really are."

"Like time," Mitchell suggested.

"Now you're thinking boy. Like I told you once before, you see time like some kind of linear stream, all runnin' in one direction. But I'm gonna help you see it more like an ocean of currents, with folks like us just buzzin' away like strings on a fiddle—some slow an' some too fast to see."

Mitchell shrugged. "You should be talking with Sarah or Susan," he suggested. "They're the ones with all the schooling."

The old man scowled, waving one hand as though the idea buzzed about his head like a pesky fly. "Ain't so," he argued. "I know where you been schooled. Besides, the voice says you're the reason I'm here."

"Why me?"

"Can't say, yet. But I'll let you know when the time comes."

Mitchell frowned unhappily, wondering what mischief the old man was up to. All his talk of callings and the even stranger talk of currents of time and vibrating strings was disconcerting to say the least. It was as if the old man expected Mitchell to see some logic in his twisted conception of reality—a conception that was often mystifying and incomprehensible.

"Just give me a little warning if you decide to try shootin' me again."

"Reckon we're beyond that," the old man conceded.

"What do I owe you," Mitchell asked as Murphy's wife returned to the counter with a small sack of sugar.

The woman set the sack on the counter and checked off the items with her pencil.

"There's more to be gathered, but with the clothing and all, it will come to about forty dollars."

Mitchell nodded and retrieved a small leather bag from his pocket and fished out four gold coins. Dropping the coins on the counter, he pushed the pile of clothing toward the old man.

"Don't often see these up here," the woman observed, plucking two ten-dollar gold bees from the countertop.

"I reckon we'll see even fewer of them once the railroad comes through," Mitchell admitted.

"I hear they could be finished next year," the woman reported.

"They seem to be moving mighty fast," Mitchell replied. "I've seen 'em setting ties and rails about as fast as a fellow can walk."

"That would put the tracks in Ogden next week, not next year," the Murphy woman suggested.

"It would," Mitchell admitted, "but they're stuck somewhere near Devil's Gate, and I hear they have to do a lot of blasting and then clear out the debris, before they can lay the track. I guess it slows 'em down a bit."

"I heard about the blasting," the woman replied. "David Hunter was killed up at Devil's Gate just last month. He was working for the Union Pacific. I guess they were blasting some rock, and David got caught in a sand slide and smothered.

"His wife Martha took it pretty bad. They came from Scotland about eight years ago—crossed from Council Bluffs with the Stoddard Handcart Company. David Jr. has been trying to keep up their place since the accident, but I think he's looking for side jobs to bring in some extra money."

Mitchell frowned and shook his head. "Looks like the railroad ain't a kindness to everyone," he said, remembering Devil's Gate and the roar of the Weber River where the violent waters churned around the hairpin bend, gnawing relentlessly at the nearly vertical cliffs less than five miles east of the canyon's mouth.

The railroad itself had run straight past the hairpin turn of the river, but the straighter path hadn't saved the railroad from the necessity of blasting a path through three or four miles of rugged canyon rock. In a few short weeks, a few hundred men had done more to wreck the mountainside than erosion had done in more than a thousand years.

"Brother Hunter was one of the first to work for the railroad when the Brethren called for it," the woman explained. "I wonder if it was such a good idea."

Mitchell nodded, remembering the debate in the School of the Prophets and the vote to encourage Mormon workmen to hire on with the railroad. "It wasn't an easy decision," he offered, knowing his own vote had been cast in favor of the proposition, hoping that with Mormons taking railroad jobs and contracts, the undesirable elements following the railroad would drift away for lack of business.

Mort grabbed up the bundle of clothing. "Got a room where I can change into my new duds?"

The woman waggled a finger toward the back of the room. "Storeroom's all we got," she said. "There's no window and no light in there, so you'll need to leave the door cracked open a bit or it'll be too dark to see what you're doing."

The old man nodded and gathered up the clothing. "Thank you, ma'am."

"Is this two pounds of flour or three?" The woman asked, turning the list toward Mitchell.

Mitchell leaned over the counter and peered closely at the offending line. "Kind of smudged, ain't it.... Better call it three, just to be safe."

Mitchell pushed the list back across the counter just as the front door opened to the ringing of the overhead bell.

The big man who strode into the store stood nearly a hand taller than Mitchell and must have topped the scales at more than two-hundred and fifty pounds—pounds that had the look of muscle gone soft, rather than an over abundance of fat.

"Hello, Sister Murphy," he greeted noisily.

"Afternoon, Brother Kelson," she answered coldly.

Mitchell watched as the woman turned her back to the man with hardly a glance in his direction.

"I see you dropped the price of your shovels to two-fifty apiece," Kelson blustered loudly.

The Murphy woman ignored the comment and continued pulling Mitchell's order from the shelves.

"Is two-fifty a good price?" Mitchell asked congenially.

"Fair," Kelson replied, "but these are made down in the valley and they've got pine handles, and the spade itself isn't quality metal. That handle isn't going to hold up if you're doing any real work—too soft.

"Now, I just brought in a shipment of factory made shovels—right out of Colorado… hickory handles and a good steel spade that'll last for years if a fellow takes care of it… all for two-fifty apiece."

"Sounds like a quality tool," Mitchell suggested.

"You bet!" Kelson blustered. "You won't find that kind of quality down in the valley. Not at that price anyway. Name's Kelson," he said, suddenly sticking out a meaty hand. "Edward Kelson."

"Collin Mitchell."

"Name sounds familiar," Kelson acknowledged with a grin, "but I'm no good with names. Lucky I can remember my own some days."

For a moment, Kelson stared into the sunburned face of a man who looked and dressed like a clod-kicking farmer from down in the valley—a man who looked as though he would be at home with both feet in a furrow, yet packed a Navy Colt in a tied-down holster.

Mitchell ignored Kelson's searching gaze, knowing the man's eyes had focused on the worn grips of the Colt.

"New to the valley?" Kelson asked thoughtfully.

"Lookin' things over," Mitchell responded congenially. "Haven't decided how long we'll stay, but I hear there's property over toward Center Creek that might be worth a look."

"Might be," Kelson replied noncommittally. "I don't get over that way much. Not since Blackhawk started raiding, and folks out that way pulled up stakes and moved closer to town."

"I wouldn't want to jump anyone's claim," Mitchell said quietly.

Kelson shook his head and twisted the shovel handles until each of the spades faced neatly in the same direction. "I wouldn't worry about that," he conceded. "The folks who lived out there don't seem all that anxious to get back, and I suppose some of them never will. Besides, you know as well as I do, the U.S. Congress hasn't ratified any property claims in the territory. It may be years before anyone really owns the land they're farming."

"Most folks will be going back to their homes as soon as they feel it's safe," the Murphy woman interjected.

"I hear a fellow named Stokes has abandoned a claim over in that direction," Mitchell suggested.

Kelson flushed angrily. The smile left his face, but when he finally spoke, his voice was tight, yet calm. "I suppose you're talking about Aaron Stokes. He ran off about a year ago. I suppose his place is up for grabs by now."

"Ran off?"

"He was supposed to marry that Campbell girl, but it appears he got cold feet and ran off…. And good riddance too. He was a bad lot."

"He was no such thing," the Murphy woman objected as she thumped a small bag of salt on the counter. "You just didn't like him because he had big plans to form a co-operative."

"That was nothing but big talk," Kelson argued.

"Not just talk, Brother Kelson," the woman countered. "Aaron Stokes had quite a few folks convinced he could help them market their handmade goods if they would just give him a chance."

"Stokes had no money and no idea what to do with it if he had," Kelson affirmed stiffly.

The Murphy woman shook her head. "That's not what I've been hearing," she insisted calmly. "My husband says the Larkin boy showed him proof that Aaron Stokes had enough money to make a go of it."

"If either of them had money, why would they want to put it into some tiny little co-operative?" Kelson muttered.

"It's called diversification," Mort announced happily as he slammed the storeroom door and strode across the room. "Like keepin' your eggs in more than one basket. Folks put their assets into several different investments with different levels of risk. The returns ain't always the same, but it makes it so you don't lose everything if one investment takes a turn for the worse…"

"I know what diversification is," Kelson grouched. "And I don't need some old clod kicker trying to explain the high finance of barnyard investments."

At that moment, the bell above the door jingled and a young woman entered the shop, followed closely by a dark haired young man. The young woman glanced quickly around the shop, until her eyes came to rest on Kelson.

"Are you boring everyone with business talk, father?" She asked, ignoring the silence pervading the shop.

"Business is not a subject that boors an intelligent mind," Kelson blustered.

"So those of us who prefer other conversation are unintelligent?" the girl countered.

"I didn't say that."

"But you implied it," she pressed, "infering by extension that only you are intelligent, because no one else desires to discuss business."

"I'll not argue with you, girl."

"Yes, father."

"I'll need a coat," Mort announced suddenly. "Mitchell thinks my old one an' me should part ways."

"I have a few," the Murphy woman responded. "One of them ought to fit. They're made of good, heavy wool. My husband has one and likes it real well for winter time."

"Thank you, ma'am." With only a brief glance at Kelson, the old man retired in the direction of the woman's pointing finger.

"I hope my father hasn't been pestering you with talk of business." The dark haired girl told Mitchell casually. "He has a tendency to get caught up in the subject whenever he finds a new victim for his lectures on 'business as the foundation of social and cultural relations.'"

"I don't lecture," Kelson protested.

"Are you new in town," the girl asked, ignoring her father.

"We're just looking around a bit," Mitchell replied evasively. "A friend asked us to come up for a visit."

"Mitchell is looking at land over near Center Creek," Kelson reported as he meandered through the shop hefting tools and checking prices as he progressed deeper into the room. "It seems he's interested in that piece the Stokes kid was trying to build on."

"Mitchell?" The girl's dark haired companion asked quietly. He popped the lid from a glass jar, fished-out two pieces of hard candy and laid them on the counter.

"That name sounds familiar," the girl suggested thoughtfully. She was silent for a moment; then suddenly her hand shot out. "You're the fellow Lynne Campbell sent for," she said congenially. "I'm Jean Kelson."

Mitchell smiled and took her hand, noting the strong grip and the keenly intelligent look of a woman whose auburn hair, brown eyes, and wasp-like waist gave Mitchell visions of a water-soaked, half-starved wildcat. For a moment, he felt sorry for the blustering Kelson, whose cocky, rooster-like personality, would never be a match for the razor-like wit of his daughter.

"Pleased to meet you, Miss Kelson."

"The girl looked up and smiled disarmingly. "Call me Jean," she said casually. "Lynne has talked of nothing else for several days. I feel as though I know you already."

Mitchell nodded and let go of the girl's hand.

The girl turned slightly, indicating the young man standing beside her. "This is Bradley Hunter," she said. "We're both friends of Lynne Campbell. And we both knew Aaron Stokes."

Mitchell nodded at the youth. "Pleased to meet you, Hunter," he said, pointing a thumb over his shoulder toward the back of the shop. "The fellow back there in the new coat is my friend Mort."

Hunter plunged a hand into a pocket withdrew a handful of mixed junk and plopped the lot on the counter. "Lynne says you're going to find Aaron and drag his sorry butt back for a wedding," he said as he plucked a jackknife from his pile of loot and jammed it back in his pocket.

Mitchell shook his head and watched the boy shift a few coins to one side, pick up a battered pocket watch, and thrust it into the pocket. For a moment, an intricately braided strip of leather and the sparkling chunk of quartz attached to it dangled from the pocket, until Hunter grabbed the bit of mineral and stuffed it down with the watch and the knife.

"Lynne said no such thing," the girl objected.

"Well, that's what ought to be done," Hunter muttered. "It ain't right for a fellow to run off like that and not say a word to anybody."

"You're just irritated because neither Aaron nor Nathan would confide in you," the girl responded.

"Wouldn't have hurt 'em none," Hunter grumbled, as he pushed three pennies across the counter.

"Aaron is a selfish, worthless, skunk," the girl announced stiffly," and Nathan Larkin was no better."

"Sounds like you don't care for either of them," Mitchell suggested, noting the girl's sudden change of attitude.

The girl shrugged. "In a way, my father is right about both of them," she acknowledged thoughtfully. "Just a couple of farm boys with big ideas."

"Sister Murphy says they had the money to back their big ideas," Mitchell suggested.

Hunter glanced furtively around the shop. "Aaron told me they found an old Spanish gold mine," he said quietly. "I never seen any gold, but the two of them was always sneaking off into the mountains to the south. Sometimes they rode up Lake Creek and disappeared—sometimes it was Daniel's Creek or Center Creek. I tried following a few times, but it didn't do no good. I lost track of 'em every time."

"Hah!" Kelson barked. "You couldn't find horse crap if you were standing in it."

"I ain't that bad at trackin'," Hunter insisted. "They was just real careful—walkin' their horses up stream beds and on hard ground. They even doubled back and rode in circles. Besides, Black Hawk and them renegade Utes of his was traipsin' all over the territory. It wasn't smart to be wanderin' alone up there anyway."

"You wouldn't be here now if you had run into any Utes," Kelson said.

"Don't I know it. That's why I quit followin' Stokes and Larkin. Say! Maybe that's why nobody has seen hide nor hair of the two of 'em! May the Utes got hold of 'em."

Hunter scooped the remainder of his loot from the counter and dropped it back into his pocket.

"Maybe Stokes just got cold feet and took off, and Larkin tagged along for the hell of it," Kelson interjected. "Anybody with a lick of sense would get out of this valley if they had half a chance."

"Aw… Stokes is probably dead," Hunter grumbled. "They say one of the Taggart kids was out huntin' rabbits and found some human bones. Utes probably killed Stokes and left 'im lay."

"I wouldn't wish such a cruel death on anyone," Jean said quietly.

"Too bad they wouldn't say anything about that old mine," Hunter grumbled. "That gold ain't doing either of them any good, if they're dead."

"Dead...."

The Kelson girl repeated the word in a kind of hollow, disassociated way, then stood quietly staring at a colorful bolt of cloth as though all else in the room had ceased to exist.

"Are you all right, Miss Kelson?" Mitchell asked.

Startled, the girl dropped the trailing edge of the cloth. "Quite," she answered. "I was just admiring these colors. I've never seen anything quite like it. The colors seem so brilliant, almost luminous. Where did you find such a bolt Sister Murphy?"

"It came with the last order," the older woman replied. "I'm not certain there's anything special about it though."

The Kelson girl frowned and brushed her fingers across the surface of the bolt. "A trick of the light, I suppose," she murmured quietly.

Several minutes later, when the Kelson girl and Bradley Hunter had gone, Mitchell leaned forward, searching the shelves behind the counter. "Got any caps for a Navy Colt?"

The Murphy woman opened her mouth, but no sound issued from her lips as one small pane in the front window shattered and a fiery projectile scorched a path past Mitchell's face and plunged into the wall at the back of the shop.

"What in the hell!" Mort squawked.

For a moment, Mitchell stared as a fist size patch of flame erupted into a man-sized wall of fire. An instant later, a table loaded with cloth flared up with a muffled roar. The odor of kerosene was heavy in the air when Murphy's wife brought Mitchell back to his senses with a bellow that nearly burst his eardrums.

"Sand!" She yelled, pointing at two buckets near the end of the counter.

Mitchell lunged for the buckets, snatched one from the counter, and heaved sand and half-a-dozen wooden tops at the burning wall.

While the blazing floor at the base of the wall smothered beneath the cascading sand, the wall itself continued to burn, filling the shop with a dark acrid smoke. Sand from the second bucket hit the wall, and for a moment the flames dwindled to nothing.

"It ain't out yet!" Mitchell bellowed, flinging the empty buckets toward the door where Murphy stood staring at the disaster.

"Get water!" Mitchell yelled.

Murphy grabbed the buckets and disappeared into the street, where Mitchell could hear voices raising the alarm.

"Smother it!" Mort exclaimed. The old man dragged the burning table away from the wall and began pounding the flames with a woolen blanket. Mitchell snatched a blanket from the table and attacked the flames threatening to engulf the wall. For a moment, he held his own against the fire's progress, then water slammed the wall in an almost steady stream from the hands of the bucket brigade. Gradually, the flames gave way and finally died.

Murphy dropped an empty bucket to the floor and wiped a sleeve across his soot covered face.

"What the hell started that?" he groaned unhappily.

Mitchell stepped to the fire-blackened wall. He pulled a jackknife from a pocket, levered it open, and gouged the blade into the ruined wood. A moment later, he turned back to Murphy and held out a sharply pointed piece of iron attached to the end of a charred wooden rod.

"What the hell is that?" Murphy demanded.

Mitchell dropped the offending object on the counter and wiped his hand on a pant leg. "It's a crossbow bolt," he explained.

"Crossbow?"

"Like a bow and arrow."

"I know what a crossbow is," Murphy growled. "What the hell is that thing doing in my wall?"

"Someone shot it through the front window," Mitchell said. "Someone tied a kerosene soaked rag to it, set fire to it, and shot it through the window."

Murphy shook his head and frowned angrily. His wife took his arm and watched as two of the bucket brigade dragged Mort's table and its soggy contents through the door and into the street. "Why on earth would anyone want to burn down our store?" she asked bleakly. "We've tried to be good neighbors to everyone; we've never even had harsh words with anyone."

"It doesn't make any sense," Murphy protested unhappily.

"Maybe I can help there," Turner announced from the open doorway.

"What do you know about this," Murphy demanded.

"I'm takin' a guess," Turner admitted, "but it looks like your fire was just a distraction."

"What are you talking about?"

"I think someone wanted me out of the office. The fire may have been a way to get everyone's attention and keep me occupied so they would have time to find that skull and smash it into little pieces."

"How bad?" Mitchell wondered.

"Not quite powdered," Turner admitted," but close enough it don't matter."

CHAPTER 4

22 September

The sun was just past its zenith when Mitchell emerged from Murphy's store. Up and down the street, people still watched intently as though awaiting a fresh outbreak of fire, while those who had heard the alarm and joined the fight marched, buckets in hand, back to their homes and shops.

"Seems a shame my new duds smell like smoke," Mort complained as he sniffed at the sleeve of his new shirt.

"If you hang 'em out somewhere and let 'em air out, most of that smoky smell will go away," Mitchell suggested.

"I suppose you're right," the old man admitted. "Can't say as much for Murphy's store."

Mitchell looked back toward the shop then turned and crossed the street, headed for the nearest water trough.

"I think Sister Murphy will have everything back to normal in a day or two," he called over his shoulder.

At the water trough, Mitchell swept the surface of the water with one hand, clearing away a skim of floating debris. He shucked off his smoke saturated shirt and began rinsing it out.

"Don't know which is worse," Mort commented as he looked on.

"Worse than what?"

"The smoke or the horse spit in that water," Mort concluded, pointing to the drifting debris.

Mitchell ignored the old man and continued rinsing the shirt. "Guess I'm used to horse spit," he muttered."

"Too bad someone smashed that skull," Mort said suddenly.

"Good thing I took a good look at it first thing," Mitchell responded. He took the shirt from the trough and began wringing the water from it.

"Learn anything?" The old man asked.

"Not enough."

Mort frowned and shook his head. "Folks ain't all that easy to recognize when there ain't no meat on 'em," he admitted.

"The county deputy is going to show me where those boys found it." Mitchell replied. "Maybe we can find something helpful out there."

"I imagine you'll find plenty," the old man muttered unhappily as Mitchell shrugged into the damp shirt.

"You sound down right gloomy for a fellow with a brand new outfit," Mitchell observed.

"Murder is a gloomy kind of thing," Mort responded.

"You're thinkin' this fellow was murdered?" Mitchell asked.

For a moment, the old man looked into the hazel eyes of the younger man. "It's murder," he said finally. "No reason for you and me to be here if it weren't."

"You still think God has his finger on you and me—pushing us around like a couple of pawns on a chess board?"

"Sorta."

"What do you mean, sorta?"

"Well …. You're sorta like a pawn—me … I'm more like a knight."

"Thanks."

"Ain't nothin' personal."

Mitchell frowned and looked north to where several riders slowly made their way down a dusty Main Street.

"So, where do we go now?" he asked casually.

Mort shrugged. "Hell if I know. I'm just along for the ride."

The riders were now less than a hundred yards distant, too far to distinguish anything more than dust covered clothing and tired, plodding horses, yet near enough for an uncomfortable feeling of recognition.

"Mean lookin' bunch," Mort observed as Mitchell stepped onto the boardwalk and moved into the shade of a canvas awning.

"Mean ain't the half of it," Mitchell grumbled as the lead rider drew close, revealing a slouched figure in a worn hat, dust covered jeans, and down-at-the-heel boots.

The riders advanced slowly, their horses plodding, heads hanging, hoof-tips flicking the dust covered ground into miniature storms of wind-tossed powder.

The lead rider glanced at the two men standing on the boardwalk then turned his horse to the water trough.

"You boys know where we can buy a few supplies?" he asked.

Mort stepped to the edge of the walk and pointed across the street. "Murphy's probably got anything within reason," he said congenially.

While his horse drank, the rider removed his hat and slapped at his dust covered clothing. "Don't guess we'll be too unreasonable," he growled. He drew the back of a dusty sleeve across his face and set a battered hat back on his head. Dark, unkempt hair threatened to dislodge the hat, but the rider grabbed the rim of the hat with both hands and snugged it down tight. He let his horse drink for a moment longer then turned the animal and headed for Murphy's store.

"You boys water the animals while I see about the supplies. Dunford, you see if you can find a bottle of something worth drinking."

The man called Dunford frowned. "Now where the hell am I gonna to find liquor in a Mormon run town?"

The dark hared rider turned in the saddle. "Just ask around. Find yourself a jack-Mormon. Maybe He'll have a little corn mash hid out in the barn!"

Dunford dismounted and let his horse at the water. "You fellows know where there's any liquor in this town?"

"Can't help you there," Mort answered. "We're new around here. Lucky if we can find our way out of town."

"Ain't much of a town," Dunford grumbled.

Mitchell watched quietly as the remaining four men dismounted and led their horses to the trough. The thirsty animals plunged their muzzles into the water while the riders slapped at their dust covered clothing. One of the riders peered intently at Mitchell. The man's face was weathered from exposure to the elements and hardened from something more subtle and evil.

"You fellows come far?" Mort asked casually.

"Far enough," Dunford muttered. "Thought there might be a little work with the railroad, up near Devil's gate, but the Mormons got some kind of contract, and we come away with nothin'."

"Can't see there'd be much work around here," Mort reasoned.

"We figure to do a little prosepectin'." Dunford answered. "Biggs says there's talk that the Mormons are getting gold outa the Uintahs. We figure to get some of it for ourselves…. Coleman's got other business," Dunford added, pointing toward the man who kept his eyes on Mitchell. "But he ain't told *us* what it is."

"Them mountains ain't exactly safe these days," Mort suggested cryptically.

Dunford snorted derisively. "We can take care of ourselves," he growled harshly.

"Lots of folks think that—until they run across some of them renegades who was riding with Black Hawk."

"Who's this Black Hawk?"

"Ute war chief. Him and a couple hundred warriors have been raisin' hell hereabouts for nearly three years."

"Ain't heard nothin' about it," Dunford admitted.

"Been plenty of trouble all the same."

"None of our affair," Dunford concluded. "We'll avoid 'em if we can—kill 'em if we can't."

Dunford turned away from the old man and looked toward Murphy's store on the east side of the street. "Find some shade, and let them horses rest awhile," he told the others. "And be ready to ride in an hour or so. And if anybody asks, we're headed into the mountains to do some prospecting."

Mitchell watched as the men finished watering their animals and scattered up and down the street. Dry and dusty as they appeared, he had no doubts that each of them was hunting for anything resembling the local equivalent of a saloon.

"You acted a mite un-neighborly toward them fellows," Mort suggested accusingly, when the five men had drifted to the nether regions of the town.

"Never liked Biggs or Dunford," Mitchell admitted.

"Thought maybe you knew them fellers," the old man answered. "That Coleman fellow looks like a mean cuss. Looked like he ate nails for breakfast, and they're still pokin' his insides."

Mitchell frowned. "Only Jackman, Biggs, and Dunford," he explained. "Don't know any of the others, although that Coleman fellow seems familiar somehow. I got tangled up with Biggs and Dunford about fifteen years ago. I was hurtin' for money, and I got dragged into one of their schemes to rob a bank over in Illinois, but I got out before they pulled it off.

"The county sheriff was a good sort, and when I told him what they had planned, he got a bunch of locals together and waited for Biggs and his friends to try taking the bank.

"The sheriff had the place loaded up with deputies and a dozen men hidden around outside. Biggs and Dunford went into the bank with Tom Jackman. They pulled guns and threw sacks for the teller to fill with cash. Those sacks didn't even hit the counter before the teller was on the floor and the Sheriff hollered for the three of them to drop their guns and surrender. Biggs didn't even hesitate. He just turned around and started shooting; wounded the sheriff and one deputy, before someone shot the legs out from under him.

"Jackman and Dunford were smarter. They realized they were out-gunned and ran for the street. Dunford got hit and went down in the doorway, but Jackman made it to the horses and got away clean with the two fellows who were holding the horses."

Mitchell frowned at the retreating riders. "I ain't seen 'em since," he added.

Mort grinned suddenly. "Do they know you was the one that shot 'em?"

"Oh, they know all right."

"Good thing neither of 'em recognized you."

Mitchell scowled. "I think Dunford noticed. He just wasn't sure if he wanted to start anything."

Mitchell nodded toward the opposite side of the street and Murphy's store. "The two of them are probably chewing nails about now."

"Do your womenfolk know these fellows are after your hide?"

"Not exactly."

"Probably ought a give 'em some warning," the old man suggested. "Speakin' of which…" he added, pointing down the boardwalk to where Susan hurried toward them.

When Susan reached the two men, she took a moment to catch her breath. "Sarah has disappeared!" She panted. "Daniel and Lynne are searching for her near the Campbell place. Lynne's mother says Sarah went into the backyard and just disappeared."

It was nearly noon when Sarah raised one of Amelia Campbell's good china cups to her lips and sipped cautiously at the hot yarrow tea.

"I have green tea or coffee, if you prefer," Sister Campbell offered.

Sarah shook her head reassuringly. "No, Sister Campbell, the yarrow is fine."

"You must be tired, if you came all the way from Provo this morning," Amelia Campbell observed as she shifted uncomfortably on a hard kitchen chair.

Sarah's eyes swept the room quickly, noting the size of the room and the fact that like many homes in the territory, the room did triple-duty as kitchen, dining room and living room.

"I am a little weary," she responded as she leaned back, absorbing the warmth radiating from the flat-topped stove at the back of the room.

Amelia Campbell picked up her knitting, working the thin, handmade needles with the deft swiftness of long practice. Sarah closed her eyes and listened to the gentle, rhythmic hiss of needle brushing needle.

"What are you working on?" she asked dreamily.

"It's a shawl," the older woman replied, spreading the nearly finished piece so that it fanned across her lap and dangled to the floor on three sides. "We sheared in the spring; and one little fellow had the softest fleece.... I couldn't resist, so I kept back the rovings to make a shawl." She lifted two corners of the triangular-shaped mass so Sarah could get a better look at the pattern.

Sarah leaned forward, examining the stitches. "Lynne never really said much in her letter...," she said quietly, "about her engagement to Aaron Stokes, I mean."

Amelia Campbell shook her head and laid her knitting in her lap. "She was quite excited at first," she said thoughtfully. "But after a while, it seemed as though the excitement was gone. She stopped talking about the wedding and refused to make any plans at all."

"That doesn't sound like a woman in love and about to be married," Sarah responded.

"That's what *I* told her, but she just got more morose every day. Then Aaron disappeared and she was suddenly talking about him again and 'why hadn't he come back from Salt

Lake'… and 'wasn't he with Nathanial Larkin?' Just on and on until I like to have swatted her behind for acting so scatterbrained."

"Larkin?"

"Nathan Larkin… Aaron Stokes' cousin."

"And the two of them went to Salt Lake?"

"Yes. Lynne didn't tell you that in her letter?"

Sarah shook her head. For a moment, she tried to remember the exact contents of the letter.

"I'm sure she mentioned that Aaron had gone to Salt Lake, but I thought he had gone alone to buy some of the things they needed to set up the household after the wedding."

"Good heavens, no. I don't think that was the case at all, dear."   Mrs. Campbell shook her head thoughtfully and picked up her knitting." I wonder why she wrote that. That's not the impression I had at all, and after talking with Sister Stokes, I'm almost certain that Lynne had broken off the engagement. Lynne never actually told me she had broken the engagement, but I'm sure the relationship was over before Nathan and Aaron left for Salt Lake."

"Why do you think she ended the relationship?"

The older woman frowned at her knitting, slipped the stitches from one needle and unraveled the row she had just completed. "My dear, I haven't a clue—which surprises me almost as much as Lynne's refusal to talk about it. This is a small town, and I should have heard some gossip about it by now, but everyone is strangely quiet about the whole thing."

Sarah smiled and set her empty cup on the table. "I'm sure people are talking," she offered dryly. "They're just being discreet for the moment. The gossip will catch up to you, I'm sure."

She watched as the older woman set to work with her needles again.

"I dropped a stitch," Mrs. Campbell offered when she saw Sarah's watchful eye.

"I thought as much," Sarah admitted. "I have trouble concentrating on the pattern *myself* when someone is talking to me. Sometimes, I end up unraveling the same row again and again, until I just put the whole thing down and wait for a quieter time to work on the project."

Mrs. Campbell snorted and shook her head. "If I waited for quiet times around this house, I would never even start a project."

"That's probably why I never seem to finish any of the projects I start," Sarah admitted quietly.

For a moment, she watched the older woman's hands as she deftly threw stitch after stitch onto the slender needles. "Lynne must have had some reason to break off the engagement," she suggested. "Did they quarrel?"

"Not that I know of… Although right after we announced the engagement in the spring, there was a terrible rumor going around that the Kelson girl was pregnant. The whole town was rife with speculation about who the father was. I don't believe any of the young men in town were spared suspicion."

"What an awful thing to do. The poor girl must have been humiliated."

"She seemed to stand up to the situation well enough. And she certainly put the gossip mongers to shame when all signs of a pregnancy failed to appear. Everything seemed to settle down to normal, everyday things for a while after that."

Sarah stood and stretched, easing the growing tension in the back of her legs.

"I see you have trouble with hard chairs too," Mrs. Campbell said as she stood and mimicked Sarah's stretching motions.

Sarah moved to the window and gazed into the tree-shaded yard at the back of the house.

"I'm sorry," she apologized. "It's just that some chairs seem to cut off the circulation, and my legs just stop functioning, if I don't get up and move around now and then. Susan says I'm just getting old."

"Nonsense. Some chairs are worse than others, and these have never been particularly comfortable."

Sarah turned her back on the window and watched the woman gather her knitting and tuck it away in a large bag.

"That *is* a beautiful shawl," she said. "Have you written out the pattern?"

"I hadn't until a few months ago. It's just something I worked out in my head, but Lynne said some of the Relief Society sisters wanted the pattern, and I should write it down so it wouldn't be forgotten. Lynne made several copies so I wouldn't have to lend the original, would you like one?"

"I would love a copy," Sarah said. She waited quietly as Mrs. Campbell went to a bookcase in the family's small living room and retrieved a large sheet of carefully folded paper. Almost lovingly, Sarah took the proffered gift and unfolded it to a single page nearly half a yard square.

"Lynne decided it needed something more than 'knit one, purl two' instructions," the older woman advised as Sarah stared at the carefully detailed drawing, occupying nearly three quarters of the page.

"The drawing itself is absolutely wonderful!" Sarah exclaimed. "I had no idea Lynne was such a skilled artist."

"It is beautifully done. Isn't it? Lynne spent literally hours on each one."

"You shouldn't just give these away," Sarah chided. "The pattern could easily be sold in the valley. Women in town are always looking for a new pattern to knit, and to see such a beautiful drawing of the original… I should think you could easily sell fifty or a hundred of these in Salt Lake."

"My goodness… I wouldn't have thought they were worth anything at all."

Sarah shook her head. "The pattern alone may have been hard to sell, but the drawing really lets you see what you're getting. Something like this might sell for as much as ten cents each, for just the pattern. With a drawing as nice as this—perhaps twenty cents each."

"I couldn't ask Lynne to spend all those hours on a drawing for only twenty cents," Mrs. Campbell protested.

"Good heavens, no," Sarah agreed. "You would need someone who knows the printing business. I'm thinking they could be printed like a small pamphlet."

"I'm afraid I wouldn't have the faintest idea how to go about such a thing," Mrs. Campbell objected, "but it would be wonderful if it would bring a little extra money into the household."

Sarah held the pattern in front of her and studied the drawing. "This could be a gold mine for you. You just need the money to start up and develop it. Have you done any other patterns, with drawings?"

"We've done five. Lynne is working on the sixth now."

"Do you have paper and pen?" Sarah asked suddenly.

She waited while the older woman rummaged about a small desk, then carefully inscribed a name and address on the proffered sheet. "When you get a moment, send a letter explaining what we've talked about to Brother Whitney, at this address. He knows about the printing business and should be able to advise you on how to proceed, if you're interested."

"Oh, we're definitely interested. Money is in such short supply around here; it would be foolish to ignore any prospect of making a little extra."

"My thought, exactly," Sarah agreed.

"Why don't we go out back and sit in the shade?" Mrs. Campbell offered. "It's growing too warm in here to be comfortable."

Sarah arose and started for the back door.

"Right now, the shade sounds wonderful, Sister Campbell."

"You call me Amelia, just like all my friends. Now, go find a chair and a nice spot in the shade, and I'll get us some cold water and a few of the cookies Lynne made yesterday."

Sarah left the house and wandered the yard until she found three wicker chairs tucked in a far corner, in the shade of a sprawling willow. Gratefully, she sank into one of the chairs, absorbing the coolness beneath the willow. She reached for her bag, felt something hard strike the back of her head, and fell mercifully into darkness.

Sarah lifted her head and struggled to bring the world into focus. Everything seemed oddly distorted, green and wet. And her head hurt. That was the worst of it. Her thoughts were a jumble, and instinct alone caused her limbs to function, dragging her out of the water onto a dryer fragment of the ditch bank.

Ditch?

The thought moved haltingly through an unnatural fog.

How? Campbell house...?

The memory of a white clapboard house and a hand pumped well rose through the fog and turned into dream and the sound of someone calling her name....

Sarah opened her eyes to the dimness of a small bedroom and the sensuous embrace of a feather mattress. The delicious feel of the hand-made bed was a far cry from the grimy dampness and the foul odor of stagnant mud and rotting vegetation that seemed so prevalent in her dreams—dreams that had been punctuated by the thundering of cannon fire and pain.

The pain still thundered, but the dampness and the stench of mud were welcome exclusions from her current situation.

"How are you feeling?"

Susan's voice registered through the thunder as a soft contralto loaded with concern.

Sarah turned her head slightly to see Collin and Susan standing beside the bed. "My head hurts," she complained quietly. "I think someone hit me."

"I think you're right," Mitchell agreed as he took her by the hand. "We found you in the ditch behind the house. It looked like someone knocked you on the head, and dragged you into the ditch."

"Did you see who did it?" Susan asked anxiously.

Sarah held tightly to Mitchell's hand, comforted by the strength she felt in him and the knowledge that no one intending her harm would come near, now that he was watching over her.

"I didn't see anyone," she answered, easing her tortured head back to the center of the down pillow. "I remember going out into the yard and the shade under a tree... other that that, I don't remember anything."

Susan frowned and bent over to brush Sarah's hair back from her face. "I don't understand why anyone would want to knock you on the head," she complained unhappily. "We've only been here a few hours. Hardly anyone knows we're here or why."

Mitchell gave Sarah's hand a reassuring squeeze. "Someone thought you had a map to a gold mine," he explained grimly. "You didn't have it so they left you in the ditch and took the opportunity to tear this room apart while everyone was out looking for you. "Lynne told Susan that a fellow named Nathan Larkin gave her a map that he and Aaron Stokes found and told her to keep quiet about it. Apparently, someone got wind of it and came after the map today."

Sarah glanced around the room, but saw no evidence that anything had been torn apart in a search for the map. "Did they find it?" she asked quietly.

"Lynne says the map is gone," Mitchell replied.

Susan waved a folded sheet of paper in the air. "They must have been watching when Lynne's mother gave you one of these patterns and thought it was the map."

"Someone thought my knitting pattern was a map to a gold mine?" Sarah moaned unhappily.

"Might even be the same person who started the fire at Murphy's store and smashed that skull into little pieces," Mitchell added.

Sarah closed her eyes and sighed deeply. She had hoped this trip would amount to a quiet week or two in a small mountain town—time away from the everyday concerns of raising children and running a household on too little money.

She knew the children were safe enough with her parents, in Ogden, and the family's financial situation had changed swiftly in the last few weeks—so swiftly and so radically for the better that she and Susan both had difficulty remembering that they actually had money in the bank—money that might occasionally be spent on something more than necessities.

This trip was a bit of an extravagance—the holiday they could never afford in the past. It was a holiday, yet it was not. For the first time in ten years, Collin was out of a job. When Collin had lost his job in town, the lack of an income had scared both women senseless for several weeks, until Collin had revealed his partnership in a Colorado silver mine.

The partnership with Collin's uncle, William, had been a bit of information Collin had forgotten completely, and the sudden flow of cash into their bank account had been a shock for everyone. But it wasn't just the money. Neither was it the sudden change in lifestyle that colored her thoughts with unrest. Her unease came from the knowledge that violence was once again haunting the family.

For years, she had wrestled with her fears for Collin's safety—fears that his work with the territorial marshal would bring violence not only to himself but to the family as well. Those fears had never come to fruition—until the last few weeks.

"I looked at that skull first thing," Mitchell said, interrupting her thoughts.

"And what did you discover," she asked quietly.

"It could be Stokes... could be anyone. But I'm almost certain it was a man who had been hit in the face before he died. His left cheekbone had been cracked. I think he was a young man too."

"If it isn't Aaron Stokes, who else could it be?" Susan asked.

"I'm not sure," Mitchell responded. "I need to go out to where those boys found the thing and see if Deputy Turner missed anything. Then, I suppose I should check around and see if anyone else is missing."

"That could make quite a long list," Susan suggested, "Even if you consider only the people from the nearest towns and ignore the possibility that the man came from outside the area and got himself killed by the Utes."

"I'm not sure how far we need to go with this," Mitchell responded thoughtfully. "If we can satisfy your friend that it's not Stokes... That's all we really said we would try to discover anyway. Are we obligated to anything more?"

Sarah pondered the question for a moment then answered. "Why don't we start with the assumption that it *is* Aaron Stokes and then try proving that it *isn't* him," she suggested.

"That may sound like an odd way of approaching the problem, but it would at least give us a place to start. You could still make a list of people who are missing, but I think we should concentrate on discovering what happened to Aaron Stokes."

Susan nodded in agreement. "I think that makes good sense," she offered. "If we don't concentrate on Aaron Stokes, we could end up chasing all over the territory and never really accomplish anything."

Sarah brushed a stray lock of hair from her face. "I don't think I'm ready for another ride in that wagon just yet," she confided. "My head feels like an over-ripe melon, ready to explode."

Mitchell frowned and shook his head. "You're not doing any traveling today," he replied.

"You're in that bed for the rest of the day," Susan explained. "Lynne will stay with me in the wagon, for now. If you're feeling better tomorrow, we'll consider letting you get out of bed.

"We had the doctor look at you, while you were still unconscious. He says nothing is broken, but you might be unsteady on your feet or become nauseated if you try to get up and move around too soon."

Sarah scowled unhappily. "I don't intend to be left behind while the rest of you are having all the fun," she complained sulkily.

"We are not leaving you behind," Mitchell promised. "In the morning, we'll take the wagon out near Center Creek, not far from where the boys found the skull. We'll set up camp, take a quick look around, and then I'll come back for you. If you're able, we'll ride back to camp."

Sarah tugged on Mitchell's hand, drawing him down until his lips touched her own. "Promise," she murmured softly.

"Promise," he responded.

"I'll take that as your word, *Brother Mitchell*," she whispered in his ear.

Sarah heard Mitchell groan as he drew away and knew that her *Brother Mitchell* had struck a responsive cord—just as she had intended. Collin would not dare to shut her away in the safety of the Campbell house.

CHAPTER 5

23 September

*I*t was late in the morning when Mitchell lowered himself from the saddle and gouged the heel of his boot at the hard-packed soil of the hillside. Surface fragments flaked away at the impact; while the deeper, hard-packed mix of fragmented rock and clay resisted the intrusion.

"Dammed hard job, digging a grave in this stuff," he concluded.

Turner shifted in the saddle and walked his mount a few steps higher on the slope.

"That's what finally made me give up," he admitted. "I scuffed around up here, kickin' dirt for four or five hours. I couldn't find any signs of a freshly dug grave. Not a hint of loose dirt anywhere. I finally decided the bones had to be somewhere else, and some coyote dragged that skull up here and left it."

Mitchell took a moment to survey the hillside and its sparse covering of sagebrush and cheek grass.

"Where was the skull, exactly?" he asked.

"Over near that pile of rocks," Turner responded. "I piled 'em up first thing, so I could find the exact spot again if I had to."

Mitchell walked to the small cairn and stared at the hard-packed ground surrounding it.

"You're sure those boys didn't kick it around or move it any?"

"The Taggart boy said they never touched it," Turner answered. "The Parks kid got down on his hands and knees to get a closer look—got his face real close when the Taggart kid poked that skull with a stick and howled like a ghost. Scared the shit out of the Parks kid, I guess."

Mitchell grinned and shifted the hat on his head. "Would have scared the shit out of me too," he admitted. He took the hat from his head and let the morning breeze blow through his hair.

"I have to agree," he said, pushing his hair back and clapping the hat back in place. "This isn't the kind of place you would expect to find a burial... But it is the kind of place a dead body could be left, and in a couple of weeks there wouldn't be much left except bones and clothing. And it wouldn't take long for coyotes and rodents to scatter that."

"So we're back to the idea some coyote drug it in?"

Mitchell raised an eyebrow. "Your idea," he pointed out.

"Aah!" Turner squawked. Slowly, he swung down from the saddle. "There were no tooth marks on that thing, and you know it. Any dog that picked it up would be gnawing it like some old soup bone."

Mitchell grinned. "I'll go along with that, but the wind didn't blow it up here."

Turner frowned. "Maybe them boys did more than poke at it with a stick."

Mitchell studied the hillside. It was not a particularly steep incline. They were still in the lower foothills south of town, and the mountains themselves were still a mile or two away—too far, for a couple of young boys to pack such a grisly trophy.

Kick it around a bit or poke it with a stick maybe; maybe even roll it down the hill.

"Did either of the boys seem curious enough to handle it or carry it around?" he asked.

"I doubt it," Turner answered. "The Parks kid was talking some nonsense about monsters made from the parts of dead bodies. By the time they got into town and told me what they had found, they had themselves so scared they didn't even want to come back out here."

Mitchell smiled. "Frankenstein's monster," he explained. "English gal named Mary Shelley wrote the story about fifty years ago."

"You're pullin' my leg."

"Nope. Story's about some crazy doctor who gets the idea he can make dead folks live again. So he takes all these parts of dead bodies and sews 'em together like a patch-work quilt. When he brings the monster to life, it goes crazy and kills the doctor."

"Where in the hell did you read a story like that?"

Mitchell frowned and peered closely at the deputy. "Can you keep your mouth shut, if I tell you?"

"I suppose I can," Turner answered. "It ain't like folks are goin' to come rushing up to me askin' 'hey Turner, where did Mitchell read that Frankenstein story?'"

"Hah!" Mitchell exploded. "You just keep quiet about it nonetheless."

"Fine. I'll keep quiet. So, where'd you read it?"

"Harvard," Mitchell muttered.

"Harvard? The school?"

"Yep, the school."

"What was you doin' there?"

"Reading law among other things."

"Good lord! You're one of them parasite lawyers!"

"I ain't a lawyer."

"Ain't that what they teach there?"

"Among other things. I just didn't have any interest in law, so I quit."

"So how long was you there?"

"Three years... almost four."

"Damn!"

"So, that's where I read Frankenstein. And you keep quiet about it, 'cause I ain't told anybody—not even Sarah and Susan."

"Seems strange you ain't told your women folk..."

"Not strange at all. I figured to see if they could still care about me if they knew most all of the bad stuff and only a little of the good. If they didn't cut and run like a couple of young doe's with a wolf on their trail, I figured I could start letting them in on some of my better qualities. So, I've been holding back on the Harvard thing."

Turner grinned. "Maybe I should have held back on my cow milkin' education. Then the wife could get up before daybreak and milk them cows... I could fill her in on the details when my boys are old enough to take over the job."

"Might get yourself smacked up side the head with a frying pan too," Mitchell warned.

"Like the fellow we're looking for," Turner suggested.

"Maybe break your nose instead of your cheekbone," Mitchell advised.

"Selma wouldn't bash me in the face for something as petty as cow milking."

Mitchell turned his thoughts back to the now pulverized skull and its cracked cheekbone. "This just doesn't seem like a likely place," he grumbled.

"Think we should start scuffing through the brush lookin' for soft spots?" Turner asked.

"I'm not sure we'll find anything you didn't see already," Mitchell countered.

Turner surveyed the hillside again, letting his gaze pause here and there as if trying to remember each step he had taken in his earlier search. "Ain't that your motley colored dog hiding out there?

"She's mine," Mitchell admitted. "We've got this game we play. She sneaks around and every now and again, when I ain't lookin', she sidles-up and grabs my pant leg and starts tugging and growling like some vicious animal. Then I throw a piece of jerky at her and she snaps it out of the air. Then we start all over—unless I catch her at it first. Like now."

Mitchell whistled loudly, and the dog leaped to its feet and trotted to his side. He patted the dogs head, rubbed her ears, and fed her a small piece of jerky. "Stay out of trouble," he told the animal.

"It don't make any sense," Turner muttered. "I sent that Taggart kid back to town for a big ball of twine. Then I tied one end of the twine to a stick and wedged it in that pile of rocks.

"Hell, I walked circles around that pile every two feet, looking for anything—bones, clothing, soft dirt… I didn't find anything."

"Maybe you didn't look in the right place," Mitchell suggested abruptly.

"Hell, I know that already!"

"Did you look there?" Mitchell asked, pointing to where the motley-colored dog rooted happily at the base of Turner's rock pile.

"That spot ain't big enough for a grave," Turner objected. "She's probably after a mouse."

"Let's move some rocks and see," Mitchell suggested.

Susan lifted the hinged footrest that served as a lid for the small grain bin on the front of the wagon. Deftly, she untied a heavy string and opened the mouth of a fifty pound sack.

"Looks like Collin has two sacks of grain and a sack of oats in here," she said as Lynne handed her one of the four feedbags hanging from the side of the wagon. Susan took the bag, scooped it one-quarter full and traded it for a second. When the fourth bag was finished, she closed the lid and latched it in place.

"Do you think it will take long for Brother Mitchell to discover what happened to Aaron?" Lynne asked as they fed the team.

Susan shrugged, wishing that even now she were with Collin and investigating the site where the boys had found the skull. "I don't know. I guess it will depend on how difficult it is to track his movements and find the people who have had contact with him," she replied.

"I really think he's dead," the girl said bleakly, "and I feel so guilty."

"I don't see why you should feel guilty at all," Susan responded tartly. "The engagement was off. If anything happened to him, it was because of his own choices... not yours."

"I still feel guilty."

"Well, stop feeling guilty and start putting your life back together."

"*Your* life seems to have gone well. Salt Lake must be a wonderful place," the younger woman said congenially. Her eyes followed the Pratt kid as he hobbled the saddle horses and watered each of them from a large wooden bucket.

Susan rolled her eyes and brushed her hair back over one shoulder. "Until last month, things were normal enough," she admitted. "Collin was working for the territorial marshal two years ago when trouble started with Black Hawk. When things got bad about a year ago, Collin went south with his regiment of the Nauvoo Legion. He came back early this summer."

"And things haven't been the same?"

"Not quite. Some awful things must have happened while he was with the Legion. He told me about Nine Mile Canyon and how they were ambushed there. But when he came home, his job was gone and the marshal was taking a hard stance on plural marriage and arresting any cohabs he could find. Collin had to stay out of sight or be arrested. That went on for several weeks, until Brother Brigham asked Collin to go to Ogden and look for a missing girl."

"But at least you've had a life outside this valley," Lynne responded. "You've lived down in the valley. I'm only seventeen, but it's a whole different world up here. I'll bet there aren't more than fifteen hundred people between here and Park City. There's not a thing to do, and if I marry one of the eligible males up here, I'll just end up trapped on a farm somewhere."

"A farm isn't such a bad thing," Susan responded.

"Maybe not in Salt Lake or Provo," Lynne sighed, "but up here the season is short and winters are long and cold. It's not unusual to see snow in June and forty-below almost any winter night.

"I'm just not anxious to spend the rest of my life up here, and most of the girls I know feel the same way. It's hard to explain, but that's why I couldn't marry Aaron. He had no intention of giving me a life outside this valley. He and Nathan had already made a claim on half a section of land and were planning to go partners on a sheep ranch. Even if they had found that mine, they were going to build homes here and raise sheep."

Susan sighed wearily. "I wish I could help," she said thoughtfully. "But I'm not sure I understand what it is you're trying to tell me."

The girl frowned unhappily. "I don't know," she murmured quietly. "I guess I just don't want to marry and spend the rest of my life in this valley."

"Then don't," Susan said firmly. "I don't think anyone is going to force you into a life you don't want."

"I'd like to marry and have a family," the girl offered bleakly.

Susan thought for a moment. "How about this," she suggested suddenly. "You come to work for Sarah and me— help with the children and the housework... If you find the situation intolerable, we could help you find another more to you liking."

The girl's face broke into a grin. "That would be wonderful!"

"Don't count on it," Susan warned. "Collin has promised to build a house for each of us, and while there are only three children at the moment, there will be more. You could grow to hate us very quickly."

"Never! This is like an answer to my prayers."

"Very well... I think Collin will agree to set your pay at twenty-five dollars a month—you can have weekends off."

"Twenty-five dollars a month!"

"It's not as much as they pay at some of the lumber mills. Of course, you will have room and board as well..."

"It's more than fair," the girl objected. "I just didn't expect so much."

"If you save carefully," Susan suggested, "You might have a very nice dowry when you meet the right young man."

"If I can convince mother and father...."

"I'll talk with your mother," Susan offered. "She can convince your father."

"When shall I start?"

"How about now?" Susan suggested.

"Now?"

"Of course we're living out of this wagon at the moment," Susan admitted. "Sarah and I are looking at it as an extended holiday. The children are with our parents in Ogden, and we've been living like gypsies for the past week."

"It must be uncomfortably crowded," Lynne suggested as she eyed the narrow wagon.

"I think we're going to need another wagon and a second team," Susan responded. "I'll have Daniel take care of that tomorrow. Then we'll talk with your parents and get your things together."

Susan looked eastward, wondering how Collin and Deputy Turner were getting along.

"Tell me what you can remember about the day Aaron and Nathaniel left for Salt Lake," she told the girl.

Lynne stood thoughtfully for a moment then pointed east. "We were all having a picnic over near Lake Creek—not far from here, actually."

"Who is *we*?"

"Aaron, Nathan, Bradley Hunter, Jean Kelson, Steven Taggart, Zina Wilcox, Silvie Murdoc, and me."

"I'm surprised Nathan and Aaron didn't want to make an early start," Susan suggested.

"They did. But they were going down to Provo first. They planned to spend the night with family then go on to Salt Lake.

"It's only about twenty miles to Provo; so we talked them into having a picnic before they left. They didn't seem to mind, although Bradley Hunter was acting strangely, and Jean Kelson would hardly speak to anyone.

"Things went well enough I suppose… until Aaron said something awkward. I could see that Jean was upset, and finally, she just climbed on her horse and left. No one stayed long after that. Aaron and Nathan left for Provo, and the rest of us rode back to town."

"And no one saw either of them after that?"

"Deputy Turner says he talked with anyone who might have seen them along the way, but no one saw anything."

Susan shaded her eyes with one hand and gazed into the distance. To the West, the valley sloped into the foothills where the heights of the Wasatch Mountains rose like a wall of sheer, granite-like cliffs against the western sky. At the southern extent of the cliffs, Provo Canyon slashed the mountain range in two, leaving Timpanogos Peak and its formidable cliffs to the north. "I wonder if anyone might have been traveling up the canyon that day," she said.

Lynne drew back one of the nosebags and peered into its empty depths. "Brother Turner probably checked into that," she replied, "but if he found anyone who had, I never heard of it."

Susan looked at the younger woman thoughtfully. "It would be nearly impossible for anyone on the canyon road to have missed them, and they had no reason to leave the road or avoid other travelers.

"*If* there were other travelers," the girl advised.

"And if they actually ever intended to go to Provo or Salt Lake," Susan suggested suddenly.

"What do you mean?" Lynne demanded. "They said they were going to Salt Lake. Why would they do differently?"

"Any number of reasons," Susan replied. "Think about it… Nathan gives you a map and tells you it leads to a gold mine and warns you to keep quiet about it. That sounds like a man who is trying to protect a secret by placing it in the hands of someone he trusts. If they were concerned enough to do that, they may have tried to conceal their movements whenever they went looking for the mine."

The younger woman frowned and looked doubtful. "You think they never intended to go to Salt Lake…"

"I think it's possible. They may have thought they were close to discovering the location of the mine and made up the story about going to Salt Lake so no one would suspect what they were really doing."

"I suppose they could have," Lynne admitted reluctantly. "Nathan told me they had an old journal that they had found with the map. He said the journal held the key to the map and that neither was any good without the other.

"Aaron took the journal and hid it somewhere after he had memorized a few of the keys to the map. Nathan took the map and hid it until he gave it to me. But if all they did was go looking for their mine, why didn't they come back?"

Susan took her empty feedbag and hung it from the side of the wagon. "I don't know," she answered as they each took a second bag and grained the last two horses. "Maybe they were bushwhacked by the Utes, like Sheriff Hamilton thinks...."

"Maybe they struck the mother lode and never looked back," the girl suggested.

Susan frowned. "I don't think so," she answered thoughtfully.

Old Tom, the eight-year old roan gelding yanked on the nosebag, nearly dragging her to her knees. Susan yanked backward and cuffed the animal's muzzle. "You old bonehead," she barked.

"I should have let Daniel take care of this one," she told the girl. "He gets impatient, and if you're not careful he can pull your arms right out of the sockets."

"Your foreman seems like a rather placid fellow."

Susan looked up, realizing the girl's tone of voice suggested an interest that transcended idle curiosity. "Placid...," she parroted. "I'm not sure I would label Brother Pratt as a *placid fellow.*"

The girl glanced toward the creek where the Pratt kid had tied the riding horses and was now busy brushing down Mitchell's grulla. "He seems a lot like the boys up here— content to feed the animals and hoe the weeds in the fields."

Susan heard the sarcasm in the younger woman's voice and found herself frowning in spite of the sudden urge to laugh. "I don't think Brother Pratt fits your image of the typical farm boy," She responded. "Why don't we fix some lunch and take it out to Collin and Brother Turner?"

CHAPTER 6

23 September

*T*wo hours later, the Pratt kid tossed another shovel full of gravelly soil across the sage covered hillside. It was well past noon, and the kid was discovering blisters on an unprotected pair of hands.

"We ain't found nothin' but neck bones," he complained.

"That's because this fellow was buried standing straight up in this hole," Mitchell explained as he knelt in the shallow hole and with a smaller shovel, worked at removing the tightly packed soil from the exposed vertebrae. "You go careful, or you'll be cutting into other bones right soon," he warned.

The Pratt kid frowned and jogged the spade free of the soil. "I think I already did," he admitted reluctantly.

"Well don't stop digging," Mitchell commanded. "You can't make him any deader than he already is."

"I don't see why you're being so careful anyway," Turner grumbled. "Just dig him up and be done with it. It's too hot to be out here digging holes and frying our brains."

Mitchell paused, took his hat from his head and wiped his face and the back of his neck with a damp bandana.

"He's looking for more than bones," Susan explained. "He's looking for anything unusual."

"Whole damned thing is unusual, if you ask me," Turner complained. He tugged at his sweat soaked collar and turned his back to the afternoon sun. "Why would you stand a fellow up like that. Why not just bury him and toss a little dirt over him? It would be a lot less work."

"That's something I'd like to find out," Mitchell answered. "This ground is loose now, but when this hole was first dug, the ground was packed hard. You couldn't just come out here and shovel out a hole deep enough to stand a fellow in. This would have been hard pick and shovel work."

"Don't make any sense," Turner muttered.

"No, it doesn't," Mitchell agreed.

Susan stood quietly to one side, with her parasol shading the upper half of her body from the heat of the sun and her shadow cast upon Mitchell's sweat soaked back.

"It may have been dug at an earlier time for some other purpose," she offered. She stepped slightly to the west, keeping her shadow on the moving form of her husband.

"There's no reason to dig a well on this side of the hill, if that's what you're thinking," Turner objected.

Susan shook her head. "That's not what I'm thinking," she responded. She turned toward Lynne and called out to the girl who sat twenty feet away steadfastly refusing to watch as the digging proceeded to unearth the remains she was certain belonged to Aaron Stokes.

"You told me Aaron had started building a house," Susan reminded the girl. "Was it near here?"

Lynne glanced at the hole where Mitchell and Daniel worked and shook her head. "No; it was about a quarter of a mile west of here."

"Oh."

"But Nathan's house was only two or three-hundred feet south of here."

"Mitchell looked up. He felt the heat of the sun on his back and the sweat pouring from beneath his hat onto the back of his neck. "I didn't see any signs of a house," he responded, thinking the steepness of the hill made it an unlikely place for a house.

"Around the curve of the hill… There's a natural depression in the hillside. Nathan had only put in a few foundation stones."

Mitchell looked up at Susan. "What are you thinking," he asked tiredly.

"Just an idea," she responded cryptically.

"So tell us," Mitchell prompted.

Susan smiled and brushed a stray lock of hair back from her face. "It could be the privy," she suggested casually.

"The privy!" Turner exclaimed.

"It's close enough," Susan defended.

"She's right," Mitchell concluded suddenly. "No one would dig a hole in ground this hard, unless they had a good reason, Larkin must have dug the pit as a makeshift privy while he was building the house. It's out of sight and far enough away from the house for some privacy. Once the house was finished, he could fill in the hole and dig a new one in a better location."

"Whoever killed this fellow must have discovered the hole and made use of it," Turner suggested.

"Or they knew right where to find it," Susan countered.

Mitchell kept silent, letting his thoughts return to the excavation and the oddities suddenly revealed by the two probing shovels. "Now don't that beat all," he murmured quietly.

* * *

"I don't understand what you found," the Campbell girl complained as the group rode back to Mitchell's camp.

"Quick lime," Mitchell responded. "That hole wasn't very deep, and the bottom half of it was filled with quick lime."

"I don't know what that means," the girl admitted.

"Powdered lime, mixed with water," the Pratt kid explained. "Folks mix it in mortar; it helps the mortar set up."

"It's a chemical reaction," Mitchell added. "Water and lime mixed like pancake batter. Some people say the quick lime heats up to about five-hundred degrees, and lime is very caustic."

"Why would you put quick lime in a grave?" the girl asked cautiously.

Turner frowned and shifted uneasily in the saddle. "Probably trying to destroy the body or evidence of the crime," he suggested.

Mitchell's glance tightened into a scowl as he shook his head in disagreement. "I don't think so," he answered. "I think this fellow was alive when he was put into that hole."

"That's crazy!" Tuner exclaimed.

"I don't understand," Lynne objected.

"It was the spikes, wasn't it," the Pratt kid suggested. The kid's upper lip curled in a snarl of distaste as he realized the direction Mitchell's thoughts had taken. "You think that fellow was tortured, don't you."

Mitchell frowned and looked at the two women. Susan and Sarah would hound him until he gave them every detail they felt necessary to solve the puzzle, but he wondered about the Campbell girl.

The girl was still too young to be involved in such a hideous affair and her life in the Heber Valley had been secluded and insulated from some of the more gruesome aspects of human nature.

Susan edged her mount closer and pinched up her face in imitation of Mitchell's unfriendly squint. "What spikes?" She inquired grimly.

Mitchell glanced toward the Campbell girl. "I think we should talk about it later," he suggested.

Susan flashed a look toward the Campbell girl then smiled disarmingly. "We certainly *shall* talk about it later, *Brother Mitchell.*"

Mitchell flinched at the *Brother Mitchell* and mirrored Susan's imitation of the Mitchell squint. "Stop pinchin' up you face like that. You're scarin' the horses," he grumbled.

"I am not."

"You're scarin' me. What happens if your face gets stuck? I'd be stuck with a wife with a face like a prune!"

Susan's pent up breath, exploded from between her tightly pinched lips, as she burst into laughter.

Mitchell shifted in the saddle, searching for a more comfortable position—one that might ease the ache in his back.

"You're a fine one to be talking about prune faces," Susan objected.

Mitchell grinned and straightened himself into a caricature of a British gentleman they had once met in Salt Lake. "I scowl only when necessary; I'll have you know," he intoned, mimicking the Britton's accent.

"You scowl at everyone," Susan protested stubbornly.

Mitchell opened his mouth to reply, but stopped suddenly as he caught sight of the wagon and their camp in the distance.

Something is definitely wrong, he thought, realizing that the camp appeared as a chaotic jumble of colors and shapes rather than an organized and recognizable grouping of objects in a familiar setting.

"Something is wrong with the camp," he informed Susan.

Susan shaded her eyes and peered into the distance. "I can't see anything wrong," She replied evenly.

Mitchell heard the pensive appeal in the girl's voice, and knew that both sisters had things of value in the camp—things neither woman wanted lost or damaged.

"Too much color," he answered soberly, feeling a strong sense of unease, yet unable to explain adequately. "Usually, I can see the white canvas of the wagon top," he explained. "Everything else just blends into the background."

Susan stared toward the camp. "Too much color," she sighed reluctantly.

Mitchell reined the dun to a halt and waited for Turner and the two straggling teens to catch up.

"Something wrong?" Turner asked when he saw Mitchell standing in the stirrups, straining for a better look at the camp.

"Pretty much," Mitchell replied. "Looks like someone has busted up our camp."

He reached out and took Susan by the hand. "You wait here with Daniel and Lynne while the deputy and I see what's going on down there."

"Why don't we all look?"

Mitchell frowned, remembering that Biggs and Dunford were in town, and it would only take the mention of his name to start more trouble than the town of Heber had seen in its entire existence. "Nice people don't ride into a strange camp and wreck it," he pointed out, "and I don't want you shot because you give the benefit of a doubt to someone who doesn't deserve it."

Susan planted her fists on her hips. "You could get shot too," she objected.

Mitchell lifted his hat and wiped the sweat from his forehead. "I'm going to shoot anything that moves down there," he growled. "You stay here so it ain't you I'm shootin' at."

Five minutes later, Mitchell reined in the dun and from a distance of twenty yards, surveyed the damage. Quilts, blankets, sheets, and clothing were strewn everywhere. Pots, pans, and utensils lay scattered on the ground, while flour, oats, and grain covered everything like dust after a windstorm.

"Looks like a tornado or somethin' come through here," Turner suggested dryly.

"Or something," Mitchell echoed. "I don't see the horses," he grumbled. "If they didn't steal 'em, they run 'em off."

"They'll turn up somewhere, if they've just been run off," Turner advised. "If they been stole, we'll have a hard time findin' 'em."

Mitchell looked hard at the wreck of the camp and felt a hot anger rising up from the pit of his stomach. It flared up in an instant and burned like Dante's inferno.

For a moment he sat quietly, waiting for the rage to cool. When he spoke, his voice held an edge. "I'll get 'em back," he said grimly.

Turner's mouth tightened, but if he had anything to say he kept it to himself. He knew little of the man who rode beside him, other than the rumors that drifted through the valley from time to time—rumors of a reformed gunman—a man hard to provoke yet hard as nails when pushed too far—a man rumored to be harder to kill and more deadly than Rockwell.

Turner had heard the rumors of Nine Mile Canyon and a running gun battle that had left five legionnaires and seventeen renegade Utes dead and only Mitchell left alive amidst the carnage. Even now, he knew there were remnants of Black Hawk's renegades who would take great honor in killing the white man they called Shenabavegan. As far as Turner was concerned, a man Ute warriors believed had been touched by God's hand and rode with the angel of death was not a man to cross when he was in a snit.

Mitchell nodded toward the camp. "Ride careful through there," he advised. "Susan will knock us in the head with a fryin' pan if one of these horses tromps on a quilt."

"I hear that," Turner responded.

Slowly, the two men circled the camp.

"Nobody around," said Turner, when they had checked the inside of the wagon and dropped ropes around the necks of two of the missing horses.

Mitchell glanced back toward the camp where the Pratt kid and the two women were already trying to assess the damage.

"The other four are probably somewhere nearby," Mitchell concluded, as Turner helped him secure the two strays to a wagon wheel.

"The others may wander in, once they smell your campfire and realize there's grain and oats to be had over here," Turner suggested.

Suddenly, Mitchell realized that Turner was anxious to be on his way. What prompted the deputy, Mitchell had no idea, but the man was ready to go, and Mitchell saw no reason to keep the fellow if he had other business.

"I want to ride back and load up those bones," Turner offered. "We came here for a sack. Remember?"

Mitchell smiled. "Now that you mention it...."

Spotting the wreck of their camp had driven all thought of the bones from his mind, and it had been nearly an hour since they had left that lonely grave site.

"I need a gunnysack or something to put 'em in, so I can get 'em back to town," Turner prompted.

Mitchell glanced around the camp, noting the scattered grain from the wagon's feed bin. "Should be half a dozen sacks lying around," he offered. "Take what you want."

"Two or three oughta be plenty."

Mitchell glanced around the camp and spotted the Pratt kid as he moved about the camp, gathering household goods and sorting them into several groups under Susan's watchful eye.

"Turner needs a couple of empty grain sacks," said Mitchell as the kid passed by.

"I used 'em up already," the kid reported. "Only found three of 'em anyway."

Mitchell frowned, remembering the grain that had been stored in the bin at the front of the wagon. There had been at least six bags of grain when they had started out from Provo.

"I guess I can dump a couple of 'em in the wash tub or something," the kid offered.

"The others are around somewhere," Mitchell concluded. "Empty the one's you have into the wash tub. We'll get more when we go into town."

"We'll need more than that," Susan confided as she joined them. "Lynne and I have looked over most of the damage, and it's the food that suffered most—scattered and trampled into the dirt. We might be able to salvage some of it, but it would be better to restock everything—just in case."

Mitchell glanced across the camp to where the Campbell girl stood folding one of Sarah's hand stitched quilts. "We'll need another wagon and a team," he concluded, remembering Susan's news that she had hired the girl as a housekeeper.

"Better make it two wagons and two teams," Susan advised. "We can use one wagon for our supplies. Lynne will need the other for her things."

Mitchell nodded. With Susan's statement, he realized that the Campbell girl would be bringing all of her belongings with her. The prospect didn't bother him, as they had plenty of their own belongings jammed into the restrictive confines of the first wagon. The additional wagon would simply give them all a little more room.

"Lynne and I will make a list of household things we need to replace," Susan proposed. "I think you and Daniel should decide what we need for the camp."

"Okay," Mitchell agreed, grateful that Susan was taking charge of the household needs. Counting up the broken dishes might not have been a problem, but calculating how much flour, meat, or potatoes would be needed to fill the larder was a chore he had no desire to be involved in. Probably, it was no worse than calculating how much feed they would need for the herd of new animals Susan proposed, but somehow calculating feed for the animals and deciding the exact type and quantity of new tack they would need seemed less daunting.

Mitchell watched as Turner tossed three empty sacks across his saddle horn and turned his mount east, toward the grave site and the remains of Larkin's foundation.

"I'll head back into town, after I gather up what's left of the fellow," said the Deputy. "If you need me, I'll be at the office until about four. After that, I'll be out at my place lookin' for my chickens. In fact, why don't you all come out to my place for dinner? The Campbell girl can show you the way. I'll head home a little early and let Selma know you're all coming."

Mitchell glanced around the camp. "I expect we'll be headed into town right soon," he answered. "In fact..." He turned to the Pratt kid. "Why don't you ride into town, Daniel, and rent a horse and buggy. Then come back for Susan and Lynne. We should still have time enough to look for wagons and horses."

The Pratt kid shot a quick look toward the saddle horses now tied near the creek with the two recaptured animals. Mitchell knew what the kid was thinking—that they could all just ride into town—but it was a hot, dusty ride, and Mitchell was sure the two women would prefer the relative comfort of the buggy if given a choice.

"When you rent the buggy," Mitchell cautioned, "tell Murphy what's happened and let him know we're on the way."

The Pratt kid nodded and shot a look toward the Campbell girl. "She says she's comin' to work for you," he said casually.

"That a problem?" Mitchell responded.

"Nope... just wondered."

* * *

Sarah stood quietly at the kitchen sink and watched as Selma Turner finished plucking the feathers from a plump hen and removed a round metal plate from the top of her flat-topped coal-burning stove. Immediately, heat rose upward from the burning coals below, filling the room with a new wave of heat.

"I think we're going to need at least three more birds to feed this bunch," she announced as she held the plucked bird over the flames, scorching the skin and removing any down that might have remained after the plucking.

"As soon as I get these pin-feathers out, I'll ask Jared to bring in three more."

Sarah glanced at Susan and saw the smile on her sister's face. "Why don't you ask Collin to get the chickens for you," she suggested.

Selma Turner looked up from her bird and frowned.

"You folks are our guests," she objected. "I don't even feel right about letting you wash up those dishes."

"Collin won't mind," Sarah insisted.

Susan nodded and looked out of the window to where Mitchell sat quietly in the shade of a large, full-leafed elm. He sat with his back against the trunk, his head tipped back, his eyes closed, and to all appearances, asleep.

"We have him do it all the time," Susan advised gleefully.

Selma Turner shook her head. "I'd better have Jared do it," she replied. "Those chickens are half wild, and they just run in circles all around anyone who tries to get near them. Sometimes, Jared gets hopping mad trying to catch one."

Sarah laughed. "Then you must definitely let Collin do it."

"You'll not regret it," Susan predicted.

Five minutes later, Susan led the way to the southwest corner of Jared Turner's barn. The five women crowded up near the splintery, sun-dried planks of one wall, as Susan peeked around the corner to spy on Mitchell's activities near the hen house.

"There are about a dozen hens milling about," she whispered to the others. "He's just deciding which three he wants."

"They'll go mad the second he tries to grab one of them," Selma whispered.

Susan shook her head. "You'll see...."

For several long moments, Mitchell watched the flock mill about in a chaotic dance. Their stuttering, head-thrusting walk seemed almost humorous as they marched about, pecking mindlessly at the dusty ground. Yet, not mindless—there was intelligence there, and a sense of purpose. What that purpose might be, was not all that clear at the moment, unless it included meat for the table.

He watched, feeling the world grow quiet and distant, yet hearing Mort's voice like a familiar whisper on the air.

"There is a purpose in everything. Life is like a garden path" the old man had said. *"God looks around and says: 'Here's a little bit of intelligence. I think I can make something of this fellow.'*

"So he stands a fellow up on his hind legs in front of this big gate an' says: 'You got the smarts to handle this, so here's what you do. Go through this gate and walk the path straight through to the next gate. You can sniff the flowers and play, but don't wander around in the weeds or you'll get all dirty. We're gonna have dinner in a while, an' if you're all dirty, I'll have to send you to your room with no dinner. You don't have a lot of time, but it will be all you need. I'll call you in when it's time, an' you come on through that next gate. Be good. Don't be mean to the other folks in the garden, or I might have to send someone to bring you home early.'"

The old man's whisper faded from Mitchell's mind, and the world was silent. The chickens stood still, as though waiting. Three of them cocked their heads and looked Mitchell in the eye as though offering themselves.

"Come home," Mitchell whispered gently.

Life fled from three sets of eyes, and Mitchell snatched the Colt from its holster. Fire leaped from the muzzle in a flare just a heartbeat long.

Selma Turner stared at the chickens that would soon be in her frying pan.

"He shot their heads off," she whispered. "I never saw anyone move so fast. Why did he shoot them?"

Susan shrugged. "He says he hates wringing their necks and taking an axe to them."

Selma Turner stared at the chickens a moment longer. "I think I can understand that," she admitted gravely. "I've never liked killing them myself."

The women watched as Mitchell stooped and retrieved the birds.

"We'd better get back to the house." Sarah suggested.

But as the others turned and hurried back to the house, Sarah caught Susan by the sleeve and held her back.

"I noticed something odd," she said anxiously.

"What was that?" Susan prompted.

"I thought...."

"Good heavens!" Susan laughed. "What did you think?"

Sarah sighed. "Those birds were dead before Collin even fired a shot!" She hissed.

For a moment, Susan stared quietly into her sister's eyes.

"Of course they were."

CHAPTER 7

24 September

*L*ate the next morning, Mitchell removed his hat and wiped the sweat from his forehead with a dry sleeve. Quietly, he replaced the hat and glared at Feldman. The dark haired farmer stood bare headed in the sun and leaned against the wooden fence of the pig pen. The raw stench of the pen stung Mitchell's nostrils like a handful of pins fresh from one of Sarah's bobbin lace pillows.

"I guess it's plain to see that I ain't no great shakes as a farmer," Feldman muttered.

Mitchell glanced quickly around the farmyard. "I'd say fifty percent of the job is just feeding your stock and keeping your pens clean and repaired. May not seem like it, but a fellow is always feeding someone or mucking out the pens.

"I've got a personal dislike for pig crap myself. That stuff will burn the hairs right out of your nose. But cows are the worst for filling up a pen. I swear a cow can drop its own weight in crap every day. You feed 'em hay from a trough and they'll fill the area around it damn quick."

Feldman shook his head. "I ain't doin' very well," he admitted.

"You built all this," Mitchell suggested, nodding toward the house and the out-buildings in general.

"Naw... I bought it all from a fellow named Davis about two years ago. Him and his boys started the place back in sixty-three. By the time I come along they'd had enough of the winters up here, and I didn't know no better. Now I'm stuck here, unless I can sell out. You ain't interested, are you?"

Mitchell shook his head. "Nice enough place, but winters at forty below ain't my idea of a happy home. I'd spend all my time cutting and hauling firewood."

"That ain't no lie," Feldman agreed.

"That why you wanted in with Stokes and Larkin? The money I mean... a little gold would go along way toward getting you out of here and set up somewhere else."

"I offered 'em the farm to buy in at ten percent. They just laughed at me. I went down to five percent before I realized they had their minds made up and nothin' would change, no matter what I offered."

"So you followed them."

"I tried, but I ain't much good with a horse, and I could never keep up with 'em. Once I lost sight of 'em it was no use goin' on."

"Did you ever go out to the Larkin boy's place?"

"You mean that pile of rocks he was tryin' to turn into a house?"

"That's the place."

"Yeah, I been there."

Mitchell nodded. "I'm curious," he confided.

"About what?"

"About Nathan Larkin and his house building... Was he making any progress?"

"Not much from what I could tell. He dug down a couple of feet and leveled everything out and started hauling in a bunch of rocks. Best I could see... he was makin' a tight little pad of rocks to set the house on. Looked real sturdy to me, but then I don't know much about that sort of thing."

Mitchell studied the farmer from the corner of his eye. "Was he using lime for the mortar?"

Feldman frowned and looked at the ground. "Could be... He had a few bags of something stacked over near one end of the pad. I suppose that could have been lime."

Mitchell leaned forward, resting his forearms on the top rail of the pen. "You ever help with the stone work?"

Feldman grunted humorlessly. "Hell no. I ain't no good at that sort of thing. Any help he got came from his brothers or that Stokes kid."

"And they helped with the mortar?"

"How the hell would I know? Why are you askin' anyway?"

"Just curious about what was going on up there. It seems a little odd that a fellow who was putting all that effort into building a house should just drop everything and run off like that."

"They figured to find that mine. I guess that's all they cared about by then, 'cause neither one of 'em did much of anything once they found that old map."

Mitchell's eyes narrowed at the mention of the map. "They had a map?" He asked casually.

"Sure. They found the map and an old journal at some old Spanish camp back in the mountains somewhere."

"You saw the map and the journal?"

"Naw. Ed Kelson told us about 'em one time."

"Kelson?"

"Yep. He come snooping around here one time, gettin' all friendly like. Askin' how I was doin'. After a while, he got down to what he was really after. He started askin' if I knew about the map or the journal and did the two of 'em ever let me get a look at the map.

"I told him that pair wasn't about to show me or anybody else a map, if they even had one. After that, Kelson just climbed on his horse and left. Since then, he ain't spoke more than two words to me unless he can't avoid it."

Feldman frowned unhappily. "Now, you answer me a question... What the hell is goin' on? You ain't askin' all these questions 'cause you think they got all religious on the way down to Provo and headed off to save some gentiles from their wicked ways."

Mitchell shook his head. "No," he replied. "I don't think they went off on a mission. I never even thought of it. I did telegraph Provo and Salt Lake to see if they got themselves thrown in jail, but no one had ever heard of them."

"You think they got themselves bushwhacked don't you?"

"Did you know Larkin had started digging a privy near that foundation?"

"No, but it don't surprise me none. It don't take long to get tired of running for the trees whenever nature calls."

"We found a man's bones buried in that hole," Mitchell responded.

Feldman groaned loudly and shook his head. "That's bad," he muttered. "Which one?"

Mitchell shook his head. "Larkin, maybe. But there was no way to be certain."

"Accident?"

"Not a chance. His cheekbone was broken. There was no sign of any clothing. Someone had thrown him naked into the hole, nailed his wrists to a couple of chunks of wood, and then poured quick lime in the hole."

Feldman swallowed hard and cursed under his breath. "Trying to destroy the body?" He asked bleakly.

"I doubt it. It looked like he was deliberately tortured."

"The gold mine," Feldman hissed.

Mitchell shrugged. "Looks like it. I don't know how long a fellow would last—up to his waist in quick lime. That stuff will burn your skin anyway, and it gets hotter than hell when you mix it with water and the chemical reaction gets going."

"Who the hell would do something like that!"

"That's what I'd like to find out."

"Look!" Feldman objected. "I admit I wanted in on the deal and I tried following them a couple of times, but I never had nothin' to do with this. A fellow would have to be insane to do something' like that."

"Quite likely."

"Well, I didn't!" Feldman snapped. "And I don't know anybody who would! Even old Kelson ain't that sick!"

"I never said you had anything to do with it," advised Mitchell. "I'm just trying to get a feel for what might have been going on and who might have wanted that mine bad enough to kill for it."

"Nobody I know," muttered Feldman.

"It's possible someone from outside the valley got wind of what they were up to," suggested Mitchell. "Did you ever notice any outsiders talking with them or following them?"

"I don't think so."

"What about that bunch hanging around over on Lake Creek?"

"I don't think they showed up 'til early last spring... At least I never seen any of 'em 'til then."

"What about folks in the valley?"

"I already told you," Feldman snapped angrily. "Why don't you go pester somebody else."

"I plan on it," Mitchell growled. "I plan on pestering everyone I can, until I find out who killed Larkin and what happened to Stokes."

"Maybe Stokes done it."

"Maybe... maybe not. Mostly, I don't see any reason why Stokes would go to all that trouble.

"You say no one else up here had reason to do it, but I don't know folks up here, so as far as I'm concerned anyone might have had a reason. The point being that someone did kill him and they did a damn hard job of it.

"Most likely, those bones are what's left of Nathan Larkin. That means he never left the valley the day of the picnic. If he did, he came back and was killed before anyone knew he was back.

"I like the second scenario better than the first, but that raises the question of where they went that day and what brought Larkin back. Half a dozen people or more had some suspicion that the two of them were headed into the mountains again, and any one of them could have followed them and bushwhacked them, including you."

"The hell I did!"

"But let's suppose for a minute that you didn't do it. Who are we left with? The kids who were at the picnic? Kelson? Some stranger? The Utes maybe?

"I think we can forget the Utes. It isn't their style. They might ambush a fellow and cut him to ribbons, but I don't think they would fiddle around with quick lime.

"Now, a stranger might have done it, if he happened to find the lime *and* the privy. But that seems to be stretching coincidence a little far—don't you think?"

"I wouldn't know. I don't even like thinkin' about it."

Mitchell shrugged and looked the unhappy Feldman in the eye. "Well… you should think about *this*, whoever killed Larkin probably wanted the map, and it's likely they've killed Stokes as well. If they didn't get the map, who do you think they will be watching now? You and the Hunter kid seem to be the only ones who were ever able to follow Stokes and Larkin. Suppose the killer gets the notion you know more than you've let on?"

"That's crazy. If I knew how to find that gold, I would have got it before now and got the hell out of the valley!"

Mitchell unhitched the dun and climbed into the saddle. "You know anyone who owns a crossbow?"

"Crossbow?"

"Yep; looks like a bow on a rifle stock."

"I know what a crossbow is."

"Do you know anyone who owns one?"

"No. I don't."

Sarah awoke to the gentle stroking of Mitchell's fingers through her hair. The intensity of the sunlight pouring past the open canvas at the back of the wagon and the fact that Mitchell was fully dressed told her it was late in the morning, and the random clatter of metal against metal told her that someone was busily making a late breakfast or an early lunch.

The smell of cooking food, mingled with the smoke of a campfire, made her mouth water and her stomach complain, and for the first time in two days she wanted to be up and doing. Her first day of recuperating at the Campbell house had been one filled with odd dreams, fitful sleep, and an aching head.

The ache in her head had calmed to a distant, yet bearable pain, and she had slept deeply through the night, after Collin had settled her within a deep nest of quilts in the family's newly acquired wagon.

"Feeling better?"

Mitchell's voice was low and gentle, and Sarah felt a sudden surge of gladness at his presence.

"Much better," she answered quietly.

"I was afraid the trip from town would be too much for your bruised head."

"In a pile of quilts like this? I hardly felt anything. I think I slept most of the way."

"Sleep is good for you."

"I think I've slept enough for a while. I smell food, and I'm half starved."

Mitchell smiled. "Susan and Lynne will have lunch ready in just a few minutes. We all decided to let you sleep and feed you when you were ready."

Sarah let Mitchell help her to a sitting position and shift some of the pile behind her. When she had eased back into the newly arranged softness, she looked into his hazel eyes. "What have you been up to, Brother Mitchell, and what have I missed while you and everyone else got to play detective?"

Mitchell barked out a humorless laugh. "My dear, I don't think the Mitchell's are welcome in this part of the territory."

"I get the feeling we're not just talking about the knot on the back of my head."

"No we're not."

Sarah sat quietly and listened as Mitchell brought her up to date on the events of the past two days. When the tale came to its conclusion, Sarah tipped her head back and stared at the inside of the wagon's canvas top.

"You've been very busy," she concluded.

"More running back and forth to town than anything else," Mitchell replied. "I'm not sure we've discovered anything remotely useful."

"But you have some ideas," she prompted.

"A few."

Sarah waited while Mitchell gathered his thoughts. She knew her husband as a quiet, thinking sort of man—a man who generally kept his thoughts to himself—thereby giving the impression, to those who didn't know better, that he was a man who took little interest in anything beyond the price of seed corn, or how many sacks of potatoes he should hold back for next year's planting.

"I don't think the fire at Murphy's store was intended to hurt anyone," Mitchell said thoughtfully. "That bolt shot right past my face. Close enough to singe my eyebrows, but it hit the one place in that store where it would do the least amount of damage and still keep us occupied putting it out."

Sarah nodded in agreement. "To draw Deputy Turner away from the sheriff's office," she conceded.

"And to warn me off," Mitchell added.

"And being a typical male, you failed to heed the warning, inciting the culprit to destroy our camp."

"It's possible."

"I hear reluctant agreement in your voice."

"Yesterday, some fellows rode into town," Mitchell admitted. "*They* might have wrecked the camp."

"And why would these fellows want to destroy our belongings?" Sarah asked quietly, dreading the answer she thought she already knew.

Mitchell frowned unhappily. "I knew these fellows a while back. They would be extremely happy to wreck my life in any way they can."

"You really think they saw you in town, then somehow found our camp and destroyed it?"

"Seems a little far fetched," Mitchell admitted.

"Still possible," Sarah conceded doubtfully. "Tell me about the bones you found."

"Now *that* sounds even more far fetched," Mitchell confided. "We found the bones in a shallow pit. I don't know if it was good luck or bad, but Turner had piled some rocks right on top of it the day he went out to pick up the skull. We never would have found it, if your dog hadn't taken an interest in that rock pile."

Sarah smiled. "Such a smart little doggie."

"Smart enough to eat all my jerky," Mitchell complained. "That animal is a bottomless pit."

"You were telling me about another pit," Sarah prompted.

"Yeah... Well, there was bones in it all right."

"Were bones," Susan corrected as she climbed into the back of the wagon and smiled disarmingly at Mitchell. "You were supposed to be telling me this too. Remember?"

"Sorry. I got carried away. I should have waited."

"Don't stop now; I want to know what you found and didn't let me see."

Mitchell scowled, remembering how he had blocked Susan's view of the excavation for the few critical moments it had taken to hand the offending implements over into Turner's waiting hands.

"Lime," he said, hesitating to tackle either of the grisly discoveries. "That pit was only three feet deep and just big enough to drop that fellow in on his knees.

That left him just about neck deep. The killer filled the hole about halfway with quick lime, then stretched the fellow's arms out on top of the ground and drove a couple of twenty-penny nails through his wrists and into a couple of chunks of wood.

"Both arms were broken. I don't know if that happened before of after the fellow died."

Susan's face lost its color. "That's what Daniel meant when he said *torture*. You think the man was still alive when he was dropped in that hole!"

"Yes, I do."

Sarah sat quietly for a moment, her face as pale as her sister's. "Do you think it was Aaron Stokes?" she asked reluctantly.

"Or Larkin," Mitchell admitted grimly. "The killer must have known about the mine and his victim wouldn't tell."

"Twisted sort of way to get someone to talk," Susan muttered darkly.

Mitchell scowled and looked out of the back of the wagon toward the brush covered hills to the south. "Twisted, yes," he agreed. "But it gives us a little more information about the killer. That's more than we had before."

The two women looked at one another then turned on Mitchell. "What information about the killer? They demanded in unison.

"Just little things. Two things to begin with."

"Such as?" Susan prodded.

"The quick lime for one thing. I think it definitely suggests a white man—someone who knew prolonged contact with quicklime would be very painful. And someone who knew Larkin."

"How so?" Sarah prompted.

"Most Indians around here are Utes, and I doubt many of them are familiar with quick lime. They have their own ways. They might throw him in a hole and leave him buried up to his neck, but I don't think they would take the time to haul lime and water up there.

"Whoever killed Larkin, if it *was* Larkin, must have known him well enough to know where he had dug the privy—someone who knew about the lime and had a willingness to torture a man to death."

"That should limit the number of people who could have done it to several dozen." Susan muttered dryly.

"Probably," Mitchell admitted. "But there is one person who easily fits the parameters and had ample opportunity and possibly even the motivation to kill Larkin."

The two women flashed surprised looks at one another. "Whom do you propose as the best fit for these *parameters?*" Sarah asked, emphasizing her last word.

Mitchell frowned, realizing his mistake in using a word consisting of more than three syllables.

"Stokes!" Susan exclaimed. "I hadn't ever considered him. But he might have had the *motivation*. They could have had a falling out."

Sarah knitted her eyebrows in thought. "You're suggesting that Stokes tortured Larkin. Why?"

Mitchell shook his head. "I don't know," he admitted. "Lynne said Larkin left a map and a small bag of gold with her for safekeeping. That bag of gold suggests they had found something. Stokes may have thought Larkin had found the mine and was holding out on him."

Sarah frowned and shook her head in disbelief. "Lynne said Larkin and Stokes are cousins and have been friends since they were little boys. I have a hard time believing that either one of them could do such a thing. I can imagine them knocking one another all around the barnyard, but not this...."

Susan hesitated for a moment then climbed into the wagon. "If it wasn't Stokes, then it had to be someone who knew what Larkin and Stokes were up to, and if the killer got the information he wanted by killing Larkin, he's either looking for the mine or he's already found it."

Sarah nodded in agreement. "Susan's right," she concluded. "But I think there is something we can look for that the killer may not be able to hide."

Mitchell leaned forward, anticipating Sarah's thought. "Unfinished work?" he asked.

"Yes.... It's plain to see how little either Stokes or Larkin accomplished on the homes they were building. It seems evident that anyone caught up in treasure hunting devotes less and less time to their everyday chores. Their fields might be planted or watered erratically. Crops or animals might go untended. It certainly seems to be the pattern that took hold of Larkin and Stokes."

With a sigh, Mitchell picked up his hat and brushed at the dust it had collected. "You both make good sense," he admitted.

For a moment, the three were silent, until Susan raised one finger and shifted her attention to the open farmlands beyond the camp. "Rider coming in," she said casually. "Looks like Mort."

The old man reached the camp just as Sarah finished dressing and climbed down from the wagon.

"Hoped I'd catch you before everyone was out and about for the day," he said cheerfully. "I brought back your feed sacks, plus two of the ones that were missing."

He draped the sacks over the rear wheel of the new chuck wagon and drew in a chest full of air. "Smelled that food half a mile away," he groaned happily. "Mind if I have breakfast with you? Or should I call it lunch?"

Sarah smiled and took the old man by the arm. "It's lunch," she answered, "and you're welcome to eat with us any time. And you know it."

"Where'd you get those sacks?" asked Mitchell, when the old man was seated on a log near the fire and happily shoveling eggs into his mouth.

"Turner asked me to bring 'em out," the old man responded between scoops. "Said the bones was gone, and he didn't need 'em after all. Said he found two of your missing sacks near the pit, and he figured the other was used to haul off the bones."

Mitchell scowled in disbelief. "Someone stole those bones?"

"Every one of 'em."

CHAPTER 8

2 September

Susan stood at the edge of the boardwalk and drew her cloak a little closer at the throat. Not another woman in town seemed to be dressed for colder weather, but the late afternoon breeze held the chill of an early autumn and gave her goose bumps whenever it forced its way beneath her cloak and caressed her with its cold fingers.

On the opposite boardwalk, near Murphy's store, the wind grabbed at the skirts of four gossiping women and lashed the hand-woven cloth against their legs like four flags tethered and dancing against eight stout poles. The quartet ignored the flapping skirts, grabbing instead for the bonnets that threatened to leap from their heads and skip down the dusty street into the oblivion of sagebrush and tumbleweeds.

For a moment, Susan watched the women, realizing how alike they seemed in their dress and in their mannerisms—a hand raised in a careless gesture, to be mirrored moments later—four matched pairs of black, high-button shoes—each shiny and new. The similarities were striking, yet at the same time revealing. The young women were in their late teens or early twenties. They were unmarried. Their families had money, or at least wanted people to think they did, and they considered themselves to be the cream of the valley's crop of eligible females.

To Susan, these characteristics were the self-evident behavioral traits tied to Mormon culture throughout the territory. Intuitively, she realized that her own behavior was intricately interwoven with those same cultural patterns—patterns instilled in her childhood, accepted in her youth, and now part of the tightly woven fabric of her faith and her very existence.

Silently, she smiled, feeling the contentment of familiarity and a sense of *home*. She knew some women in the territory struggled with their culture and the hardships of life in the Great Basin, but for Susan life had been good, and she had neither regrets for the past nor any desire to change the present or the future it might conceive.

Her thoughts had hardly touched upon the future and the wonders that might lie ahead, when two of the young women broke off their conversation and steered a course directly toward her watch point on the edge of the boardwalk. The pair was nearly upon her before she realized their intent was to make contact.

"You sound as though you have a strong dislike for Aaron Stokes," Susan suggested minutes later.

Jean Kelson looked up and fixed her brown eyes on Susan's face. "Not at all," she responded thoughtfully. "We were good friends."

"A friendship that survived all the rumors...." Susan offered.

"And why shouldn't it? Aaron wasn't responsible for the rumors. And he was certainly more supportive than anyone else in this godforsaken hole."

"Was Nathan Larkin a friend too?"

"Just a friendly acquaintance. His family owns a small farm about three miles north of town. They're quite poor, and the farm has slowly gone to pieces since Nathan's father fell with his horse."

"I understand the sons are taking care of the place."

"The boys are doing the best they can; I suppose.... But Nathan is the oldest and the family relied heavily on him. When he left, the burden fell on the younger boys. They do the best they can, but not all the chores on a farm can be done by children or crippled old men."

"Did Nathan or Aaron ever talk to you about their plans or what they were up to when they went off on one of their trips?"

"Why should they? I'm just a girl. Why would they tell me anything about their manly pursuits?" The girl's voice had taken a slight edge.

"They must have talked to someone," Susan replied disarmingly. "If they didn't talk to you about it, who might they have taken into their confidence? I find it hard to believe they didn't let something slip about what they were up to."

"They didn't have to tell anyone. Everyone knew they were looking for some old gold mine. We all thought they were being silly... acting like little boys when they should have been taking care of their responsibilities at home. I told them so, but they wouldn't listen. They both had land they were going to farm, and they were both setting the foundations for the homes they were building. But they were always running off and nothing was getting done. The Larkin farm very nearly went under last spring. If mother hadn't sent our hired help over to the Larkin place to help with the planting, they never would have gotten their seed planted. Nathan's little brothers were working like dogs trying to get everything done, but they needed Nathan's help and he was never around."

Susan raked her fingers through her hair, brushing it back from her face. "And then they just rode off and never came back," she concluded. "Did either of them have any enemies?"

"Enemies? What are you suggesting?"

"I'm suggesting that they never came back because they came to harm and couldn't return."

"That's ridiculous. They had no enemies. Nathan and Bradley Hunter never got along, but they were hardly enemies."

Susan shook her head, frowning at the auburn haired girl who seemed frozen in concentrated thought. "The idea that they have come to harm is not as ridiculous as you seem to think," she argued. "Those mountains can be dangerous of themselves… not to mention the fact that there are still some of Black Hawk's renegades who refused to make peace when Black Hawk did. They've been all over these mountains, and they would have no compunctions about killing a couple of foolish young men if they happened to discover them alone up there."

"You're suggesting they've been killed by Ute renegades?"

"Possibly."

"But you asked about their enemies.…"

"And you said they had none." Susan watched the girl closely. "Did you know that a man's remains were found near the foundation on Nathan Larkin's property?"

The girl's head turned sharply as she looked piercingly into Susan's eyes. "Remains?"

"Yes, a skeleton—at least part of one, and it appears he was deliberately tortured and killed."

The girl's face drained of color. "It's like a bad dream," she whispered. "Utes would do such a thing?"

"That's what we're trying to discover."

"Was it Nathan?"

"Possibly... we can't be sure at the moment, but it is possible."

"I think I knew something terrible had happened to them—like seeing it all in a dream, yet not being able to accept it as real."

Susan felt her sympathies go out to the girl, realizing that in a community so small, friendships could be closer than they might seem. "You said Nathan and Bradley didn't get along. Did they ever fight?"

"Once or twice.... When they were younger.... Bradley has a temper and he's rather possessive. He thinks he's in love with me. I suppose they fought over me at one time, but I never encouraged either of them."

"Did Aaron and Nathan ever disagree or fight with one another?"

"Oh, they were always arguing about something or other. It never amounted to much as far as I know."

"But the day of the picnic, did they seem to get along with one another?"

"As well as ever."

"Tell me what happened that day."

"I hardly remember. It's been so long now."

"I understand. Just do the best you can."

"I hardly know where to begin."

"Tell me who was there and what you did."

"There were eight of us I think. "Four boys and four girls...
Yes, that seems right—Aaron, Bradley, Nathan, Steven Taggart,
Zina Wilcox, Silvie Murdock, Lynne Campbell, and me.

"We each took a little something for a picnic lunch, and
everyone met at our place because it was the closest to the
pond over on Lake Creek where we had decided to have
lunch."

"You all rode out to the pond together?"

"Yes. We had the devil of a time convincing Sister Campbell
to let Lynne go out there at all. Some folks around here still
consider that area unsafe. But we finally convinced the adults,
and they let us go on condition that the boys went armed. I
don't think any of them really thought we would run into any
renegade Utes. They just didn't want to admit we were all old
enough to make our own decisions."

"So you went to the pond?"

"Yes. We got there almost exactly at noon. I remember
because the sun was almost directly overhead and we had to
find trees big enough to give us enough shade for the whole
group.

"We took about an hour to eat and then we all left. Aaron
and Nathan said they were going down to Provo, and they
were anxious to leave. The party sort of fizzled out because of
it, so we packed up and left."

"Lynne told me that Bradley was acting strangely," Susan
prompted.

"I don't remember that," the girl replied thoughtfully.
"Lynne sometimes exaggerates things. Bradley might have
been a little frustrated, because he thought Nathan and Aaron
were headed off into the mountains again, and he wanted to
go with them. He was a little upset when they told him no."

"Upset enough to follow them when they left?"

"Good heavens, no!"

Susan waited as the girls' eyes darted to one side as though following a swift movement.

"Lynne told me you left before the others… when Aaron said something that bothered you."

"I may have left a little before the others, but they were right behind me."

"What was it that Aaron said to make you leave?"

"Aaron was always saying things that were rude. I left because I was tired of listening to him."

Susan smiled disarmingly. "So everyone went home, except Aaron and Nathan, and they rode off toward Provo?"

"Exactly."

"And no one followed them?"

"No one."

"I understand your father sent you back east when the rumors started, and you had only been home a few days before the picnic."

"My father thought the rumors would hurt his business, so he sent me to a school in Denver. I was gone less than six months when my dear father decided the cost was too high and brought me back. If I had my way, I would never have come back."

With that, the girl's focus shifted to something beyond the front window of Murphy's store, dismissing Susan completely from her mind.

"Don't you dare bang that chest around, Brother Pratt!"

The Pratt kid frowned and under the watchful eye of the Campbell girl, he helped her tow-headed younger brother lift the girl's hope chest into one of the new wagons.

"She always this bossy?" he complained glumly.

"Bosses *me* all the time," the younger boy replied unhappily.

The Pratt kid leaned hip-shot against the wagon, like a horse resting placidly in a pasture. "Kinda skinny too. She ain't sickly, is she?"

"I am neither skinny nor sickly, Brother Pratt. And if I am bossy, it's only because some men are naturally lazy and need constant supervision, or they never finish anything they put their hand to."

The Pratt kid spun around to face the girl and grinned sheepishly. "Reckon them lazy fellows could use some of your attention, so us hard-workin' types could finish loadin' this wagon."

"You *are* one of those lazy fellows, Brother Pratt. Have you no ambition or desire to better yourself?"

The Pratt kid frowned and shook his head. "I got ambition," he objected. "I been savin' up my money, and when I got enough, I'm gonna buy me a little place and a couple of pigs and some chickens. I figure a fellow can't go wrong raising pigs and chickens. Pigs ain't much work and they eat almost anything."

The girl planted both fists on her hips. "A pig farmer," she hissed. She turned and walked toward the house. "You should be wary of setting unreasonably high goals," she advised.

When the girl had disappeared from sight, the tow-headed boy looked at the Pratt kid and grimaced. "You really want a pig farm," he demanded, disgust thick in his voice.

The Pratt kid snorted abruptly. "Hell, no! I hate pigs. I just said that to get her goat. She seems to have made up her mind that I'm some kind of good-for-nothing!"

The younger boy frowned. "Girls make me sick. I seen her ride rough shod over nearly every fellow I know. She's playin' some kinda game. She's got a sharp tongue too. Maybe she'll leave me alone if she's pickin' at you."

"A game...."

"Seems like."

"You fellows got that thing loaded up?"

Mitchell's query startled the pair into a rush to close up the tailgate and lash down the canvas flap at the rear of the wagon.

"We're done as far as I know," the Pratt kid responded, "unless that gal finds a way to cram more junk in here."

"I'd say you're finished," Mitchell advised quietly. He looked quickly toward the house then turned back to the Pratt kid.

"You got your pistol handy?"

The Pratt kid frowned unhappily at the question, but nodded. "In my saddle bags," he replied, noting that Mitchell was packing his own hardware.

"Strap it on," Mitchell instructed, "and break out those two cartridge rifles and a couple of boxes of shells."

"Sister Mitchell won't be happy to see me wearin' that pistol again," the kid grumbled.

"You let me handle Sarah," Mitchell advised. "There are several fellows in town who might decide to cause trouble. They've got no reason to like me, and if they know you're connected to me in any way, they're likely to shoot you out of pure meanness."

"You must have treated 'em pretty bad to make 'em want to shoot *me*," the kid muttered. "They ain't disgruntled former employees are they? 'Cause if they are, I might do well to give notice now and avoid being in the same predicament."

The kid stifled a grin as Mitchell scowled. "They ain't former employees," Mitchell growled, "and if *they* don't shoot you, I just might do it for them."

"Aw, you won't do that. Who's gonna run your ranch and be your right hand man? There ain't two fellows like me around. Your whole enterprise could fall apart without a fellow like me to keep things running smooth."

"We've got no ranch," Mitchell retorted.

The Pratt kid sighed and crossed the yard to the railing where his horse was tied. "How many of these old friends of yours do I need to watch for?" he asked as he dug into his saddle bags and fetched out the gunbelt and the Navy Colt he had stashed there less than a week earlier.

Mitchell thought for a moment then shook his head. "Don't know for certain," he admitted. "Biggs, Dunford, and four or five others.... But if Biggs and Dunford are here, it's likely Baldy Jackman is hanging around somewhere with half a dozen of his cronies."

The smile left the Pratt kid's face. "That's just *dandy*," he groaned.

"Just keep your eyes open and don't let anyone corner you," Mitchell advised.

The Pratt kid strode to the front of the wagon and climbed onto the seat. For a moment, he leaned headfirst over the back of the seat and rummaged about in one corner. A moment later, he handed out the rifles and two boxes of shells. "Hope we don't need any of this," he grumbled.

Mitchell studied the Pratt kid's face for a moment, sensing the boy's concern. "I hope we can save it all for that hunting trip we were planning," he replied evenly. "But you'll be glad to have it, if Biggs and his cronies come after you. They wouldn't care if you were unarmed. They'd just shoot you down and think you stupid for not being ready to defend yourself.

"Of course you could go unarmed and hope Deputy Turner could run across town and save your ass before Biggs could shoot you, but we both know Turner ain't that swift of foot."

The Pratt kid raised an eyebrow. "That's a tough choice," he muttered. "Shot by Biggs or a tongue lashing by Sister Mitchell. I almost think I'd rather be shot. Did you know she lectured me for nearly half an hour the last time she saw me packin' that Colt. And me just 'yes ma'am, yes ma'am' from Kaysville clear to Centerville. I think my ears was bleedin' before she decided I had enough."

Mitchell smiled, realizing that the Pratt kid's dilemma was real enough. In the kid's mind, Biggs was a distant and unsubstantial threat, while Sarah had already demonstrated the ability to give a fellow hell if she thought he deserved it.

"I'll try explaining to Sarah," he conceded. "Just watch out for Biggs."

Mitchell shoved the rifle into the boot on the grulla's saddle and tied the animal beside the Pratt kid's horse.

"Where's the dun?" asked the kid.

"Dropped him over to the blacksmith's for some new shoes. One of 'em had a big old crack and looked like it might go bad any time."

The Pratt kid nodded. "Just wondered," he confided. "Seems like you prefer the dun; though I don't know why."

"Nah…" grunted Mitchell. "I like 'em about the same. The dun's got a little more bottom, but the grulla here is a little more amiable. The dun likes to spit on me."

The Pratt kid grinned. "I seen him do it," he squawked. "You teach him to do that or did he come by it natural?"

"I'd allow it's nothing but natural born orneriness," observed Mitchell. "You'd think Sarah and Susan would get tired of washing horse snot and spit out of my shirts, but every time it happens, they just laugh like a wagon load of circus clowns walked in the door."

"At least he ain't trying to nip you all the time. My old man had a horse one time—you couldn't get near him without him takin' a nip at you. Found out he didn't like men. Women and little girls… hell, they could walk right up to him and he'd sidle up to 'em a beggin' for treats like they was long lost friends. But let a *man* get near him and it was nip, nip, nip 'til you had to swat him to get him to stop."

"The dun ain't tried to bite me yet," Mitchell admitted. "I'd probably get rid of him if he did."

The conversation ground to a halt as both men realized they were avoiding the subject of Walt Biggs and his cronies. The Pratt kid inclined his head toward the house. "They was talking about going over to Murphy's place after we got the wagon loaded. Seems they heard some fellow named Hunter got into an argument with another fellow over a chunk of gold ore.

"Just the mention of gold got all three of 'em fired up and ready to rush right over to Murphy's, until I reminded 'em about how you said for them to stay out of town until you could go with 'em."

"Wouldn't be the first time they ignored *my* advice," Mitchell responded.

Silently, he watched as the three under discussion flew from the house in a rustle of petticoats and skirts, leaving the screen door with its aged and peeling white paint to slam with a jarring *crash* that startled the two dozing horses into sudden wakefulness.

Mitchell stood petrified with curiosity as the trio fluttered across the yard to take him captive by the shirt sleeves.

"There has been a fight at Brother Murphy's store!" Sarah exclaimed. "Sister Murphy came as soon as she could. She knew we would want to know about it, because it started when a Mr. Feldman tried to buy some supplies with a small handful of gold ore!"

In her excitement, Susan grasped one arm so tightly Mitchell squawked.

"Hey!"

"Sorry," she blurted. "Bradley Hunter went crazy when Mr. Feldman put the ore on the counter. He leaped on his back and started punching his fist into the side of Mr. Feldman's head!"

"Mr. Feldman finally threw Hunter to the floor and stomped him in the ribs with the heel of his boot," Sarah added. Brother Murphy started around the counter to break it up, but before he could get there, Mr. Feldman snatched up his supplies and ran from the store. Bradley Hunter was right on his heels, and the last anyone saw of either one of them, they were riding hell-bent toward Mr. Feldman's farm."

Mitchell's face tightened into a scowl as he led the three women toward the rented buggy. "Sounds like we should have a talk with both of those fellows," he suggested as he helped each of the women into the buggy.

For a moment, the women fluttered their skirts as they settled themselves. When they were comfortable, the Campbell girl turned toward Mitchell. "I don't understand why Bradley Hunter would attack Mr. Feldman. He hardly knows the man."

"It had to be the gold ore that set him off," offered Susan. "Jean Kelson told me Bradley Hunter was trying to get Stokes and Larkin to let him in on their deal."

"Maybe he thought Mr. Feldman had something to do with Nathan's death," Sarah suggested.

"I don't see why that would make Bradley attack Mr. Feldman," the Campbell girl objected. "Bradley and Aaron were not good friends."

CHAPTER 9

24 September

*T*wo hours later, Sarah found the Hunter boy on the boardwalk in front of Kelson's Dry Goods. Bradley Hunter was a young man of average height, average build, and average mentality. His mediocrity of height and build were readily discernable by anyone who cared to note his physical merits, but his mental capacity was not so easily discovered — unless one took the time for more than a passing conversation. Sarah was fully five minutes with the boy when she suddenly realized her questions had gained her nothing.

"Surely you remember something about the day of that picnic…."

"Not really. A bunch of us went over to some pond and had us some lunch."

"I suppose you remember who was there."

"Yeah. There was me and Stokes, Larkin, Jean Kelson, and couple of other girls."

"That was the day Aaron and Nathan rode down to Provo?"

"Yeah. I guess so… least wise that's what they told everyone. I never believed 'em though. I knew they was headed off lookin' for that mine again. All that business about goin' to Salt Lake was just a lot of talk so nobody would know what they was really up to.

"I knew they was lookin' for an old gold mine, 'cause I heard 'em talkin' about it one time when they thought no one was around."

Sarah smiled. "I've never heard of anyone finding gold in these mountains," she offered.

"Oh, there's stories enough. There's stories say old Tom Rhodes got gold for the church from some old Spanish mine up in the Uintahs. Nobody knows where it's at, 'cept old Rhodes and the Utes, an' none of them are gonna tell."

"Is that the mine Aaron and Nathan were hunting?"

"Naw. They was lookin' for somethin' around here. If they was goin' off into the Uintahs, they wouldn't have been packin' so light as they were. They never had no pack horse an' they never took nothin' for a long stay."

Sarah nodded thoughtfully. "Did you ever see anyone follow them when they went on one of these trips?"

"Most folks just ignored the both of 'em. A couple of us followed 'em one time, but they must have caught sight of us, 'cause they started coverin' their trail and wandered all over the mountain. We lost 'em over on Coop Creek an' never did figure out where they went. When they come back, they come ridin' up from Provo Canyon. Made us look pretty stupid losin' 'em that way."

"Who was with you the time you followed them?" Sarah asked patiently.

"Just Mr. Feldman an' me."

"Did anyone else ever show enough interest to try following them?"

"Well…"

"Who?"

"I thought I saw old man Kelson one time. I was a ways off, but I'm sure it was him."

Sarah frowned. "I thought he spent all his time down in Salt Lake?"

"Maybe so, but I seen him that time, an' he was followin' their back trail mighty close. I figure they left him eaten' their dust just like they did me an' Mr. Feldman."

"Did anyone follow them after the picnic that day?"

"Yeah… that's when I saw old man Kelson."

"Where were they when you saw Mr. Kelson?"

"They was all out near that foundation Nathan was buildin'."

"How long after the picnic was this?"

"About an hour."

"Did they talk with Mr. Kelson?"

"Nope… At least I never seen 'em talkin'. Old man Kelson was sittin' on his horse way back in some trees. Seemed like he was just watchin' the two of 'em. I only seen him 'cause I was on the other side of the trees an' he couldn't see so good from his side."

"Did you talk to him?"

"Nope. I was headed out to his farm to see Jean. I don't like her old man anyways, so there wasn't no reason to talk with him."

"What about Mr. Feldman? Did he ever follow either Stokes or Larkin other than the time he was with you?"

Hunter thought for a moment. Finally, he shook his head. "Mr. Feldman ain't much of a hand when it comes to the outdoors," he replied. "Him an' me had trouble followin' them two—mostly 'cause Mr. Feldman ain't much when it comes to ridin' a horse. He says it's 'cause they're so big they make him nervous.

"I figure he ain't got any guts… Sorry, ma'am. I figure he's chicken, an' a horse can tell when a fellow is scared. That makes it even worse. Mr. Feldman can do okay at a walk, but at a gallop, he's all over a saddle like a rag doll in a tornado. It's a wonder he don't break his neck. That's why we couldn't keep up with those two, an' that ain't a lie. They spotted us an' left us eatin' their dust. I wouldn't ride with Mr. Feldman after that, an' I don't figure anyone who knows him would."

Sarah nodded, sensing the boy was holding something back. "What made you attack Mr. Feldman today? From what you've told me, it seems unlikely that you would have reason to be so angry with him."

"That's between him an' me."

"You know Deputy Turner will be coming to talk to you. Mr. Feldman will probably file a complaint."

The boy gritted his teeth, but remained stubbornly silent.

Sarah smiled disarmingly. "I can understand how you feel," she said reassuringly. "I would have been angry too."

The boy frowned. "You would?"

Sarah nodded. "Certainly. Mr. Feldman should have known better," she confided.

The boy shook his head. "I thought I could trust him," he said, letting a bitterness creep into the tone of his voice. "He seemed like a decent sort."

"Even decent people can make bad decisions," Sarah suggested.

"He should have been more careful, like he said he would," the boy complained.

Sarah smiled. "Maybe he was," she answered.

The Hunter boy had been sitting hunched over, with his head down and his eyes on the boardwalk. At Sarah's suggestion, he looked up. "You think he set my share aside?"

"Did you ask him?"

"Naw. I just saw him payin' for his stuff with that gold and figured he was tryin' to spend it all before I found out he done it." The boy shifted his gaze, avoiding contact with Sarah's eyes.

Sarah leaned back and sighed with the sudden realization that the boy had been lying. "Why are you lying to me?" she asked crossly. "What possible harm could come of telling me the truth? You didn't kill Stokes or Larkin, did you?"

"No."

"Do you know who did?"

"No."

"Then why all the lies?"

The boy was sweating now, beads of perspiration gathering on his forehead. "He told me he would kill me, if I said anything."

"Mr. Feldman?"

"Naw. He ain't a bad sort. It was that Coleman fellow. Leastwise, that's what he calls himself."

"Coleman?"

"He's been hangin' around town for about a month. I think he spends most of his time over on Lake Creek."

"And this Mr. Coleman threatened to kill you?"

"Yes, ma'am."

"Why?"

"He said he heard about me and Mr. Feldman followin' Aaron and Nate. Said he'd kill me if I didn't tell him the minute we found anything. Now, every time I turn around he's there, watchin' me."

"And you attacked Mr. Feldman because this man Coleman threatened you?"

"I did it because that Coleman fellow said we shouldn't let anybody know about the gold. He said it would just upset everybody and they would start asking a bunch of questions about where we got it."

"Where did you get it?"

"Found it," the boy answered reluctantly.

"You found the mine?"

"I wish."

"What did you find?"

Hunter glanced nervously up and down the street. "We found a dead horse and some saddle bags. They must have been Aaron's. I recognized the saddle bags, and they had this little bag of gold ore inside."

"And that's what you thought Mr. Feldman was spending at Brother Murphy's store."

"He was!" Hunter squawked. "He admitted it when I followed him back to his place!"

"And the saddle bags?"

Hunter frowned. "I don't know. Feldman has 'em someplace, I guess. Look, I got to go."

Sarah grabbed the boy by the shirt sleeve. "Where did you find the horse?" She demanded.

"South of town," Hunter grumbled, "near the mouth of Center Creek canyon."

Sarah nodded, remembering the dead horse Collin had found in the trees just outside of town. "I suppose we had better talk to Mr. Feldman," she said quietly.

CHAPTER 10

25 September

By nine in the morning, the air inside the wagon was stifling hot. Sarah pushed at the dream, trying to force herself into reality. She knew she was on the verge of wakefulness, yet her body felt as though it weighed a thousand pounds. Every move was an effort requiring all of her will, and every second brought four conquistadors closer to camp with the steady clatter of horseshoes. Their armor glinted in the glare of the afternoon sun, and the sound of metal against metal seemed harsh amid the silence of the mountains.

Their leader was a short, hard-faced man, bearded, dirty, and staring intently forward as though something ahead held all his attention. The others were similar in features and build, their personal natures invisible and hidden deeply beneath the outward show of armor and past violence. But of them all, the last in line bore the look of a man to whom evil was a passion and violence a malignant growth that had eaten his soul. The conquistadors were nearly upon her when she forced her eyes open and snatched up the shotgun.

The four men rode the trail south from town with little conversation and little more than the sound of horseshoes on rocky ground to disturb the solitude of the ride. They said little, three of them having exhausted any topic of common interest in the distant past. The fourth man was hardly new to the group, but he seldom spoke with anyone and seemed to have a streak of meanness that intimidated everyone who knew him.

Jackman, Biggs, and Dunford had ridden together for nearly twenty years, herding cattle, working odd jobs, and stealing whatever they could lay their hands on. Their preoccupation with theft, more often than not, had resulted in their swift departure to far places and an ever shorter list of refuges that might offer even a temporary welcome—a welcome that was nonexistent as they entered the Mitchell camp.

The first man in line swung down from his horse without invitation and stepped toward the campfire and the redheaded spitfire who stood defiantly in the center of the camp.

"Missy, that pistol ain't goin' to do you much good against four of us," he warned. "Besides, we ain't gonna hurt you none. We just saw your camp and smelled your cook fire. We thought maybe you'd offer us a bite to eat."

The short man took a step closer to Susan and let his hand fall casually to the butt of the pistol tucked in the waistband of his trousers. With the other hand, he reached up and swept the battered hat from his head. "Like I said Ma'am, we just stopped by to be friendly."

"If you're so friendly, take your hand off that pistol," Sarah advised as she stepped from behind the wagon and leveled the twin muzzles of her scattergun on the man's chest.

The man stiffened then carefully drew his hand away from the butt of his pistol. "You be careful now, ma'am. You pull that trigger and you're likely to hit this little lady too."

Sarah shook her head and took half a step forward. "I've shot this thing at least fifty times in the last two weeks, and I'll tell you for a fact, it's loaded with double-aught buckshot, and at this range every bit of shot is going to hit an area about the size of your head. Whatever misses you will probably tear some nasty holes in that fellow behind you."

"Don't do anything stupid, Baldy! She means business."

"Shut up, Biggs!"

"You friend is right," Sarah advised. "I do mean business."

"Most women would be home knittin' or cookin' dinner right now, and here's the two of you shuckin' that Colt and shovin' that ten-gage in my face! Mighty strange pair, if you ask me."

"No one's asking," Susan responded.

"Where's your men folk?" The short man demanded suddenly.

"Dragging some deadfall back here, for the fire," Sarah answered suddenly, realizing that the short man believed they were alone and neither woman would have the nerve to shoot.

"Jackman!"

"Shut up Biggs! Lots of folks drag deadfall for firewood!"

"Collin might even be watching us right now," Susan suggested thoughtfully.

"Shit!" Biggs turned angrily and stalked back to his horse. He mounted and without another word spurred his horse east toward Lake Creek. The three remaining riders watched as their partner crested a ridge and disappeared.

"Let's go, Baldy," one of them muttered unhappily.

Jackman frowned as the second rider nudged his horse and headed east at a walk. Suddenly, Jackman smiled. "Guess we ain't stayin' to dinner." He announced stiffly. Angrily, he slapped his hat on his balding head and climbed into the saddle. The two men turned their horses eastward, and within minutes, they crossed the ridge and disappeared.

Quietly, Sarah lowered the shotgun. She walked to the log Collin had dragged into camp. She seated herself on the area Collin had flattened with an axe and stared at the surrounding foothills and the pine covered ridges of the farthest mountain. Collin was there—somewhere, and at the moment she wanted him beside her more than anything.

"What was that all about?" Susan demanded as she rotated the Colt's cylinder and eased the hammer down on its one empty chamber.

Sarah sighed deeply and shook her head. "I haven't a clue," she admitted.

Susan peered at her sister and the cocked ten-gage she held in her lap, "You better let the hammers down on that thing. You're liable to shoot one of us the way your hands are shaking.

Sarah lowered her eyes and stared at the gun reposing quietly on her lap. Her hands were definitely trembling. It was a small thing, when she felt as though her whole body should be shaking furiously, like a leaf beaten by the winds of a mountain storm.

Susan moved close and placed a comforting hand on her sister's shoulder. "I knew they'd back off when you shoved that ten-gage in his face."

Glumly, Sarah shook her head. "It's not what you think," she said quietly as she yanked both triggers on the shotgun.

The twin hammers dropped, but no ear-shattering roar broke the stillness, only the loud popping of the caps as the hammers struck.

"I didn't have time to load it," she announced bleakly.

Susan groaned and dropped to a seat beside her sister. "I'm glad I didn't know," she confided. She glanced at her older sister, suddenly realizing what they had just done. "Collin isn't going to be happy about this," she warned.

Two hours later, Mitchell looked out over fields overgrown with weeds and sun bleached buildings and pens badly in need of cleaning.

"Doesn't look like Mr. Feldman spends much time taking care of his farm," Sarah said quietly.

"Animals have been fed recently," Mitchell observed, "but that's about all."

"Do you think he had anything to do with Aaron Stokes' disappearance?"

"Possibly, but if he is involved, he's kept this place up—until the last few months. Most of the disrepair has taken more than a year, but the pens have been cleaned and taken care of until recently."

Mitchell surveyed the unkempt pens, noting that it had been more than a month since any of the pens had been cleaned. The animals had been fed, but the troughs for the pigs and sheep had new feed dumped on top of older, inedible leavings—leavings now pressed into the bottom of the troughs and rank with the smell of mold and decay.

"Those pigs look rather thin," Sarah reported as she leaned both forearms on the top rail of the enclosure and took stock of the poorly fed animals gathered tightly in one corner of the pen.

"Not enough feed and no salt," Mitchell suggested. "I don't see any salt blocks in any of these pens. Most farmers know you get better weight gains if your animals get the salt they need. Feed ain't enough by itself."

"Someone should talk with Mr. Feldman and get him to take better care of his animals or sell them to someone who will," Sarah suggested.

Mitchell scowled and let his eyes search the farmyard.

"Might as well be us," he reasoned. "It doesn't look as though Mr. Feldman has many visitors."

"I think you should have a talk with Bradley Hunter too," Sarah suggested. "His account of the matter seems very strange."

Mitchell nodded his agreement. "The Campbell girl seems certain that Hunter and Feldman hardly know one another," he observed. "But an unprovoked attack…. Hunter's behavior makes me think that he and Feldman are more than just casual acquaintances. That would seem to fit better with the story he told you."

Sarah stepped back from the fence and glanced toward the farmhouse. Less than a hundred yards away, a single horse stood hitched to a stout railing near the front of the house. "Maybe we'll have the opportunity to talk with both of them now. That horse fits the description Lynne gave of the one Bradley Hunter owns."

Mitchell looked toward the house. "He must have ridden here like his tail was on fire as soon as you finished talking with him. Let's wander on up to the house and have a chat, shall we?"

The walk to the house was over quickly, and while there seemed to be a normal abundance of domestic animals roaming about the place, human activity was distinctly limited.

Mitchell took the porch in two steps and rapped sharply on the face of the door.

"Suddenly there came a tapping…" Sarah quoted gloomily.

Mitchell raised an eyebrow at her. He struck the door three sharp blows. "'As of someone gently rapping…'" he added.

Sarah smiled slyly. "'Rapping at my chamber door.'"

Mitchell grinned. "'Tis some visitor. I muttered, tapping at my chamber door—only this and nothing more.'"

"You've been reading my books. Haven't you?"

"No one seems to be at home," Mitchell replied, avoiding the question.

"They must be around somewhere, Sarah insisted. "Hunter wouldn't leave without his horse."

Mitchell stepped across the porch and peered through the front window.

"You shouldn't do that!" Sarah hissed.

"Too late," Mitchell replied dryly, letting his eyes sweep the room beyond the window.

"I think we should take a closer look," he confided a moment later.

"Go inside?"

"I think we must, but you had better let me go first. It may not be pleasant."

"It will certainly be *unpleasant* if Mr. Feldman finds us wandering about his house uninvited."

Mitchell shook his head in disagreement. "Judging by the amount of blood—what looks like blood—on the floor in there, Mr. Feldman might not be in a condition to care if we brought the whole town with us."

Sarah shifted uneasily. "I hope you're not suggesting that Mr. Feldman is lying there dead. I'm not entirely at my best when confronted with violent bloodshed and death."

Mitchell turned from the window and raised a quizzical brow at the woman whose handbag even now concealed a short-barreled Colt's pocket pistol—a woman who had already proven herself equal to the task of putting lead into a villain who had deserved nothing less.

"You wait here while I take a look," he instructed.

With that, he lifted the door latch and entered the room beyond the window. There was no body, only the blood pooled on the floor, soaking the edge of a badly worn rug.

Quickly, he searched the house, but found no sign of either man and no further evidence of violence. When he again reached the front door, he was perplexed.

"No one inside," he said quietly. "Beats me how there could be so much blood and no body to go with it."

"Maybe it was carried off," Sarah suggested.

"Should have left some kind of blood trail," Mitchell insisted.

"Not if it was rolled up in a rug or blankets."

Mitchell frowned. "There were some blankets missing from a bed in the back room."

"What do you suggest we do now?" asked Sarah.

"I suppose we should go back to town and let Turner know about the blood," Mitchell suggested.

Sarah waggled a finger in the general direction of the outbuildings and the animal pens. "Maybe we should make sure no one is lying out there bleeding to death," she proposed.

Mitchell leaned forward and kissed her on the forehead. "On one condition."

"*Brother Mitchell….*"

"On the condition that you stay with me, and I check into anything that looks suspicious. No wandering off by yourself. Understood?"

For a moment Sarah hesitated as she searched for a logical reason to object to Mitchell's demand; then she saw his face harden and his eyes narrow into the squint she knew so well.

"Very well," she conceded. "I will stay within reach at all times. Is that good enough?"

"Good enough. How about we start with the barn?"

The tall, weathered structure stood a hundred feet south of the house and looked as though Feldman had cobbled it together in a patchwork of leftover wagon slats. Gaps and holes marred every wall as though an army of tomahawk flinging Indians had used it for target practice on a dark, moonless night. The roof alone looked as though it might do its job and keep out the weather, and it was only a season's worth of alfalfa hay chopped and piled high against the inside walls that kept the winds from howling through the structure with nary a pause.

Sarah paused at the barn's large double door. "What is that odor?" She demanded. She took the kerchief Mitchell offered and covered her mouth and nose. "Something smells awful," she muttered from beneath the bright red and white bandanna.

"It's the hay," said Mitchell as he cracked one door and squeezed through the narrow opening. "Stay outside," he called. "Feldman cut this stuff and didn't let it cure long enough."

"Why does it smell so bad?"

"You should have stayed outside," Mitchell growled.

"I promised to stay within reach. Remember?"

"Devious woman."

"Why are you worried? It just smells bad."

"The hay is damp and it's fermenting," explained Mitchell. "Feldman should have known better."

"And now his crop is ruined…" Sarah suggested.

"And now his crop is about to catch fire and burn down his barn—his house too if the wind is wrong."

"Catch fire?"

Mitchell grabbed up a wisp of hay and held it where Sarah could plainly see that the stems were still green and pliable. Mitchell twisted the wisp in his hands and a thin film of moisture appeared on the stems.

"Alfalfa hay needs to be dry and a little bit brittle when you store it," Mitchell explained. "It doesn't matter if it's tossed in a big pile like this or baled and stacked. If it's at all damp, it'll start fermenting. Then it gets hot—real hot… It starts putting off a real pungent odor and vapors. You feel how warm it is in here… well, that ain't 'cause it's a sunny day outside. The heat's coming from the hay. And somewhere down in that pile, it's hot and getting hotter every minute.

"When the worst of the pocket in there gets to about a hundred and seventy, maybe a hundred and eighty degrees, it's already smoldering—folks have been calling it spontaneous combustion, and this stack is ready to go off like a torch."

Sarah's eyes widened as she looked at the small mountain waiting to roar into a conflagration that could engulf them in seconds. "Maybe we should leave," she suggested grimly.

Mitchell paused at the edge of the fermenting mass and snatched up a worn-looking set of saddle bags. "I think now is a good time!" he exclaimed. "I smell smoke!"

Within seconds, the barn filled with an eye searing smoke. The pair forced their way through the space between the doors, coughing and rubbing at their eyes.

Sarah backed away from the barn until her back pressed against the railing of the pig sty. "That was awful timing!" She shouted as the barn exploded in flames.

Hastily, the pair rushed down the fence line, striving for greater distance between themselves and the inferno behind them. On the opposite side of the railing, the entire herd of swine broke from the corner of the pen and fled, snorting and squealing their dismay.

Near the house, Hunter's terrified horse lunged against the hitching rail then heaved backward, snapping the rein near the bit. Within moments, the animal was galloping madly away from the smoke and the flames.

"That wasn't just bad timing," Mitchell replied as he watched the flames roar skyward.

"What do you mean?"

"When we opened that door, we let fresh air into the barn. It was like pumping a bellows on hot coals."

Sarah's face was grave as she watched the flames consume the barn. "Now that we've destroyed the barn, what do we do?"

Mitchell frowned unhappily and stepped closer to the railing and stared into the corner of the pen where the herd of starving swine had been happily rooting just moments before. The heat from the burning barn was intense as he edged along the fence line until he stood near the corner of the pen. Quickly, he glanced back toward Sarah who stood clutching her handbag and watching him curiously.

"Gather up our horses," he instructed. "Then we'll go back to town and let Turner know we've found Bradley Hunter."

Sarah turned away, and Mitchell climbed the fence and began the grisly task of removing Bradley Hunter's half eaten remains from the pen.

Jared Turner had the look of a very unhappy man when he entered the sheriff's office and pointedly shut the door.

"Our regular doctor has gone to Provo for a couple of days, so I had Bob Jenkins examine the body."

Mitchell watched as Turner strode to the desk, dropped a chunk of iron and a short wooden shaft on its top and planted himself in the chair behind the desk. It was just after noon and sweat had turned his collar from a faded blue to a shade closer to its original color.

"Jenkins knew the Hunter kid well enough to identify the remains," he explained. "He pulled that thing out of the kid's back." Turner fished around in the desk then dropped a second quarrel on the desktop. "Looks like they match up pretty good, don't you think?"

Mitchell took a closer look. "Look the same to me," he admitted. "Seems our friend has gone beyond the flaming arrow stage."

"Moved right up to murder," Turner muttered.

Mitchell felt Sarah shudder as she peered closely at the two quarrels. He knew what she was seeing, and thought he had a glimpse of her thoughts.

The quarrels were identical. From the hand cut nock of the shafts to the wedge-cut tip of the rust pitted heads, both quarrels were perfect copies. Only the soot staining one and the blood staining the other made it possible to tell the two apart.

"Got any ideas?" asked Turner.

Mitchell dug into the pocket of his coat and dropped a rusty chunk of iron beside the two already on the desk top.

"Questions," he affirmed. "No answers."

Turner frowned and picked up the quarrel point. "How did you come by this," he demanded.

Mitchell smiled. "Thought that would make you curious," he responded.

"Damned right it does!"

"Found it southwest of here; stuck in the trunk of an old pine tree."

"A pine tree?" Turner hefted the chisel point and shook his head in disbelief. "How did you ever find it when it was stuck in a tree out in the middle of nowhere?"

"That was a curious thing," admitted Mitchell. "I was looking for conquistadors."

"Conquistadors? You talking Spanish soldiers and armor and such?"

"Sounds odd, doesn't it?"

"Damned strange, if you ask me."

"But I found one, Mitchell confided.

"You're pulling my leg."

"Not a bit. The dog actually found the conquistador, but I spotted the tree and what was left of the fellow pinned to it with that quarrel.

"The dog found the rest of the Spaniard in the leaves and brush at the foot of the tree."

Turner leaned forward and dropped the iron point on the desk. "Strange coincidence," he conceded, but how does it have anything to do with Hunter's death. If Spanish soldiers ever came this far north, it was long before the Saints ever got here."

Mitchell pushed the rusty point across the top of the desk until the three chisel-shaped points touched one another. "Take a look at those points," he suggested. "Notice anything about them?"

"They all look the same," Turner admitted.

"They *are* the same," corrected Mitchell. "Rusty, pitted, same chisel point… made to punch through steel armor—the same."

Turner frowned. "What are you getting at?"

"I'm getting at the fact that these points are identical—all from a set."

"That don't make any sense," objected Turner. "Those two are new, and that one has been stuck in that tree since who knows when."

Mitchell shook his head. "Just an observation," he admitted. "I don't know what it means."

"Well, if you figure it out, let me know."

Turner paused and gestured toward one corner of the room. "Those saddlebags you brought in ain't no mystery," he reported grimly. "A couple of folks recognized 'em right off, and some of Aaron Stokes personal belongings were still inside, so there ain't no doubt they were his."

Mitchell crossed the room and joined Sarah, who stood at the window, watching the flow of wagons, horses, and people along the town's main street.

"It seems more and more like Aaron Stokes *is* dead, and those were his bones we dug up," Mitchell said thoughtfully.

"Seems like," Turner agreed, "but we've got nothing to prove it, and I've got no time to waste trying to figure it out, A lot of folks disappear out here. Sometimes it's because they want to. They just wander off without a word, and no one ever sees 'em again.

"I have to spend my time on things I have half a chance of figuring out. Like that Hunter kid and the fire at Murphy's store. Might even spend some time on those bones we found, but that's only because it looks to be a murder—like you said. But traipsin' around the territory askin' folks if they know anything about Aaron Stokes is something I just ain't got time for."

Mitchell kept his eyes on the street outside and the sudden commotion surrounding a small building two blocks away on the west side of the street.

"I wonder what's going on down there," he muttered.

Sarah leaned closer to the glass. "I saw a team and wagon come racing down the street from the south end of town," she offered. "They stopped right there, and it looked like a couple of men carried someone inside."

"That's the doctor's place," Turner advised as he pushed the door open and stepped onto the boardwalk. "I just come from there after Bob Jenkins examined Hunter's body."

"Maybe someone is hurt," Sarah offered.

Turner nodded. "Must be more than the usual busted arm to attract so many folks."

Mitchell watched as the crowd near the dust covered team parted and two men strode purposefully toward the sheriff's office.

"Looks like you've got company coming," he suggested.

"More trouble by the look of 'em," Turner replied.

As the men approached, Mitchell took Sarah by the hand and led her out of the office. "It might be better if we're not here when Mr. Turner talks with those fellows," he told her as Biggs and Dunford came close enough to recognize. They were several steps away when Biggs confronted the deputy.

"We don't need no help!" Biggs shouted a moment later.

The deputy's reply was indiscernible as Biggs gave a terse and angry recounting of what had happened in the mountains south of town. When Biggs finally spun on his heel and stalked away, Turner ambled down the boardwalk to where Mitchell and Sarah stood waiting.

"Unpleasant sort of fellows," observed the deputy.

"No doubt of that," Mitchell agreed.

"He says they were riding the Center Creek trail up near Bald Knoll when someone started a big old chunk of rock rolling down the mountain. It came a hoppin' and a jumpin' like a jackrabbit with its tail on fire. Guess it jumped once too many and knocked a fellow named Franklin right off his horse. Busted him up pretty good, according to Bob Jenkins—broke his arm and four ribs. I told that Biggs fellow I would ride up there and see what I could find, if he was sure someone done it on purpose."

"Would it do any good?" Sarah asked.

"I doubt it," Turner responded. "Bald Knoll is about ten miles south of here, and even if Mr. Biggs could lead me to the exact spot, it ain't likely whoever done it is hangin' around waitin' for me to come after 'em. Besides, I ain't much of a mountain man.

"That area up there must cover nearly five-hundred square miles of high mountain country. Some places are so thick with pines and quakies you can't see more than fifty feet.

And if you get into the oak brush… well just forget it, 'cause that stuff is like a jungle it gets so thick.

"Besides, the nights get butt-freezing cold up there this time of year, and I ain't interested in spending even one night up there huntin' for a fellow who may or may not exist. Biggs says someone set that rock to rolling on purpose, but they never saw anyone, and that rock could have come loose without any help."

"So what's you plan?" asked Mitchell.

"I'm going after Feldman. It looks like he killed the Hunter boy, and he has some questions to answer about them saddle bags and the whereabouts of Nate Larkin and Aaron Stokes."

"You think he killed Stokes?" Sarah asked thoughtfully.

Turner frowned unhappily and looked west to where the Campbell house was barely discernable among the tall elm trees growing in front of the house.

"I hope not," he replied sadly. "Stokes wasn't a bad sort, and I hope he ain't dead. And if he is dead, I hope it was some gentile passing through that done it and not Feldman."

Mitchell studied the rough-cut surface of the boardwalk and found his own sentiments echoing those of the deputy. It was much easier to acknowledge the misdeeds or death of a total stranger. The involvement of friends, neighbors, or even family in such goings on brought things too close to home, and could result in a bilious stomach and a nervous condition.

"Someone is dead," he advised, "and whoever killed him has done a pretty good job of destroying any evidence we might have found. It seems to me that your killer is still around."

Mitchell left the deputy and joined Sarah who had met Jean Kelson and wandered across the street to the ice cream parlor.

The auburn haired girl smiled as Mitchell joined them. "Hello, Brother Mitchell," she greeted happily. "I was just waiting for Bradley when Sister Mitchell came along."

"You've made friends then?" asked Mitchell.

"Certainly," the girl responded. "We've discovered that we both have a fondness for vanilla with no extras."

Mitchell nodded. "That's a good start."

"Brother Hunter appears to be late," Sarah said casually.

"He'll be along soon," the girl replied. "He's late for everything, so you just get used to waiting."

"He seemed like a nice enough fellow," offered Mitchell.

"Nice enough," the girl echoed.

For a long while, the girl stood staring through the window of the shop. She made no sound, but stood caught in her thoughts for so long that Mitchell began to feel uncomfortable and wondered if he had said something to offend the girl.

Surreptitiously, Sarah shook her head, warning Mitchell away from the subject of Hunter's death. "We were talking about the Stokes boy when you came up just now," she explained.

"Jean was telling me an interesting story about how Aaron Stokes found a ruined and very old crossbow somewhere on Center Creek and used it as a pattern to make one for himself. It seems he found quite a few rusty old quarrel points too."

"That is very interesting," Mitchell agreed. "I wonder what became of the bow he made?"

"I was wondering the same thing myself."

"I'm tired of waiting," the Kelson girl said suddenly. "Bradley should have been here half an hour ago."

Without another word, the girl turned and walked away, crossing the street and disappearing down the alley between Murphy's store and the barber shop.

"A rather precipitous departure," observed Mitchell.

"A *precipitous* departure…," echoed Sarah.

Mitchell frowned and kept his eye on the alley. He could feel Sarah's questioning look and felt the heat of her curiosity. It was not curiosity about the girl's departure.

"You surprise me, Brother Mitchell," she said quietly. "It seems you've been reading from my dictionary as well as the works of Mr. Poe. How do you account for it?"

Mitchell smiled suddenly and took Sarah by the hand.

"Who is Mr. Poe?" he asked dryly.

CHAPTER 11

25 September

*L*ater that afternoon, Susan sat quietly in the Larkin's tiny log home and waited as Nathaniel Larkin's mother dried her eyes on one corner of a faded apron. It was obvious the family was struggling to survive and had been for some time. Everything in sight was handmade and had the well worn look of a necessary and often used tool. From the straw broom standing in a corner behind the front door to the drab and worn table cloth draped over a rough-cut kitchen table, the entire place reeked of hard work and little return.

Sister Larkin finished daubing at her eyes and let the damp corner of the apron fall from her fingers. "Things have gone from bad to worse since Nathan went away," she confided unhappily. "The younger boys are a big help, but Nathan took on the lion's share of the work after his father hurt his leg two years ago."

Brother Larkin leaned forward in his chair and slapped his right leg. "Horse fell with me, busted my leg in three places below the knee; been lame ever since. I can get around okay, but not like I used to. Nathan took up the work while I was laid up, but we've had a rough go for the last while. The younger boys and I do what we can, and the neighbors have been good enough to help when they can, but as you can see, we're barely hangin' on. Shames me to admit it, but the Lord knows it's the truth."

Susan felt her stomach churn as she contemplated how desperate the family's circumstances must have been for the past year. "It doesn't sound as though your son is the kind of man who would just walk away and leave the family in such dire circumstances," she concluded.

"It isn't like him at all," Sister Larkin protested unhappily.

"We lost some of the harvest last fall," Larkin confided. "Nathan's leaving caught us by surprise."

"He didn't tell you he was going?"

"Not a word," Larkin replied.

"He said he was going to a picnic with some friends," Sister Larkin protested. "He never said a word about going to Salt Lake."

Susan frowned and clasped her hands together in her lap. "It seems awfully strange that he told everyone at the picnic he was going to Salt Lake with Aaron Stokes, but told his family nothing about it."

Larkin snorted in disgust. "I never believed that nonsense for one minute," he said bitterly. "And I told Sheriff Hamilton it was a cock and bull story."

"You don't believe Nathan's friends are telling the truth?" Susan asked.

"That's not what I said," protested Larkin. "They're probably repeating exactly what Nathan and his cousin told them. But I doubt either of them had any intention of going to Salt lake."

Susan leaned forward and studied Larkin's weathered face. "If they had no intention of going to Salt Lake, why did they tell their friends such a thing?"

"Because they didn't want anyone to suspect where they were really going," Larkin replied. "I got after Nathan about neglecting some of the chores, and he just laughed and told me he wasn't worried about the crops at all. He said that he and Aaron had found the stairway that led to a lost cache of Spanish gold. He said he knew they would find it soon and we would all be rich."

"Lynne Campbell told us Nathan and Aaron had a map with directions to an old gold mine," Susan replied thoughtfully.

"Nothing but foolishness!" Larkin responded vehemently. "Any flimflam artist will sell you a *genuine* map to a lost Spanish mine."

"I don't think they bought this map," Susan explained quietly. "I think they found the map and an old journal somewhere, and they were convinced they were authentic."

"Nathan never said anything to me about finding those things," Larkin admitted. "He just started letting the chores go… at first just a day or two now and then, but after a while he was gone for several days at a time. That went on for several months."

"You think something terrible has happened to my son, don't you?" Sister Larkin groaned.

Susan started as the woman snatched up the corner of her apron and burst into a flood of tears. "I have no idea what has happened to your son or Aaron Stokes," she replied awkwardly.

Larkin shook his head unhappily. "I figure the Utes killed both of them," he muttered. "They would have been in them mountains while Black Hawk and his renegades were thievin' cattle and killin' folks."

For a moment, Susan considered telling the couple of the skeletal remains Mitchell had found near the foundation of the home their son had been building, but she quickly decided against revealing anything of that discovery for fear they would leap to the conclusion that their son was dead and the bones were his.

Best to leave that can of worms unopened, she thought.

"Did your son and Aaron Stokes get along with one another?" she asked suddenly.

"As far as I know, they got along fine," Larkin replied.

"They fought over the Campbell girl not long before that picnic," Sister Larkin said bleakly.

"They argued?" asked Susan.

"Fistfight is more like it," Larkin corrected. "They were both bruised and bloodied from it."

"You said they fought over Lynne," Susan responded. "Why?"

"Nathan didn't explain," said Larkin, "but I suspect he's in love with the girl. Aaron was engaged to her earlier in the spring, so I suspect Nathan was trying to convince Aaron to stand aside, and Aaron took it badly."

Susan sat quietly, wondering to herself if either of the cousins could have been angry enough to kill. It would certainly not be the first time men had fought and killed one another over a woman or gold.

An hour later, Susan joined the Campbell girl and the Pratt kid on the boardwalk across the street from Kelson's store. The Pratt kid took her horse by the headstall and tied the rein to the nearest hitching rail.

"Did you learn anything helpful?" The girl asked.

"I'm not sure I learned anything useful," Susan replied thoughtfully.

The mile ride from the Larkin farm back to town had given her ample time to review her interview with the Larkins, yet little of that talk seemed to shed any real light on the whereabouts of Aaron Stokes or his cousin Nathan. Both seemed to have disappeared into thin air.

The Pratt kid returned to stand beside the Campbell girl and pointed to where a black haze filled the southern sky and drifted eastward with the slow afternoon wind.

"Brother and Sister Mitchell came ridin' hell bent for the sheriff's office not long after that started. Rumor up and down the street is they were actually inside Mr. Feldman's barn when it caught fire. Folks are sayin' it was spontaneous combustion."

For an instant, Susan panicked. "Were they hurt?" she demanded.

The Pratt kid shook his head. "No, but I heard they found Bradley Hunter's body out there. Looks like Feldman killed him."

Susan watched the drifting haze from Feldman's barn. Suddenly, she wondered if Hunter's death was somehow connected to the disappearance of Stokes and Larkin and if Feldman was involved in all of it. Abruptly, her train of thought came to a halt as the door of Kelson's store opened and Edward Kelson emerged to stand on the boardwalk with two very dirty and unsavory looking characters.

"I'll bet those are the fellows Bother Mitchell wants us to avoid," said the Pratt kid.

The kid's voice was low and filled with a harsh vehemence that took Susan by surprise, and the sudden tenseness she felt in the boy filled her with a sense of foreboding.

"What are you up to, Daniel?" She hissed. She watched as Kelson said something inaudible and the two men glanced quickly in her direction.

"I think we've got trouble," the kid muttered.

The Campbell girl grabbed at the kid's shirt sleeve. "What's going on?" she hissed as the kid jerked his arm free of her grasp. "Brother Mitchell told me those fellows would shoot us in the blink of an eye," the kid said crossly. "You can hang on my arm anytime you want—but not right now. You and Sister Mitchell start walkin' up toward the bank right now. And don't dawdle. I'll be right behind you. When you get near enough to do it, signal Brother Mitchell that you need help."

Susan took the younger woman by the arm and started walking briskly toward the bank. Immediately she lost track of the Pratt kid as the clatter of their heels on the boardwalk erased any trace of the kid's progress.

"What's going on?" the younger woman demanded.

"We are trying to keep Brother Pratt and ourselves from being killed."

"I don't understand."

"Perhaps not, but now is not the time for explanations."

With that, Susan loosed the girl's arm and shoved her free hand into the open mouth of her handbag. Her fingers had barely closed on the rosewood grips of the Colt inside, when she heard Daniel's angry challenge to the two men angling swiftly across the street on a course set to intercept her.

The reaction of the pair in the street was so swift that neither woman had time to do more than turn and witness the ear splitting eruption of gunfire as the two outlaws yanked pistols from their gunbelts and poured a barrage of lead toward the Pratt kid who now stood forty feet away at the edge of the boardwalk.

Horrified, Susan watched as the Pratt kid snatched at his own pistol and fired twice. A heartbeat later the kid's pistol bellowed again, filling the air with the sulfurous stench of burnt powder. The Campbell girl screamed and made as though she would run toward the Pratt kid, but Susan grabbed at the girl's arm and held her fast. Abruptly, the thunder died, the sound of it rushing away toward the distant peaks of the Timpanogos.

The Pratt kid stood for a moment, the smoking bore of his Colt trained on the two men lying prone in the dusty street then slowly he settled downward to sit in the dust beside the boardwalk.

Both women rushed to the kid's side and knelt beside him. Susan frowned at the blood soaking one pant leg.

"You have no more sense than Bother Mitchell," she muttered irately as she wadded her kerchief and pressed it tightly into the wound. The Pratt kid flinched at the pressure against wounded flesh.

"Damn it, woman! Be a little gentle!"

"Stop fidgeting!" Susan commanded. "Hold this," she ordered the Campbell girl.

"What in the hell just happened?" The younger woman demanded as she took Susan's place and held the kerchief tightly against the Pratt kid's leg.

For a moment, nothing was said; then a tall man in a butcher's apron looked down on the girl. "I think this young fellow just saved your lives," he said quietly.

Across the street, Edward Kelson stepped quickly away as the door of his shop slammed open and a hot tempered

Mitchell stormed across the room and backed him tightly into a corner.

"What the hell were you thinking when you pointed out my wife to a man like Kyle Dunford!" He demanded angrily.

"I don't know what you're talking about…"

"I'm talking about that dead piece of shit lying in the street. You told him Susan was my wife, didn't you."

"He said he was an old friend and heard you were in town. How was I to know he would start shooting at everyone?"

"Not everyone; just my wife. If it hadn't been for that Pratt kid, she'd probably be dead right now."

"It's not my fault the man went berserk."

"I suppose you've been talking to Walt Biggs too."

"Mr. Biggs seems like a decent fellow."

"You're either a poor judge of character or just plain stupid. Walt Biggs has never been a decent fellow, and most people with any sense can recognize the fact without a second glance at the man. And Kyle Dunford was cut from the same bolt of cloth."

"I saw nothing of that in either man… In fact, they were both quite affable and expressed a great deal of interest in my investment ideas."

"Mister, you got rocks in you head. Biggs is a damned outlaw."

"So you say…."

Frustrated, Mitchell stepped back a pace, giving Kelson room to breathe. The big man took a deep breath and puffed out his chest. "I'm a respected citizen here, Mitchell, and I see no reason why I should allow you or anyone else to insult me.

I suggest you leave my store before I'm forced to send for the sheriff."

Abruptly, Mitchell turned and left the store. He had been angry enough to kill the man when he had discovered Kelson's duplicity in the shooting, but the anger had quickly dissipated when he realized what a pompous fool Kelson really was.

"You didn't do anything you would regret, did you?"

Mitchell paused as Sarah took his arm and steered him across the street to where the Pratt kid now lay on the boardwalk. "Are you sure you're not hurt?" Mitchell demanded grimly as Susan pushed though a small crowd of gawkers. He took her by the hand and drew her close. In his arms, he could feel her tremble even as she struggled to hide her reaction to the sudden violence.

"I'm fine... really," she murmured bravely. "None of the shots came close enough to Lynne or me to notice."

"How is Daniel?"

"He's lucky it isn't worse. The bullet went though his thigh, but didn't hit the bone or any major blood vessels. Mr. Jenkins has already cleaned and dressed the wound. He says Daniel should be fine in a week or two."

Satisfied that the Pratt kid was not in any grave danger and that his own presence would not interfere with Jenkins' work on the kid, Mitchell pushed through the crowd and hunkered down beside the kid. The kid's face was pale as he looked up at Mitchell.

"Hurts like hell... especially when I try to move my leg," he groaned.

"So stop flopping around, you nitwit. You ain't going to die."

At Mitchell's words, the kid seemed to relax, or at least some of the tenseness drained from his face. "You was right," the kid grumbled. "They didn't hesitate one second. That storekeeper pointed us out, and they was on the street grabbin' pistols and ready to shoot before Sister Mitchell had gone ten steps. There wasn't nothin' I could do but try and change their minds. I reckon they didn't like the interference."

Mitchell looked toward the street where Turner already had men clearing away the two bodies. "Looks like you gave them a permanent change of mind," he told the boy.

The Pratt kid frowned and looked down at his leg. The blood soaked pant leg was neatly cut from knee to hip.

"Yeah, your butt's hanging out," joked Mitchell. "But nobody's lookin' except Sister Campbell."

"I am not!" exclaimed the girl, her face suddenly flushed.

Mitchell smiled suddenly and stood. "I'll leave you to Sister Campbell's kind attentions," he told the kid. To the girl, he said. "If Jenkins thinks it will be all right to move him, we'll load him in the wagon with the rest of your things and haul him back to camp when we leave. Just take good care of him."

"You make it sound like he's a piece of furniture and I own him," the girl objected.

Mitchell sighed and drew the girl aside. "I ain't nearly as dumb as I might look," he said quietly. "I know the look you had on your face, and I can tell when a woman has laid claim on a man. You just take good care of him. You're both good folks and you'll be good for each other. I won't say anything to Daniel about it; that way he can think it was all his idea when he gets up the nerve to talk about it."

CHAPTER 12

28 September

*T*hree days later, just after noon, Jared Turner walked into the Mitchell camp and dropped into a chair. He leaned forward and pulled off his boots, and Mitchell could tell the deputy was more than just trail weary. The man looked utterly unhappy.

"Funny, you never notice how rugged them mountains are when you're straddlin' a good horse. I got pains in places I didn't know was there," he grumbled.

"You look like you've been dragged though a knot hole," replied Mitchell. "What the hell have you been up to? And where's that roan gelding of yours?"

"Dead... about ten miles south... maybe eight. I'm not sure."

For a moment, Turner was silent as Sarah handed him a hot bowl of stew and a hunk of her homemade bread. "Ain't had anything to eat since yesterday," he explained, after wolfing down the stew and swabbing the bowl clean with the bread.

"I was following Feldman's trail and finally caught up with him—up high and deep in some pines. He spotted me and high-tailed it out of there as fast as he could. It was too thick in those pines to run a horse flat out, but I managed to stay with him for a while. Not for long though. Somehow, he go me twisted around until I wasn't sure which way was up. Next thing I knew, I was walking the gelding on a trail across a steep talus slope. The rock was loose and the footing real bad. Feldman was nowhere in sight.

"The gelding just slipped, and the whole side of the hill started moving. Wasn't a thing I could do for the horse; he was already up to his knees in that stuff. So I scampered out of there like a jackrabbit with his tail on fire. When I looked back, the gelding was gone and all my gear buried with him. I didn't dare walk out there to look for any of my gear. I just started walking and hoped I could get off the mountain before I froze to death.

"I had my knife, my pistol, and an old piece of flint in my coat pocket. Last night, I built a shelter, gathered up a pile of firewood, and got a little fire going. I spent the night half-froze and wishing Feldman would walk up to my fire so I could shoot him."

"And you walked out today?" asked Susan.

"More of a climb than a walk," Turner responded. "Those mountains are steep and in some places it was quicker to get off the trail and take a straight shot at getting out of there. It was more work, but it probably saved me three or four hours and another night freezing my tail off."

"Where did all this happen?" asked Mitchell.

Turner studied the ground and shook his head. "That's the odd thing," he muttered sheepishly. "I've got a vague notion that when I first spotted Feldman; he was poking around an old camp site below a bald peak..."

"A bald peak?"

"No, that ain't quite right," Turner corrected. "I was up high, so it must have been part of a ridge line—just a knob where the northern slope dropped down real steep through thick pines to a little lake at the base of the slope. Feldman was there in a clearing near the edge of the lake. I could see a few small cliffs twelve or fifteen-hundred feet up the side of the mountain. Then above that, just the rocky knob sticking out above the tree tops."

"You said Feldman was poking around an old camp site?"

"That's what it looked like—rocks piled like a fire pit in the center and a few rotten old trees laid out around the perimeter like some kind of a barricade."

"What was he looking for?" Susan demanded impatiently.

"I have no idea," Turner replied, "but I'm sure he never found anything right then 'cause he hadn't been off his horse for more than a minute or two when he spotted me coming through the trees and took off like the devil himself was after him."

Turner held out his empty bowl while Sarah filled it with a second helping of stew. "I did discover something important while I was up there," Turner declared cryptically.

Suddenly, both women turned their full attention on the deputy.

"I discovered I ain't no mountain man, and I ain't no tracker. I failed miserably at both."

"Losing your horse was just bad luck," reasoned Mitchell. "Next time you'll be better prepared and you'll stay away from trails crossing bad ground."

Turner shook his head. "There ain't goin' to be a next time. I had my fill of that crap. I got a family and a farm, and that's good enough for me. I ain't cut out for this kind of work."

"You're not going after Feldman?"

"No, I'm not."

Mitchell frowned and looked toward Center Creek and the mountains beyond. "You should at least talk to the man. You have plenty of cause to arrest him for the murder of the Hunter boy."

"Oh, I agree," Turner replied, "and if he shows up around here, I'll arrest him quick as a wink. But I ain't goin' into those mountains alone again. You're welcome to go up there and drag his ass back to town, but I've had enough mountains for awhile."

Mitchell grunted out a humorless laugh and looked up at Sarah and Susan. "Maybe I will," he replied.

Three hours later, Mitchell dismounted from the grulla's back and tightened the cinch another notch. When he was satisfied the saddle wasn't going to slip and dump him on the rocky trail, he took a long look at the surrounding slopes and felt an overpowering sense of solitude settle like an immense weight upon his shoulders.

Suddenly, it felt as though the wilderness had stretched to infinity in every direction while he himself had shrunk to miniscule proportions. The sensation left him feeling insignificant and extremely vulnerable—vulnerable enough to strike up a one-sided conversation with the grulla.

"I can see why Turner was spooked by this country," he grumbled. "Ten miles would seem like a hundred with no horse and no gear."

The grulla made no reply, seemingly more intent on the local grass than on Mitchell's company. Finally, Mitchell took the animal by the rein and started walking the narrow trail. Within moments, his thoughts had turned inward to the

questions he had pondered in front of Murphy's store—
questions of family and what they might face in the future.

Somehow, he found it hard to believe that life for the
Saints in the Great Basin would continue as it now was.
Already, political and economic forces were bringing changes
to life in the Salt Lake Valley, and he was certain the
completion of the railroad would speed the process, with the
influx of gentiles and outsiders into the Territory bringing even
more friction over plural marriage and other cultural
differences.

His own family would surely be caught in the battle over
plural marriage, and somehow they would have to find a way
to keep the family from being ground to bits in the conflict.

"You're a deep thinking fellow."

Startled, Mitchell turned to find Mort standing in the trees
not ten feet away. "You scared the crap out of me," he growled.

"Good lord, we better feed you quick. There ain't nothin'
left after a scare like that."

"Why the hell are you hiding in there?" Mitchell
grumbled.

The old man grinned and held up an oversized pan that
looked as though it had been burned in a fire. "Ain't hidin'," he
responded. "Been doin' a little gold panning whilst I waited
for you. Ain't found anything special though, just lots of open
country and damned few people; thank the good Lord. Kind
of place a fellow could live and not have a herd of folks tellin'
him what to do and how to live."

Mitchell eyed the old man and cracked a smile. "You may
have a good idea there," he said thoughtfully.

The old man grinned. "Might be a little lonely for womenfolk and kids, but a fellow could take 'em all to town every

now and again. And a couple of college taught gals oughta be able to school their own kids as well as anyone."

Mitchell watched as the old man tossed the blackened pan on the ground and led his pigeon toed horse from among the trees. "A fellow would have to find the right place for a setup like that," he reasoned, following the old man up the trail.

The old man twisted around and gave Mitchell a look of disgust. "You nuts or what? Compared to most folks, you got money coming out your ears. You don't have to *find* the right place; you just pick a good location and *make* the right place."

"I guess you're right."

"'Course I'm right. If you're isolated just enough, the world will forget you exist. 'Cept I might change the way I do *some* things, if I was you."

"Change what?"

"Well… you ain't a very low profile fellow anyways, but draggin' all your womenfolk along makes the bunch of you stick out like a sore thumb. The world ain't gonna forget you when you're trailin' a gaggle of wives everywhere you go. Rotate 'em boy and never make it obvious you got more than one."

"Makes sense," Mitchell agreed. "I've discussed a similar plan with Sarah and Susan already. They both approve the idea. I just haven't settled on where we should live."

"Wouldn't drag my feet none if I was you. This Territory is gonna become a hot potato, and lots of folks are gonna get burned before things cool down."

The old man was suddenly quiet, his eyes roving the surrounding trees with interest. "Déjà-vu," he muttered.

Mitchell scanned the area quickly, searching for signs of the missing Feldman, and judging the defensibility of their position, should they be attacked. "You been here before?" He asked.

Mort frowned, then shrugged and pointed eastward. "Long time ago," he answered. "First time with friends—last time to collect a fellow. There's a small lake just over that ridge."

When they topped the ridge twenty minutes later, Mitchell could see nothing but a long meadow below and thick pines covering the slopes beyond. "Must not be the same place," he told the old man.

The old man snorted and gave Mitchell a look of disdain. "Open your eyes, boy and look into them trees. See where the slope flattens out… Ain't that water I see sparklin' among the trees?"

Mitchell looked over his shoulder to see the sun low in the sky. In less than an hour it would be dusk and the sun would be hidden below the crest of the western mountains. "Might be a good place to set up camp," he suggested.

The old man nodded his agreement. "Oh, it's a dandy place for a camp. There's a little stream runs down and feeds into the lake… probably a spring up above someplace" he said tiredly.

"You don't sound very enthusiastic.

"It's a nice enough place. It just conjures up old memories—some good, some bad, most of which don't bother me much, but this place seems to stir some mighty strange feelings deep down in my innards. Makes me feel a little green around the gills."

"I hope you ain't going to throw up. If you are, step over by that sagebrush to do it. I got a weak stomach when it comes to that kind of thing, and I'll end up tossing my lunch right along with you."

"I ain't goin' to throw up. It's just that the idea of camping on the spot where twenty of them conquistador fellows got themselves copped to bits don't set too well. Probably wouldn't bother me none, but it weren't a pretty sight."

For a long while, Mitchell stared at the water glittering through the trees. Finally, he swung down from the saddle. "This looks like a dandy spot for a camp, don't you think?"

The old man smiled. "Mighty fine," he conceded happily. "Beats campin' on a pile of bones."

The eastern sky was still burning with red-orange fire and a rising sun when Mitchell rolled out of his bedroll and forced his feet into an ice cold pair of boots. Frost covered the ground and the leaves on the aspen seemed suddenly more colorful than they had the previous day. Mitchell knew the weather could change for the worse at any moment, and the mountain might soon be covered with snow. Quite probably, they had two or three weeks before snow became a problem, but it wouldn't take much to put an end to any real exploration of the mountains south of Heber City.

He scowled as he finished saddling the grulla and peered across the saddle to the shadow covered pines where the early morning sunlight had only begun to filter through the trees and glisten on the surface of the tiny mountain lake.

"Did you see that?" he demanded abruptly.

The old man glanced across the meadow and grunted humorlessly. "Ghosts," he responded gravely.

"Seriously," objected Mitchell.

"And what did you see? If it wasn't a ghost...."

"Just a flash of light."

"Interesting."

"And a horse," added Mitchell.

"Now that *is* strange."

"Probably Mr. Feldman...."

"Wearing a very flashy metal shirt and hat," the old man countered.

Mitchell squinted and struggled to conjure up an accurate image, but the vision eluded him. "Now you've put *that* thought in my head, all I can see is a conquistador on a gray horse."

"With spots," the old man added. "Does this ghostly fellow have a name?" he prompted.

Mitchell frowned, remembering the spots on the horse's rump. "Antonio de Guevara," he responded without thinking.

The old man's face split into a grin. "Serves the bastard right," he squawked happily. "Mean clear through, that one. Conscience like a chunk if rawhide boiled and dried out hard as a rock. Looked and acted the bookish type, but was always lookin' for ways to stab a fellow in the back."

"Sounds like you know him well."

"Knew him briefly," the old man replied. "These mountains and the gold fever snapped something inside the man. He wasn't at all happy to meet the Shinob. Sorta scared the life right out of him."

"When did you meet him?"

"Right after he killed those fellows over by the lake."

Mitchell frowned and stared at the lake. He dreaded the direction the old man was taking the conversation. "He killed twenty men?" he asked quietly.

"While they was drugged half out of their minds. He wanted the gold all to himself, so he drugged their food with some plant he found and killed every man jack of 'em. Then he ran 'cause the Shinob was coming for him. Killed his horse in a rockslide not far from here. He was a sittin' there under some pines scribblin' away in his journal when I found him."

Mitchell shuddered involuntarily as the obsidian edged war axe slashed toward the man beneath the tree and swept the head from his neck. The scene unfolded like a perfectly vivid memory from the depths of his own mind.

"Yep… Nasty fellow," the old man muttered. "Serves him right if he has to wander a bit and ponder his sins."

Mitchell shook his head in disbelief and forced himself to think of something more pleasant. "I reckon a place like Heber City would be too harsh in the wintertime for the kind of place I'd like for Sarah and Susan," he said deliberately.

The old man cracked a smile. "Look a little farther South," he counseled. "Manti… Richfield… milder winters, hotter summers."

The lake was small, cold, and crystal clear when Mitchell halted the grulla and let the animal slake its thirst from a thin stream of water trickling down from the northern face of the mountain. The animal pushed to the edge of the stream, stretched out its neck and gulped at the water until Mitchell drew him away from the icy stream and led the way into what had once been a large, yet perfectly concealed clearing near the southern edge of the lake.

The clearing had once been more than two-hundred feet in diameter, thickly surrounded by pines, and wedged between the lake and the sharply rising slope to the south.

The surrounding pines were now old, thick at the bole, and in some cases rotted, dead and crushed to the earth in a tangle of lifeless branches. New growth had sprung up where old had fallen. Aspen had seized territory once claimed by pines. And amid them both, mountain grass fought for a hold among fallen leaves and layers of long dead pine needles.

"Ain't quite so eerie, once you get right up close," Mitchell suggested.

The old man let his eyes rove the clearing. "Like I told you," he insisted, "it's a nice place for a camp, so long as you don't know about them Spanish fellers spread out all over the place."

"Looks like someone has been doing a little digging here and there," Mitchell observed.

The old man ground hitched his pigeon-toed horse, and wandered to the nearest hump of freshly dug earth and examined the hole beside it. "Kind of like a post hole, only they ain't so deep," he reported as he kicked loose soil back into the hole.

"What are they for?" asked Mitchell as he copied the old man and kicked dirt and leaves into the nearest hole.

"Treasure hunters, I reckon. Won't do 'em no good though. Guevara cached a bit of gold and anything else he wanted up in them rocks."

Mitchell wandered the clearing, kicking dirt into every hole he could find. He was hardly surprised when nearly every pile of soil proffered up odd bits of worm eaten bone and rust cankered metal.

"The Campbell girl told us Stokes and Hunter found an old journal and a map somewhere up here. They thought the map would lead them to an old Spanish gold mine."

"Not Spanish... and not really a mine," the old man corrected. "Salazar led Guevara and the others into these mountains looking for Aztec treasure."

"Aztec?"

"When Cortez laid siege to Tenochtitlan, Cuauhtémoc sent a huge part of the empire's treasury out of the city with a few hundred warriors to protect it. They traveled north to find Aztlan, the ancient home of the Aztecs, and hide portions of the treasure in various locations."

"Never heard of Cuauhtémoc."

"Motecuhzoma was killed. His nephew, Cuauhtémoc was king during the siege, and he sent Qetzalcatl and his warriors north with the treasure. They cached the treasure, and mapped every location. One warrior eventually made it back to Tenochtitlan, but Cortez had already won the city. Thousands were dead of plague and starvation and nowhere for the map to go. So the warrior kept the map and told no one where he had been except his two sons. He made copies of the map and gave one to each of his sons.

"After his death the two sons went looking for the treasure. They never returned and their maps were lost with them. The warrior's map was handed down through his daughter's family until nearly a-hundred and fifty years later, when it was sold to Salazar."

Mitchell raised an eyebrow. "And then Stokes found it," he suggested.

The old man cracked a smile. "Sorta... Guevara killed Salazar and the others almost two-hundred years go. I reckon Stokes found it last year."

Mitchell frowned and shook his head in disbelief. The whole story was so far-fetched it would have been laughable if it hadn't been for the worm eaten shards of bone and the unrecognizable bits of rusted metal scattered about the clearing.

"All of that really makes no difference," he said stubbornly. "I came up here to find Feldman and see what he has to say about Bradley Hunter's murder. He looks guilty as sin right now."

Mitchell halted his methodical refilling of holes. There were too many to deal with easily, and he found he was not in the mood to wander about the clearing kicking dirt into holes. The old man's story had been strange, unbelievable, and unnerving at the same time. Finally, he wandered back to the grulla, pausing only briefly beside the old man's horse.

"That's a good yarn!" He called out as the old man continued kicking dirt near a tangle of rotting deadfall on the far side of the clearing.

"Ain't no yarn!" came the stiff reply. "Seen every bit of it myself!"

Mitchell fished around in his saddle bags and brought out a large hunk of jerky. "Want some jerky?" he called, ignoring the old man's defense of his tale.

"You ain't listenin'!"

"Sure I am; I got a couple of tins of beans if you ain't interested in jerky."

"Beans! I tell you the bald-faced truth, and you accuse me of spinning yarns!"

"Beans sound better to me too," Mitchell responded agreeably. "I've about had a craw full of jerky."

"Damn!" squawked the old man. "My reins is tied in a big knot! Danite…."

"Ain't touched 'em," lied Mitchell. "Must have been that Guevara fellow."

"Guevara my ass! You tied my reins in a knot!" The old man tugged at the tangled leather and muttered under his breath.

Mitchell leaned forward and peered closely at the tightly woven straps. "Don't believe I've ever seen anything quite like it," he insisted. "Was that Guevara fellow ever a sailor? I hear sailors can tie some wicked knots and that sure is a wicked looking knot."

"This ain't no sailor's knot," the old man growled. "It's the kind of knot some goat roper with four thumbs would tie."

"Goat roper!"

"With four thumbs!"

The old man glanced toward the lake and groaned. "I got half a mind not to mention that fellow down by the lake."

Mitchell spun quickly toward the lake to see a man in a light brown coat dig his heals into the sides of his horse and gallop hell-bent into the pines. "That must be Feldman."

"Go!" The old man snapped. "I ain't here for Mr. Feldman. You are!"

Mitchell grabbed up the grulla's rein, threw himself into the saddle, and tagged the animal's flanks with his spurs. The animal lunged ahead in a head-long pursuit of Feldman and the roan mare.

At first, the distance between the two animals widened, as though the mare was the swifter of the two, but in less than three hundred yards, the grulla had closed the gap and was hard on the roan's heels. Then the terrain shifted. The woods changed from bristling pines to tall, closely spaced lodgepoles and back again so swiftly that Mitchell fought to keep himself from being swept from the saddle by the wild lash of pine boughs or crushed by the unyielding trunks of the lodgepoles.

Finally, Mitchell was forced to rein in the grulla, and Feldman was soon lost among the trees. Angered by his failure to overtake the man, Mitchell began the slower process of tracking the roan through the soft mountain soil. "Thought that fellow wasn't supposed to be able to ride," he hissed.

At a walk, the grulla's heavy breathing slowed to a regular and rhythmic rate, and before long, the sedate pace and the search for the roan's tracks on a well traveled game trail left Mitchell himself in a more peaceful state of mind. So peaceful, in fact, that the sudden appearance of the riderless roan among a cluster of aspen near the trail so startled Mitchell that he snatched the Navy Colt from its holster and searched for a hidden Feldman among the trees. When Feldman failed to appear, Mitchell moved cautiously ahead.

When Feldman did appear, it was not with pistol in hand, but with fist clenched upon the bloodied shaft of a broken pine branch, a branch that pierced his chest and held him firmly where his horse had thrown him upon the deadfall blocking the trail.

Feldman opened his eyes as Mitchell knelt beside him. For an instant he seemed startled; then he smiled. "My horse threw me," he said hoarsely. "I thought I might be okay, but now *you've* come—I can see, it's worse than I thought."

"It's pretty bad," Mitchell said quietly.

Feldman coughed and blood frothed at his lips. "I never hurt anyone," he confided quietly. All I ever wanted was a family and a decent place for them to live...."

Suddenly, he reached out and grabbed Mitchell by the sleeve. "Hurts," he whispered. "Take me home so it don't hurt no more."

Tears welled up in the man's eyes, and Mitchell felt his own heart wrench. He gripped the dying hand tightly and felt dampness in his own eyes. "It's okay," he said quietly. "You can go home now."

Mitchell said little on the way back down the mountain, and it was just after noon when they rounded the last bend in the trail and the white canvas tops of the wagons appeared less than a mile away.

"Feldman was still alive when I found him," he said finally. "He was hurt bad, and there wasn't a thing I could do to help him."

The old man glanced quickly at Mitchell, but made no reply.

"By then he wasn't thinking too clearly. He thought I'd come to take him home."

The old man said nothing.

"He never killed that boy, did he?"

The old man quietly shook his head.

Mitchell sighed and studied the back of the grulla's head. "He was just a quiet fellow and nobody took the time to know him."

"He's past all that now," the old man said thoughtfully.

"I sure felt useless."

"Well, you weren't. You done what you was sent to do, and you collected the poor fellow real gentle like. You done fine, so quit squawkin'. You're makin' me tired."

"I didn't do any collecting."

"Look here, boy. I've been at this callin' a long time, and it ain't at all what you think it is. But you'll learn…. You'll learn."

Mitchell scowled and reined the grulla to a halt less than a hundred yards from the camp. "What do you make of that?" he asked, pointing to where multiple horse tracks had churned the ground into dust.

The old man removed his hat and massaged the back of his neck with one hand. "Looks like you've had a visitor," he replied. "Seems like a good spot to keep an eye on your camp without being seen."

Mitchell frowned at the thought of someone watching the camp. "I don't recognize the tracks," he admitted. "Turner says Baldy Jackman and his bunch are camped over on Lake Creek somewhere. You think one of them has been hanging around?"

"You're talkin' to the wrong fellow," the old man protested. "Never had any experience trackin' horses. I tracked a Jaguar once, when I was younger. He was a fighter, that one. But I finally got the better of him and put his own sword through his heart. "Ain't Utes though. I can tell that much, unless they've got steel shod horses now days."

"I suspect it's one of Jackman's bunch," Mitchell responded unhappily.

The old man held up the reins to Feldman's horse and nodded in the direction of camp. "Why don't you go on down and check on your womenfolk while I take Mr. Feldman down to Deputy Turner. Turner can talk with you later, if he needs to know more than I can tell him about how Mr. Feldman died."

The old man was soon on his way, and when Mitchell finally dismounted, it was with a sigh of relief and the feeling of being home. At first, the feeling puzzled him, the camp was certainly nothing like home, the surroundings were neither comfortable nor familiar, and it took a moment to realize what made the place feel as it did. It had nothing to do with the location or the familiarity of things; rather, the feeling enfolded him like a warm blanket, and it came when he saw Susan rise from the chair beside the fire and come towards him, while Sarah turned and smiled in greeting from a makeshift table and a washtub full of dishes and soapy water. In an instant, Mitchell knew that home was wherever these women chose to be.

"We didn't expect to see you back so soon," Susan confided as she watched him strip the saddle from the grulla and store his gear in the back of one of the wagons. "We thought you would be gone at least a week," she added.

Mitchell looked into Susan's eyes for a moment; then took her in his arms and held her close. "I think it would have taken longer," he admitted, "but I ran across Mort up there, and somehow we ended up right where we needed to be when Feldman showed up."

"You spoke with him?"

"For a moment," he answered.

"For a moment? I don't understand."

Mitchell smiled and took her by the hand. "Let's gather up Sarah and get comfortable," he proposed. "Then I can tell both of you what happened."

An hour later, Sarah leaned forward in her camp chair and studied Mitchell's face. "You saw a conquistador?"

Mitchell shook his head. "I saw a man on a gray horse," he replied. "Mort said he was a conquistador. It could have been anyone."

"What a terrible way to die," Susan observed quietly.

Sarah frowned. "You don't believe Mr. Feldman had anything to do with Bradley Hunter's death, do you?"

Mitchell looked up at Sarah's question and shook his head. "At first, I thought he might have killed the boy, but not now. There's no earthly reason I should feel so strongly about it, but just those few words before he died convinced me that he had nothing to do with it."

"Then why did he run when you discovered him," asked Sarah. "It certainly made him look guilty enough."

"Yes, it did," Mitchell responded, "so much so that I chased him to his death."

"And it leaves us without a clue to the killer's identity," Susan concluded.

"Someone had the motivation for it," responded Sarah, "even if we can't see the reasoning behind it."

"Perhaps Bradley Hunter discovered something about Stokes and Larkin," Susan offered. "Perhaps he found some proof that Stokes is dead. Hunter could have been killed to keep him quiet."

"You're thinking of the bones in that pit, aren't you," concluded Sarah.

"Those bones belong to someone," reasoned Susan. "It seems perfectly reasonable to assume they belong to Aaron Stokes."

"They might well belong to Nathan Larkin," Sarah suggested.

"They very well may," Susan agreed readily. "In either case, we might surmise that one of them was killed because someone thought they had found gold, and Bradley Hunter was killed because he knew something that would have brought it all to light and expose the killer."

"So Hunter was silenced before he could tell anyone what he knew," Sarah concluded.

Mitchell leaned back in his own chair and let himself relax and enjoy the moment. The warmth of the fire eased the ache in his bones, and the smell of sage drifted about the camp with every shift of the breeze scattering smoke from the campfire.

"Looks like we're about out of firewood," he said absently.

"We've been getting by with bits of dead sagebrush," Sarah admitted.

"I'll go out and drag in something more substantial," he offered.

"Wait an hour or two," suggested Sarah. "Lunch should be ready soon. Lynne just put potatoes on to boil, and we have those steaks you bought from Sister Murphy."

"That rider is probably Mort coming from town," she said, pointing toward a vague figure in the distance. "He'll want that steak you promised him."

"Turner wasn't happy about Feldman," the old man reported when his plate was empty for the second time and Sarah's motley colored dog lay under the nearest wagon, gnawing on leftover steak bones.

"I'm not happy about Feldman either," advised Mitchell. "I wanted to ask him how he came by those saddlebags."

The old man nodded and waved one hand in an arch that took in the southern half of the valley and the mountains beyond.

"I reckon he found 'em somewhere and picked 'em up."

Mitchell eyed the old man suspiciously. "Is there something you're not telling us?" he demanded.

"Not me," the old man protested. "I'm a regular chatterbox. Never could keep a secret."

"I hadn't noticed."

"It's true. No one confides in me any more. It's kind of depressing. A fellow my age kind of likes a little conversation now and again, especially in the evening when everyone's sittin' around the fireplace all cozy and everything."

"I'm afraid this is as close as the Mitchell's come to having a fireplace at the moment," Sarah replied, pointing to the campfire.

"Like a family of wandering gypsies," the old man squawked happily. "Say! Did I tell you about that gypsy fellow I met in Spain last week?"

"I thought you were in Paris last week," objected Mitchell.

"Paris on Tuesday, Madrid on Wednesday. Now, this gypsy fellow, he had a real sense of humor… candle maker he was … traveled the country sellin' his candles.

"Ran into a rich old Spanish fellow who refused to pay him one year. Next time around, the rich old boy pulled the same trick, but got some special candles for his trouble. That gypsy fellow had loaded up three or four of those candles with black powder and a cannon fuse tied to a short wick.

"Burnt down half that old boy's house. He never knew what hit him." The old man paused for a moment then looked at Sarah. "Yep, you folks remind me of old Georgio the gypsy. 'Cept he burned down houses while you seem to prefer barns."

CHAPTER 13

30 September

Mitchell awoke to the sound of the Lady-dog's clamorous barking and the smell of smoke. The smell alone threw him into a sudden panic, and the dog's persistent noise provided the impetuous to bring him fully awake in an instant with his heart pounding.

A quick glance about the darkened interior of the wagon revealed no sign of flames, and the smell of smoke was definitely coming from outside the wagon. With that fact in mind, and Sarah's immediate safety assured, he snatched up his trousers and flung himself from the back of the wagon.

"It's Lynne's wagon!" bellowed the Pratt kid as he rushed past and clamored up the side of the burning wagon.

Mitchell tossed his trousers aside and ran for the back of the girl's wagon and threw down the gate.

"I've got her!" bellowed the kid as he dragged the groggy, stumbling girl from beneath the blazing canvas canopy.

Mitchell glanced quickly at the pair and then ignored them completely as he began ripping the girl's belongings from the back of the wagon.

"This town seems to have a penchant for fires!" He yelled as the Pratt kid joined him..

"Forget the rest!" the kid bellowed.

Mitchell felt the kid's rough hold drag at his arm, holding him back from the wagon. Swiftly, Mitchell surveyed the camp, gauging the distance between the other wagons and the one that had now turned itself into a large bonfire. The morning air was calm, and with no breeze to fan the flames, the canvas top had already disintegrated and fallen into the wagon bed, and for the moment the situation seemed unlikely to grow worse.

"Sorry I couldn't rescue more of your things," he told the Campbell girl.

"It's a wonder you saved anything at all," the girl replied quietly.

"We may need to go into town," Susan advised from where she stood beside the girl, examining the blackened sleeve of the girl's nightgown and the damaged flesh beneath.

"How bad?" asked Mitchell.

"Not as bad as it could have been," Susan replied. "It might have been very serious, if Daniel hadn't acted so quickly. As it is, I think she'll be fine after we get the burn cleaned up and bandaged, but we should have the doctor look at it anyway."

The Campbell girl looked down at her arm and shuddered. "It hurts," she admitted, "but I think it looks worse than it really is."

"I'm sick of fires," Mitchell complained as he scooped up his discarded trousers and pulled them on. "How in the hell did this one get started?"

The Pratt kid led the Campbell girl to one of the camp chairs and made her sit while Susan began cleaning the burn.

"The dog woke me up," he reported grimly. "I heard a horse running past the camp and then breaking glass. When I looked over this way, I could see flames on the ground beside

Lynne's wagon, and the canvas was already lit up and glowing like a lantern."

Mitchell frowned and shivered in the cold morning air. "You heard a horse," he repeated.

"And breaking glass," the kid added.

"And I smell kerosene," Mitchell concluded thoughtfully. "It must have been that damned Jackman," he growled. "He must have ridden by and smashed a kerosene lamp against the wagon."

"It's a miracle Lynne wasn't burned much worse," Sarah offered as she came to Mitchell's side and handed him his coat. "She's asking if you saved the small box that was setting on top of her hope chest."

Mitchell shrugged and shook his head. "I have no idea," he replied. "I just yanked everything out of there as fast as I could. I don't remember any small box, but it could have been dragged along with the quilts or something. If it came out at all, it's probably laying on the ground somewhere."

Sarah sighed and touched Mitchell lightly on the arm. "Look for it, please. She's beginning to react to the pain and the shock of the whole incident, and she's insistent that she have the little box. Let's try and humor her."

Mitchell nodded and turned to the task, hoping the box could be found quickly, so he could get into his boots before his feet were frozen solid. The wagon had calmed from the ferocity of its original angry blaze to a more sedate and warming kind of bonfire, but the heat of its burning did little to subdue the icy cold of frozen earth on bare feet.

His feet were painfully on the edge of numbness when his toes discovered the missing object and sent it tumbling beneath the chuck-wagon. Mitchell fetched it out and trudged stiff footed to the Campbell girl. "This what you wanted?"

The girl took the box and set it gingerly in her lap. "It is," she said quietly. "Thank you."

Mitchell waited for the girl to open the box, but the wait was unrewarded, and he finally sank into one of the camp chairs and set to massaging the life back into his frozen feet. He had brought them back to the painful tingling of pins and needles when Sarah dropped a pair of socks in his lap and his boots on the ground beside him.

"Remember your promise," she warned. "If it snows, we leave."

Mitchell looked up at a black sky lit by a billion glittering stars. "No snow today," he predicted.

"Then you have another day to play detective," she replied. "We also need another wagon."

Mitchell frowned. "Danged if I know where to find one."

"That's something you and Brother Pratt will have to work out," Sarah replied.

"Hey! I ain't done nothing' to deserve that *Brother Pratt* stuff," the kid objected.

Sarah ignored the Pratt kid's objection and looked toward the eastern skyline. "It's nearly daylight," she told the kid. "As soon as it's light enough to ride, you can take Lynne into town and have the doctor or that Jenkins fellow look at that burn."

"Brother Mitchell?"

Mitchell looked away from the fire at the sound of the Campbell girl's voice.

"I think you should see this," she confided as she opened the box and drew forth an object black as a starless night yet glittering with reflections of the flickering firelight.

"What in the world is that?" Mitchell asked as he rose from his chair and moved to the girl's side. The girl placed the object in his hands and shook her head.

"Looks like a carved snake," he observed, turning the delicately carved object in his hands.

"Nathan gave it to me along with the map and the journal," the girl answered. "He said it was the real key to finding the mine. I don't understand its significance, but Nathan thought it was the most important of the things he left with me."

Mitchell looked closely at the little carving with its square nose and fanged jaws open and ready to strike. "It's a finely crafted little thing," he admitted, "but I don't see anything about it that suggests it's anything more than a little carving."

"It's one of a kind."

Mitchell looked up to see Mort standing within the flickering light cast by the lowering flames of the burning wagon.

"A fellow named Qetzalcatl carved it. Took him nearly a year. Carved it for an old man who was his friend... fellow called Itzcoatl...."

"Obsidian Serpent," said Mitchell, holding the little serpent where firelight seemed to dance on a thousand tiny facets.

The old man moved forward and took the carving from Mitchell's hands. "This little fellow was set to guard a treasure. I wondered where he got off to."

"You've seen it before?"

At the sound of the Campbell girl's voice, the old man turned his gaze from the little serpent.

"I've seen it a time or two," he answered.

"Then you know where the mine is," the girl reasoned.

"Like I told Mitchell, it ain't really a mine. More like an old cavern… all shored up with timbers. Never was very safe. Gave me the willies every time I was there."

"You could take us there!" The Campbell girl exclaimed suddenly. "We could all be rich!"

The old man frowned and handed the little serpent back to the girl. "You keep Itzcoatl," he said quietly. "A good man made that for a friend, and it's worth more than all the gold you could stuff into that old cave."

"You won't take us there?"

The old man shook his head solemnly. "Not on your life," he said, nodding toward the obsidian serpent. "Itzcoatl guards that treasure. And he ain't real partial to visitors."

The streets were hot and dusty when Jared Turner strode down the boardwalk to Murphy's store and dropped into one of Murphy's rickety handmade chairs. "I talked to them rabbit huntin' boys again," he said.

"They remembered something about that skull?" Mitchell suggested.

"No, but it happens they were out towards Center Creek, early this morning. They were headed off from home and saw a big old fire starting out towards your camp. Not long afterwards, they saw a horse and rider walking slow and heading toward the Kelson place."

"Kelson!" Mitchell spat out the name, and forced himself to subdue the sudden urge to hunt down the blustering merchant and beat the hell out of him.

"Those kids never saw who it was," Turner continued, "but I'll have a talk with Kelson anyway."

Mitchell frowned. "Kelson was thick with Biggs and Dunford…maybe they put him up to it…"

Turner shook his head. "Kelson ain't the type," he argued. "He's a blustering bully and a sneak. If he wanted to do something like that, he might sneak out in the dark of night to meet someone and set it up, but he'd never do the deed himself. He'd hire some down-in-the-heel fellow and have him do it."

"I see your point."

"I've got my eye on a fellow I think Kelson may have paid to do it," Turner continued. "He ain't from around here, but he's been seen out toward Kelson's place. He's the shifty type, and I don't trust him an inch.

"I had a talk with him the other day, and I never in my life met anyone that could spin a yarn like this fellow. I wouldn't trust him to guard the hen house if all my chickens was down to the lake loafin' around the beach."

Mitchell nodded in agreement. "You're talking about that old boy who rode into town the other day… the one wearing that stinking old Buffalo coat. I've had my suspicions about him too."

Turner grunted humorlessly. "That's the fellow. Rode in here last night with Feldman's body, claiming he was a friend of yours. I didn't believe a word he said."

"He's been hanging around our camp," Mitchell reported grimly. "I'm not sure what he's up to."

Turner nodded. "Like I say… I got my eye on him." Turner hooked a thumb back toward Murphy's store. "How's the Campbell girl?"

Mitchell leaned back in the rickety chair and gazed down the street toward the stables where the Pratt kid stood in deep conversation with the local blacksmith.

"Jenkins says she's fine," he replied absently. "It looked worse than it was, and Jenkins thinks it will heal without any scars. "She lost a few of her things though. So my womenfolk took her inside to see what they can find to replace it all."

Turner frowned. "Lucky it didn't start the whole valley on fire," he responded. "If we hadn't had so much rain the last week or two, things would have been dry as a tinder box around here."

"Someone is trying to run us off," Mitchell replied thoughtfully. "They knew who we were the minute we rode into town, and they didn't waste any time trying to run us off. I no sooner talked with you about the skull when someone bashed Sarah on the head and set fire to Murphy's store. Now this.... And I ain't all that certain about Feldman's hay barn, now that I think about it. That hay smelled plenty ripe for spontaneous combustion, but it seems mighty coincidental that it decided to ignite the moment Sarah and I went inside to have a look around."

Turner frowned and shook his head. "Maybe it's got nothing to do with Aaron Stokes and those bones we found," he said thoughtfully. "Maybe it's those fellows out on Lake Creek. You said some of them knew you and would cause trouble if they knew where you were."

"It's possible," Mitchell admitted.

"Sure it is," Turner said decisively. "The Campbell girl told everyone in town you were coming. Kelson has had those fellows in and out of his store plenty. He could have said something that got those fellows up on Lake Creek watching for you and planning just how they would take care of you. That old boy I'm watching could be one of them."

Mitchell watched as the Pratt kid shook hands with the blacksmith and started across the street.

"I gave that idea some consideration this morning," he admitted, "but Jackman hasn't seen me for nearly twenty years. If he wanted to get back at me after all these years, seems like he'd do it himself and make sure I knew it."

"There's plenty of fellows who would stab you in the back and walk away happy, 'cause you never seen it coming or knew who done it," Turner grumbled. "This Jackman fellow could be one of 'em, and you might never know what hit you."

Mitchell scowled unhappily. Turner surely had a point. After twenty years, he knew little or nothing about Baldy Jackman or his temperament. Jackman had been hot headed and quick to strike at anyone who crossed him, but twenty years could change anyone. Still, Sarah's description of the four men who had ridden into camp the previous day left no doubt in Mitchell's mind that Jackman knew who they were and where they were camped. If Jackman still wanted revenge, he was certainly capable and had ample opportunity.

"Looks like that Pratt kid finished dickering with Nils," Turner said suddenly. "Limps a little, but he seems to be gettin' around just fine."

"The bullet went through nice and clean... doesn't seem to be infected any." Mitchell grumbled. "Hope he got a reasonable price for that wagon."

Turner snorted happily. "Don't count on it," he squawked cheerfully. "Everyone in town knows that kid works for you, and word got around real quick that you ain't strapped for cash."

Mitchell groaned inwardly at the thought, anticipating bad news from the Pratt kid. "Well?" he asked when the kid stepped onto the boardwalk.

"Well what?" countered the kid.

"Did you get a wagon?"

"Sure I got a wagon."

"How much?"

"Forty bucks."

"Forty bucks!"

Turner's face broke into a grin. "I warned you."

"That's four times what I'd pay down in the valley," Mitchell complained.

The Pratt kid cracked a smile and dropped into a chair beside the deputy.

"Nah," he replied cheerfully. "You owe him twenty. I owe him the other twenty. I'll just have to borrow twenty bucks from you until next payday."

"That's still forty bucks," Mitchell squawked.

"And *two* wagons," the kid responded glibly. "Peterson had one wagon he wanted to sell, but we got talking and I mentioned how that Feldman fellow was dead.

"Turns out Mr. Feldman had a wagon he bought from Mr. Peterson that wasn't paid for. So, I got both wagons and ten sacks of grain for the forty bucks. You get half and I get half."

"How do you plan on moving that wagon without any horses," Mitchell protested.

"Feldman had horses too," the kid replied. "He hadn't paid Mr. Peterson for them either. I got 'em for another twenty bucks, and Mr. Peterson threw in the harness 'cause I'm such a fine fellow."

"What's the grain for?" Turner snorted.

"The grain is for the horses," the kid replied. "The hay is for the sheep."

"Sheep!" exclaimed Mitchell.

"Sheep."

"How many?" Mitchell asked suspiciously. "Two rams and fifty ewes," the kid responded.

"Where in the hell do you plan on keeping fifty head of sheep?" Mitchell complained.

"Grain and hay cost me another twenty bucks," the Pratt kid answered smugly. "The sheep will cost you and me two-hundred bucks. I spent my last twenty bucks as good faith money and pasture for one month. We got to pay up by then and move the herd to our own pasture or the deal falls through and we have to renegotiate."

"You got a contract?" asked Mitchell.

"Handshake..."

"Good enough," grumbled Mitchell. "I just never thought of raising sheep."

"I just remembered what you said Brother Brigham was preachin' about self sufficiency and them plans for a woolen mill down to Provo," the kid explained.

Mitchell nodded in agreement, remembering the numerous plans now circulating through the territory. "We could trade the wool to the mill for credit on other things we could use," he suggested.

"And keep back what we need for own use," the Pratt kid added.

"I've heard of fellows who grazed their cattle ahead of sheep," suggested Mitchell.

"Makes sense," Turner conceded. "Cattle don't crop the grass as close to the ground as sheep."

"That's what I was thinkin'," said the kid. "Most folks just throw cattle and sheep out on open range and ignore them. But what if we fence off some good pasture and divide it down into six or seven sections. We could put the cattle ahead of the sheep and rotate 'em all to a new section every couple of days."

Mitchell leaned forward and looked at the Pratt kid. "Long as we don't overgraze, two days on and twelve days off should give the pasture enough time to recover."

"And it makes everything a little more manageable," said the kid. "Giving us more time to keep track of our mining operations."

"Mining operations?"

Mitchell smiled at Turner's surprise. "Mr. Pratt and I are now partners with a fellow we met in Salt Lake on the way here," he explained. "The old boy has several claims he's working, but needed funds for better equipment.

"Mr. Pratt negotiated a three-way split with the old fellow, and I put up the money for the equipment. Of course, Mr. Pratt will be my indentured servant for the rest of his life, if those claims go bust."

For a moment, the Pratt kid looked frantic. "Hey! I don't remember nothin' about indentured servants."

"You must have missed the fine print in our contract," advised Mitchell.

"I never seen no contract."

"I have a copy for you back at camp."

"Indentured servant …." The kid paused as the bell above Murphy's front door announced the emergence of the three women.

"I got me a plan for a pig farm," the kid announced suddenly. "Seems like this valley would make a right fine place for one…"

The Campbell girl made an unhappy sound—something akin to a squawk mingled with a hiss of derision—and with an abrupt toss of her head, stomped her way across the street in the direction of her father's house.

"What are you up to, Daniel?"

At the sound of Sarah's voice, the Pratt kid looked away from the girl's retreating figure and smiled. "Just keepin' her happy," he replied casually.

"Keeping her happy."

"Yes, Ma'am."

"With talk of a pig farm?"

"Yes, ma'am.

"She didn't seem very happy just now."

"That's 'cause she's startin' to like me," the kid replied.

"I don't understand."

"She thinks I'm a lazy, good-for-nothin'. And she don't think too highly of pig farmin' as a livelihood. So the more she likes me, the madder she'll get. When she finally falls in love with me, she'll really give me a tongue lashing.

"After that, I can turn over a new leaf, and stop bein' a lazy, good-for-nothin'. Then she'll be happy 'cause she showed me the light, and we can get past her bad first impression and start to likin' one another."

"I'm not certain I agree with your reasoning," counseled Sarah.

"I tried tellin' her the truth," the kid confided glumly. "But she ain't believin' it, so I got no other choice. Besides, this here plan gives me some time to get my real plans in motion before we get married."

"So, you've decided that, have you?"

"Yep. Just need a little time to get things in order."

Mitchell dropped the front legs of his chair on the boardwalk and stood as Sarah posted herself directly in front of him and planted her fists on her hips.

"Do I detect more than a hint of the Collin Mitchell philosophy on the proper care and maintenance of women?"

"No ma'am," Mitchell protested quickly. "I'm just a simple sheep farmer. I don't know anything about no maintenance philosophy."

"Sheep!"

Sarah flashed a suspicious look at the Pratt kid then turned back to Mitchell.

"First it's pigs, now sheep. The two of you are in cahoots."

"Of course they are," Susan affirmed from where she stood beside the Pratt kid's chair.

"And that leaves it to you and me to make sure Lynne has a proper trousseau when Brother Pratt finally gets the courage to discover if she'll even have him."

Sarah's manner grew even more serious as she turned her attention to the Pratt kid. "Brother Pratt is a courageous fellow," she observed thoughtfully. "I suppose we had better get to work on that trousseau, since Bother Pratt can be rather precipitous at times."

Susan smiled and took her sister by the hand. "On that note we'll take our leave, since you gentlemen appear deeply concerned with Brother Pratt's future as a pig farmer."

When the sisters were across the street and well beyond hearing, the Pratt kid leaned forward and shook his head.

"They're up to no good," he muttered bleakly.

Kelson's farm was a quarter-mile distant, and growing swiftly from a small dark blot to a more readily discernable clutch of buildings, fences, and animals. The gray, sun weathered buildings stood bleakly alone among scattered sagebrush and mountain grass. And the meandering mix of double and single posted fence looked loose and on the verge of collapsing under the constant press of animals straining to reach more desirable fodder beyond the sagging rails.

"Looks like Kelson and Feldman took a page from the same book when it comes to taking care of a farm," Mitchell observed.

"Surprises me a bit," Turner admitted. "Normally, I think he pays a couple of fellows to look after the place."

The Pratt kid nudged his mount forward until the three men rode abreast.

"I heard a couple of fellows talking over to the blacksmith's place," he offered. "They was sayin' the fellow they worked for up and let 'em go... no warning and no explanations... least wise, that's what I heard."

"Had to be Kelson," Turner reasoned "No one else in the valley has any hired help I know of."

"Must have let 'em go some time ago," reasoned Mitchell, observing the run down state of the farm.

"Possible," answered Turner. "I don't think Kelson was ever interested in the place. Seems like all he ever talks about is that store of his. He brought Sister Kelson and the daughter up here about three, maybe four years ago, set up the store and then headed back down to the valley. Never saw hide nor hair of him for nearly three months. He finally showed up with four or five wagons loaded with goods for the store.

"After that first time, he showed up more regular and stocked the store, but he never stayed for more than a few days before he high-tailed it back down to the valley and left his womenfolk to fend for themselves.

"I heard rumors Kelson took a plural wife and was keepin' the two of 'em as far from one another as he could. Don't know any more about it, other than the rumor he was keepin' the new wife in a mighty fancy home down in Salt Lake."

"Showpiece," muttered Mitchell.

"Reckon so," agreed Turner. "Probably figured he could put Sister Kelson and her daughter on a back burner up here and just forget 'em."

Turner hitched his head to the west in the general direction of the Salt Lake Valley.

"Makes me wonder sometimes how many women down there are gettin' a raw deal whenever the old man takes on a new wife," he grumbled sourly.

"A few," acknowledged Mitchell. "Probably the ones who had a raw deal to begin with, and a few more, when a fellow goes bad later on."

Turner frowned. "I guess I get a little doubtful of the whole proposition when I see folks like Sister Kelson and her girl treated badly."

"I don't blame you a bit, but I'll bet there ain't more than one man in ten down there that has more than one wife, and most of *them* got no more than two. I've seen plenty of fellows who couldn't treat one woman decent, so I don't expect being plural married makes much difference one way or another."

"Reckon so," Turner admitted somewhat reluctantly. "All I know is these two have been pretty much left on their own for the last couple of years, and the way I see it, that just ain't right."

"No, it ain't right," Mitchell agreed.

As they rode into the area between the house and the yard, Mitchell felt a growing dislike for Kelson and the man's irritating manners. It was as though the very sight of the merchant's heavy features stimulated an overwhelming urge to punch the man in the face—repeatedly.

"I'd appreciate it if you would keep a tight rein on your temper," cautioned Turner.

Mitchell scowled. "Shows that bad, does it?"

"Bad enough. Try lookin' friendly."

"That ain't such a good idea," squawked the Pratt kid. "I seen it before. It ain't pretty, and it could get us shot."

"Ignore him," Mitchell responded testily.

"Sister Kelson should be home," Turner explained as he dismounted and hitched his mount to a fence post. The gate squawked open on rusty hinges as he pushed his way past and into a yard dry and barren of vegetation. "Jean said her mother came home earlier to finish up the housework and put something together for Kelson's dinner. If Kelson ain't here, she might have an idea where we can find him."

Mitchell waited at the edge of the porch as Turner rapped smartly on the blistered paint of the front door and stepped back half a pace. For a moment, they stood, ears straining for the answering sound of footsteps. When the door finally opened, Mitchell was surprised and pleased by a friendly reception.

"You gentlemen are a long way from town," said the middle-aged woman who greeted them.

"We're here to see your husband," Turner told the woman.

For a moment, the woman studied the three men, her gray eyes considering each of them in turn. Finally, her lips tightened in a grim semblance of a smile. "He's out back," she said unhappily. "Are you going to arrest him?"

"I'm not sure," Turner admitted. "Someone set fire to Mitchell's camp this morning, just before daylight."

The woman pushed the door open and beckoned the three of them inside.

"He was gone all night," she said quietly. "He came in about eight this morning. He won't be happy to see *you,*" she confided as Mitchell stepped into the small living room. "He's been complaining about you and threatening to have you arrested since he got here."

Kelson's greeting was as cold and unfriendly as his wife had suggested it would be. He entered the room and his face grew red with anger the moment he laid eyes on Mitchell.

"I won't ask you to sit, because you aren't welcome," he snarled.

"I understand that," responded Turner, "but I have some questions for you, and I didn't feel they could wait."

"What questions?"

"Where were you just before daylight this morning?"

"This morning?"

"Just before daylight," Turner repeated.

"Kelson glanced quickly at Mitchell, before answering. "I was in bed, asleep," he replied stiffly.

"Here?"

"Yes. Why are you asking?"

"You're sure you were here?"

"Yes, I am… as if it's any of your damn business."

"Someone tossed a kerosene lamp into Mitchell's camp and burned one of his wagons to the ground," Turner said with a hint of irritation. "Someone saw you riding out that way right after the fire started."

"That's a damned lie. I was here all night. Besides, they're camped over on Center Creek, and I've never been near the place."

"That's not what *I've* been told. Several people have spotted you riding out that direction, and I know for a fact you were *not* home last night. Why don't we go have a look at your horse, there's plenty of tracks between here and Mitchell's camp. We'll just see if any of them match up to that bay mare of yours."

"That horse was stolen yesterday."

"Then you'll be happy to know she's been returned."

"What!"

"All saddled and hitched out near your barn."

"That horse was gone. I've been riding that black gelding out back of the house."

"Maybe one of your friends out on Lake Creek borrowed it," suggested Turner. "Let's gather up the mare and all of us go back to town. I can take your statement about the horse being stolen and we can talk about where you were last night."

"I'm telling you I had nothing to do with that fire." Kelson's voice was an angry hiss, and his face a red mass streaked with purple veins.

Turner held both hands palm out, motioning for Kelson to calm down. "Ease up a bit," he reasoned calmly. "I ain't sayin' you're involved."

"You're insinuating it!"

"Not a bit. I just need to check everything."

Mitchell stood to one side of the room, near the fidgeting Pratt kid. He kept his thoughts to himself, not wanting to incite Kelson into a full-fledged explosion.

The big man fumed for a moment longer then smiled unexpectedly. I'll come with you," he offered suddenly. "I can prove someone took that horse, and I can prove I was nowhere near that camp."

Turner shrugged. "Then you got nothin' to worry about."

"Let me tell my wife what's going on, and I'll get my horse."

Turner smiled and nodded toward Mitchell. "You talk to your wife. We'll let Mitchell bring your horse from around back."

Kelson frowned, and his face flared a darker shade of red.

"I'll get the horse," said the Pratt kid.

Mitchell watched as the Pratt kid left through the front door, and Kelson disappeared into another part of the house. "If he's telling the truth about that horse, then who took it? And why did they bring it back? And where are they now?" He grumbled.

Turner frowned and shook his head unhappily. "I ain't got a clue," he muttered. "I'm stumbling around just tryin' to figure who done what to who."

"Dammed if I know what's goin' on either," Mitchell admitted. I'm sure all this is tied to Stokes and Larkin somehow. If they really found gold, it wouldn't take long before the whole country knew about it."

Turner nodded and shifted his hat from hand to hand. "Seems to be takin' a while to say goodbye," he muttered anxiously.

"Daniel's got that black gelding around front," Mitchell replied. "Maybe you ought to check on Kelson."

Swiftly, Turner stepped to the doorway leading toward the back of the house. He peered into the room beyond and quickly pulled back. "No one in there," he reported, "and Pratt's got his horse."

For a moment, Mitchell considered prowling the house in search of Kelson, but quickly rejected the idea. He was only here by Turner's invitation and had no business interfering in the deputy's work. The thought had hardly been discarded when the Pratt kid appeared at the front door.

"That Kelson fellow is headed for the barn," he reported. "Looks like he's in a mighty big hurry too."

Turner rushed to the door and glared at the figure running hell-bent toward the barn. "What the hell is he up to!"

"Looks like he's runnin' away," the Pratt kid replied sarcastically.

"Probably after that mare," added Mitchell.

Turner scowled and rushed outside, leaping from the porch to the dry ground of the yard.

"Damn fool," he barked. "Where's he think he's runnin' to?"

"I'd say Lake Creek," Mitchell predicted.

Turner spun toward the Pratt Kid. "Grab your horses!" he yelled as Kelson disappeared beyond the open door of the barn.

Mitchell grabbed at the grulla's reins, but missed as the animal reared backward, tossing its head. The animal's backward surge stopped as suddenly as it began, and Mitchell snatched at the tightly stretched leather as something dark slashed the air from the barn to the deputy.

Turner's eyes widened for an instant. "What..." His voice trailed off in an awkward groan of pain. For a moment, one hand pawed ineffectually at his back, until he toppled stiffly to the ground like a felled tree.

"That came from the barn," snapped the Pratt kid.

Smoke and fire flashed at the muzzle of Mitchell's Colt, stabbing the quiet of the day with an ear splitting *crack*. Lead smacked the barn door with a solid *thump*, followed by the pounding of hooves.

"He ain't dead," said the Pratt kid.

Mitchell knelt beside the deputy, whose eyes were now open and aware. Turner groaned and tried to roll onto his side. Mitchell gripped the man's arm and held him in place.

"Hold still," he warned.

"That ain't no regular arrow," the Pratt kid announced.

"Crossbow bolt," Mitchell explained as he tore the deputy's shirt and examined the wound.

"It's high up," he told the kid. "It ain't bleeding too badly either."

The Pratt kid frowned, and Mitchell knew the kid was thinking of the half healed wound in his own leg.

"Do we pull it out, or take him into town and let Jenkins' do it?" the kid asked.

"To hell with Jenkins," Turner groaned. "Pull the damned thing out!"

For a moment, Mitchell looked at the deputy, realizing he would have felt the same.

Turner looked up. "Give me a priesthood blessing, Brother Mitchell; then take it out."

For a moment, Mitchell looked into the deputy's pain-wracked face. Every doubt he had ever felt seemed to leap from the darkest corners of his mind, screaming his faults and unworthiness. "There's better men for either job," he said quietly.

"But *you're* here," Turner hissed through clenched teeth. "I'd rather not wait 'til God sends a better man, if you don't mind."

Mitchell removed his hat and wiped a sleeve across his forehead. "Guess you're stuck with Brother Pratt and me," he concluded.

"I ain't an Elder, yet," the kid objected.

"But you *are* a priest, and you *are* here," Mitchell pointed out. "I don't see anyone else wandering around out here. "So you can stand in, and I'll do all the talking."

The Pratt kid looked down at his hands, then sighed and dried them on his pant legs. When he looked up, he shrugged. "Guess I better start payin' more attention in church."

CHAPTER 14

30 September

*T*he trail to Lake Creek began in the foothills east of town and cut its way through a thick tangle of sagebrush and scrub oak, tracing the path of the creek toward the pine covered peaks filling the southeastern sky.

"You boys followin' that Kelson fellow?"

The Pratt kid, half dozing in the saddle, started fully awake and hauled back on his horse's rein. "Dangit, Mort! You scared the crap out of me!"

The old man laughed and peered closely at the kid. "Pretty much nothin' left of you after that."

"I suppose you've been waiting for us," suggested Mitchell.

"Yep. Thought you'd be here hours ago."

"Had to haul Deputy Turner into town to see the doctor."

The old man tipped his head back and peered at a pale blue sky dotted with cotton-ball clouds.

"Forgot all about that," he confided. "Lucky he's hit up high though. Them chisel points is mean. I seen one go right through armor one time. Punched right through the front and darn near come out the back, skewered that Spanish feller like a pig on a spit; popped him off his horse like a tiddlywink.

"That was a good horse though. Never knew his breed... kind of speckled on the rump. Had a better gait than old Milo here, but then he weren't no pigee-toed critter neither. "Tasted a mite better than llama too, come to think of it—just not as tender."

The Pratt kid stared at the old man like a deer mesmerized by the light of a campfire. "You *ate* your horse," he groaned.

The old man shrugged. "Weren't no more llama's. Deer and elk was all scattered to hell an' gone, an' I tell you bark an' pine cones make a crappy soup."

"Don't think I could eat my horse," muttered the kid.

"You get hungry enough… you could eat most anything."

"Did you see Kelson come through here?" asked Mitchell.

The old man grinned happily. "Yep… In a big hurry too."

"What's he got to do with that bunch?" asked the Pratt kid.

"Reckon we'll find out real soon," the old man replied. "They're camped near a beaver pond about a mile up the trail. "I'd suggest we get off the trail an' work our way through these trees to that ridge over yonder. You can take a look at their camp from up there. Unless, of course, you just planned on ridin' right into the middle of 'em'."

Mitchell shook his head and guided the grulla into the trees. He had no desire to tangle with Jackman or any of his ilk, but he hadn't the least idea how he would manage to extract Kelson from the camp and get him back to town where Deputy Turner had a jail cell empty and waiting. The whole prospect seemed improbable in the extreme, and from the ridge-top their chances dwindled to nothing.

"Must be twenty mean lookin' fellers down there," the old man concluded as he handed a small brass telescope to the Pratt kid.

For a moment, the kid studied the camp. With the lens held tightly to his eye, he examined the camp in measured sections.

With a derisive snort, he collapsed the little instrument, and returned it to Mitchell.

"Better add a dozen Utes to that count," he advised. "They've got a separate camp about a hundred yards farther south, near the base of the ridge."

"That's not good," the old man admitted.

"They've got nearly a hundred head of cattle down there," Mitchell responded. "What do you make of that?"

The kid shrugged. "Maybe they're startin' a cattle ranch."

Mitchell shook his head and pointed toward the camp's central tent.

"Did you see that short fellow near the big tent in the middle of the camp?"

"Yep."

"How about the fellow in the brown vest standing next to him?"

"I seen him."

"Well that fellow is Dave Langley, and the one beside him is Alva Shaffer."

"Don't know none of 'em," the kid admitted.

Mitchell nodded and dropped the telescope in his coat pocket. "A couple of years ago, Orsemus Irish was superintendent of Indian affairs in the Territory. He was let go, and Franklin Head took over. Dave Langley worked for Head until folks thought he was taking stolen cattle from the Utes and running them up to Fort Bridger and selling them to folks heading west. Folks in the valley threw a fit, and Langley was dismissed. He pretty much disappeared after that.

"Then there was Bill Shaffer. He had five wives and appeared to be a church going fellow. Then about eleven years ago, one of his brothers was murdered down in Springville.

Wasn't long before Bill was rustling cattle. Folks think Bill was working with Black Hawk's brother, Mountain, and running stolen cattle over the Uintahs to Brown's Hole then up into Wyoming territory to sell. Bill Shaffer was killed last year, but it looks like Alva was in on it with Langley all along. Now, you put those fellows together with a dozen Utes and a hundred head of cattle, and what do you have?"

The Pratt kid swallowed hard and stared at the camp. "A whole ring of cattle thieves," he groaned unhappily.

"And Brother Kelson right in the thick of it," added Mort.

"And none of them happy to see us hanging around," concluded Mitchell.

The Pratt kid frowned. "So what do we do?"

Mitchell scowled. "I think we get the hell out of here and get the militia up here. We'll just get ourselves shot to pieces if we try anything on our own."

"That's a good idea," the old man conceded, "but I think we've been spotted."

For a moment, the three men watched a scrambling of men and horses in the camp below. The first shots from the camp plowed lead into the rocks ten feet below their position on the ridge, the sound of the shots trailing swiftly behind.

The Pratt kid scooted behind the thick bole of an ancient aspen and jacked a cartridge into the chamber of his rifle. "We're in a load of crap now!" he squawked.

The sound of gun-fire popped, boomed, and echoed across the narrow valley until it rolled like thunder across the ridge-top. Lead ripped through the trees, shredding twigs and leaves, pounding the rocks until the shooters below found the range and shifted their fire to hammer the trees where the three watchers lay prone.

"What now?" The Pratt kid demanded.

"Now, you sit still for a minute, so you don't get your head blown off!" snapped the old man.

As if to emphasize the old man's warning, a heavy bullet 'thwacked' the tree above the kid's head, blasting a spray of shredded bark from its trunk.

"Are you nuts!" the kid howled. "That bullet didn't even slow down!"

The old man smiled and squeezed off a shot at the men below. The heavy Sharps rifle thundered and hurled five-hundred grains of lead down slope, slamming a rustler to the ground.

"Might be a good time to make a run for it," Mitchell suggested. "About half of those fellows have got to their horses. I expect they'll be up here right soon."

"I vote we run for it," squawked the kid.

Mitchell nodded. "What do you say, Mort?"

"Jaguars and Wolves..." snapped the old man. "We should harry them from the heights, like true Eagles."

Mitchell stared at the old man, and shook his head. "We came for Kelson, not to start a shooting match with a bunch of rustlers and renegade Utes."

"The Utes have already took off," the old man protested. "And you ain't gonna fetch Kelson back to town without persuadin' his friends to give him up."

"Which they ain't going to do."

"Reckon not."

The Pratt kid poked his head to one side of his tree and peered at the camp below. "They quit shootin'," he advised. "There's a couple of 'em still there, but they're just watchin'."

"The others are trying to come up the ridge farther south," advised Mitchell.

"Which they ain't gonna be able to do," growled the old man. "They'll get to the ridge-top, but they'll have to leave their horses and come at us on foot. There's a mess of boulders up there an' no way to get through except on foot. There's a little flat spot an' no cover after that. We get up in those rocks, and we can catch 'em coming across the flats," he said, pointing toward the rocky outcropping above their position.

Mitchell frowned and studied the outcropping. "It's only seven or eight miles back to town... "We could telegraph Provo for the militia."

"An' the whole kit an' caboodle will disappear before the militia get half way up the canyon," the old man snapped.

"And Brother Kelson with them," grumbled Mitchell.

"I suspect so," the old man agreed.

From the top of the outcropping, the rocks fell away steeply on three sides, with the base of the southern face joined to a short stretch of gravelly soil caught between the outcropping and the larger *rocks* less than two-hundred yards south.

The Pratt kid studied the saddle-like expanse between the two outcroppings. "We could be in a fix, if some of 'em stay in those rocks while the rest come across," he suggested. "Some of 'em might even come through that mess of trees."

The old man nodded and hooked a thumb over his shoulder toward town. "If they do, an' things look tight, we just ride like hell back to town," he replied.

"I ain't convinced," grumbled the kid.

"Better convince *them*," Mitchell advised as the first four rustlers scrabbled from the rocks like a nest of spiders scuttling toward their prey.

"Where's the rest of 'em?" demanded the kid.

"Probably in the rocks, waiting for us to give them something to shoot at," Mitchell responded.

"I don't like it," the kid protested. "A couple of 'em could set up in them rocks and keep us busy while four or five of 'em circle around up high and come down at us through the trees."

Mitchell watched as the four men zigzagged towards them like hunched up little trolls. "If you've got a suggestion, you'd best make it quick," he warned.

"I say we put some holes in those fellows then get the hell out of here while their friends are wondering if they'll get some of the same. We could be a mile down the mountain before they can get to their horses and another mile before they get down off the ridge. Kelson ain't worth it."

Mitchell tracked a hunched figure as it scurried towards them. "Okay... Give 'em hell, and let's get out of here."

Mitchell squeezed the trigger of his rifle, and the stillness of the mountains erupted with the thunder of gun-fire.

The sun blazed high above the western mountains. A hot wind pushed up from the valley below, rattled the bright yellow leaves still clinging to the aspen, and filled the air with the taste of dust and the raw smell of sagebrush.

Mitchell reined the grulla to a stop and listened closely for the sound of pursuit. All was quiet. Only the wind, the occasional chirping of a bird, or the clatter of chipmunk feet on the dry bark of a fallen tree broke the silence.

"We should keep moving," the Pratt kid advised. "The more distance between us and them the better."

Mitchell nodded and nudged the grulla into a walk, but let his eyes rove the trees. The hair prickled on the back of his neck and he felt uneasy, as though someone or something lurked among the shadowy depths of the trees—something that slipped invisibly and silently on a course parallel to their own. Carefully, Mitchell drew the Navy forty-four.

"There's something following us," he told the Pratt kid."

"That's just great," muttered the kid. "Can you see them?"

"No… just a feeling."

"I've had them feelings a time or two," offered the old man. He leaned down and plucked up a long grass stem and began picking at his teeth. "One time I had a feeling there was this pack of Jaguars followin' us. Couldn't see nary a one, but they was there… Wasn't far from here, come to think of it… They was a bad lot. Killed ten Wolves and half a dozen Eagles before we even knew they were on us. Like to cut us to pieces…."

Mitchell caught a glimpse of movement from the corner of his eye and eased the revolver back into its holster.

"Kinda lonely up here, ain't it," the old man observed.

"Not lonely enough," the kid complained.

"You sayin' I ain't good company?"

"I'm sayin' there's a pack of rustlers up here, and that's a sight more than I want to tangle with."

"They may not give us a choice," the old man warned.

Mitchell reined the grulla to a stop in the middle of the trail and stared at the fork in the trail where a large pile of rocks held a tree branch vertically in a ridged embrace. On the tip of the branch, a woman's hat rocked lightly in the mountain breeze.

Silently, Mitchell dismounted and retrieved Sarah's hat and stuffed it into his saddle bags.

"Figured that would get your attention!"

The voice grated loudly from the trees beyond the edge of the trail, and Mitchell turned slowly, knowing the voice though he had hardly seen the man or heard his voice for nearly twenty years.

Jackman stepped from the trees, his pistol drawn and leveled at Mitchell's chest. "It's been twenty years," he growled, "and there ain't been many days in all that time that I ain't had thoughts of killin' you."

"You brought it on yourself," Mitchell replied as Jackman cocked the pistol.

"You put half a dozen birdshot into my leg," Jackman snarled. "One of 'em went into my knee cap and couldn't be took out. I figure I'll return the favor."

Jackman's eyes narrowed, and in the instant his feet shifted for a better stance, something snarled harshly and lunged from the tall grass less than a yard away, sinking its teeth into the gunman's calf.

Jackman howled in pain and smashed his fist into the dog's head, but the motley colored animal refused to let loose. For an instant, the muzzle of Jackman's pistol wavered. An instant later, the earsplitting crack of gun-fire smashed its way through the narrow valley.

At the Kelson farm, Sarah leaned forward and placed her cup on the Kelson's kitchen table. She noted that while it was a good table; it was not a *fine* table and certainly seemed to match the rest of the farm and its condition. It was quite apparent that Brother Kelson did not lavish any extras on this portion of his family.

"Jean told me you were here to find the Stokes' boy, Aaron," said Mrs. Kelson.

"I don't know that we're here to find him as much as discover what might have happened to him, and if he's still alive," she replied.

Sister Kelson set her own cup on the table and stood. "Let's go into the living room. The chairs are more forgiving there."

When they were resituated, the woman threw a woolen blanket over her knees and settled herself into the relative comfort of a padded chair. "You must think I know something about the matter; you wouldn't be here otherwise," she suggested.

Sarah smiled disarmingly. "I suspect that very few people know anything at all about the matter, but I think it wise to talk to as many people as possible. They often know more than they realize."

"I suppose, but I don't see what help I can be. I knew the Stokes boy, of course, but had little to do with him even after Jean became engaged to him. He came around, of course, but it was usually with a group of their friends, so I never really had to act as chaperone to them."

"So they were never alone?"

"Oh, I suppose they were, but it wouldn't have been often."

"So the rumors that Jean was pregnant must have come as a surprise to you."

"Awful lies!"

"Is that why you sent her away?"

"What?"

"Didn't you realize that sending her away like that would only fuel the rumors and do nothing to protect her reputation?"

"I did what was best. She was only gone a few months. Certainly people could see there was no time for her to have a child."

"But plenty of time for her to have an abortion."

"Abortion!"

"That's one of the rumors. You weren't aware?"

"That's ridiculous! I'd never put up with such a thing! How could anyone even suggest it! We're a respectable family."

"I don't doubt that, Sister Kelson, but you can be sure that Jean's reputation suffered none the less. And she felt it keenly. Her circle of friends dwindled quite perceptibly."

"Jean was ill, nothing more."

"It must have been a strange sort of illness for you to send her on such an arduous journey. Denver is a very long distance and a terrible journey for a young girl who is ill. Travel by wagon would be miserable for anyone who was ill. What kind of illness could induce you to send her on such a trip?"

For a moment, the older woman sat quietly, and Sarah knew the woman was thinking furiously.

"Funny," Sarah said quietly. "Jean told Susan she was sent to *school* in Denver."

"I…"

"She never went away, did she?"

Sarah watched as the older woman's face drained of color. "What happened?" she asked quietly.

The older woman's eyes filled with tears. "She was pregnant," she blurted suddenly, as though months of pain had burst the wall that had been holding back the secret. "Edward overheard when Jean told me. He was livid. I've never seen him so angry. He came into the room and demanded that Jean tell him who the father was. Jean refused and Edward beat her.

"I couldn't stop him," she sobbed. "He was like a monster, throwing her about the room—she was like a little rag doll being twisted and smashed against the furniture.

"When it was over, he walked out as though we no longer existed. Jean was in a terrible state. She was unconscious, bruised, and bleeding. I got her into bed and did everything I could for her. A few days later, she lost the baby. I don't know if the beating caused the miscarriage or if there was something else wrong. Either way she began to heal. That's when I started telling anyone who asked that she had gone to Denver."

Sarah frowned, feeling disgusted with the way the woman had literally swept the whole incident under the rug. "You never called the doctor?" She asked, feeling the anger creep into the tone of her voice.

The older woman stiffened defensively. "I was a midwife for several years," she said.

"You never reported the assault to the sheriff either."

"No."

"How could you not? How could you let a full grown man beat a young girl senseless and say nothing?"

The Kelson woman frowned. "He's her father. He has a right to discipline his own daughter."

"Discipline, yes," Sarah hissed, "But beat her to a pulp? I know people who wouldn't treat an animal that badly. How could anyone do such a thing to their own child?"

"She shouldn't have been so disrespectful to her father," the Kelson woman argued.

"Disrespectful!"

"She should have told him who fathered the baby!"

"So your husband could teach him some respect by beating the boy to a bloody pulp?" Sarah snapped.

The older woman stood suddenly, her face red with anger. "I think you should leave. I don't have to put up with this kind of treatment in my own home!"

Half-way to their buggy, Sarah detoured, making a beeline for the Kelson's barn. The sun weathered door screeched on rusty hinges, swung ninety degrees, and jammed its lower corner into a hump of hardened mud and straw. The two women peered into the depths of the barn and hesitated on the threshold. "I don't like this," she muttered unhappily.

"It is a bit creepy, isn't it?" Susan responded.

Sarah stood beside her sister and squinted into the darkened interior of the structure and wished Susan had been less insistent about 'having a look at the place.'

"Explain to me again why we should bother with this place. That woman was extremely upset. She made it clear she didn't want me here. You wouldn't even go inside. Besides, I'm a little leery of barns at the moment. All I need is another one exploding in flames."

Susan shook her head and shoved at the door in an attempt to force it fully open. "I wanted to look around while you were talking to her, and the barn is not going to catch fire," she grumbled as the door warped and dragged another six inches before wedging solidly. "We're looking for a crossbow," she said, dusting her hands on her skirt.

"Why?"

"Because something smells fishy about the way Deputy Turner was shot."

"What do you mean?"

The two women combined their strength on the opposite door, swinging it wide, until it slammed fully open against the outer wall.

Susan turned back to the half-opened door. "Collin said Kelson's horse was tied up in front of the barn. They saw it when they rode into the yard. But Kelson was running from the house to the barn when Collin, Daniel, and Deputy Turner came out of the house. Kelson disappeared behind this door, apparently going after his horse.

"Collin said he grabbed at the grulla's rein, and Deputy Turner was shot almost in the same instant. Collin fired one shot and it hit the door just as Kelson rode away."

"And all this means what?"

"Don't you see it?"

"See what?"

"Good grief….," Susan hissed. "How did Kelson do it all so quickly? How did he retrieve the crossbow, load it, fire it, and climb on his horse so quickly? That question bothered me form the moment Collin told us what happened."

"Kelson may have kept the thing loaded and ready," Sarah offered.

"So, in less than ten seconds, Kelson runs into the barn, grabs his bow, finds a place from which he can shoot Deputy Turner, then jumps on his horse and rides off almost as quickly as Collin can draw his pistol and put a bullet through this door," Susan squawked in one long breath.

She tapped a finger on the door just below a small round hole surrounded by freshly splintered wood.

"I suppose it's possible," Sarah replied uneasily.

"Possible, but unlikely," Susan responded. "That's why I want to look around."

Quietly, Sarah followed the younger woman into the shadows. She had no desire to be anywhere near the place, but Susan had voiced the very question that had plagued her own mind since Collin's recounting of the incident. Indeed, it seemed impossible that Kelson could have fired the bolt that had so very nearly killed Jared Turner.

In the stillness of the barn, the two women paused while their senses adjusted to the altered environment. Sunlight flooded through the doorway, and the strong smell of ammonia and horse permeated the structure, proving that no one had made the effort to clean any of the four stalls that lined the south wall.

"Probably hasn't been cleaned since Kelson fired his help," Susan suggested.

"I hope you don't expect me to tromp around the horse stalls searching for that crossbow," Sarah warned. "I've already lost my new hat, and I don't intend to ruin this dress or my shoes."

Susan smiled. "I don't think we'll find it hidden in a pile of horse manure," she responded.

Quickly, Sarah scanned the open floor and the corners nearest the doors. The missing crossbow was nowhere to be seen. "Kelson must have taken the bow with him," she offered, without conviction.

Susan frowned and probed deeper into the barn. "Search every nook and cranny. Sister Kelson says no one has been in here since her husband ran away. If it isn't here he must have taken it with him."

Sarah knitted her eyebrows in thought, realizing suddenly that there was another possibility.

"I think we're overlooking something, she confided as she retrieved a crumpled, sheet of paper from one dark corner.

"Overlooking what?"

"If Kelson didn't shoot Deputy Turner, whoever did could simply have taken the crossbow and left."

Susan frowned. "I hadn't thought of that."

"In fact..," Sarah said thoughtfully, "It's almost certain someone other than Kelson fired that shot."

"Now *you're* certain, and I'm asking how you know," Susan replied as she reached out and flipped an empty grain sack from the top of a neatly stacked pile of sacks still filled with wheat ready for planting.

Sarah frowned as she opened the crumpled paper. "Because Kelson was in Murphy's store when someone shot that bolt thought the window and started the fire. Quite likely, the same sneaking dog stole this and left me lying in the ditch behind the Campbell house."

Sarah held the wrinkled sheet aloft, revealing the Campbell girl's hand-drawn pattern.

For a moment, Susan stared thoughtfully at the damaged pattern. "Then Kelson is in cahoots with our mysterious archer," she responded, lifting the edge of another empty sack to expose the crossbow hidden beneath it.

"I think that's a fair assumption," Sarah replied unhappily.

CHAPTER 15

8 October

Mitchell opened his eyes to sunlight filtering dimly through overlapping pine boughs and the crackling of a small fire.

"About time you come around," Mort grouched as he tossed another chunk of wood on the fire. "Ain't fair—you loafing around while an old man like me builds a snug little shelter and keeps a cozy little fire going day and night so you don't catch yourself a chill."

Mitchell shifted uncomfortably, his left shoulder feeling as though he had been kicked by a mule. "What the hell hit me?"

"Hole looked about right for a forty-five caliber slug," Mort replied with a grin. "Remember much?"

"Lake Creek?"

"Lead flyin' everywhere—like a nest of mad yellow jackets."

"I remember that."

"Well… One of them chunks of lead punched a hole right through your chest and knocked you flat. Must have hit you at an angle, 'cause it missed your lung and come out under your arm pit. Pretty much hit nothing but muscle.

"Still… You're lucky I was around to fix you up. That Pratt kid would have done a credible job, but I sent him back to town so your womenfolk wouldn't worry."

"Daniel wasn't hurt?"

"Nope. Not a scratch. A bit unhappy with me for makin' him leave you and go back down the mountain, but he'll live. Susan might skin him for it, but they'll both have to get over it."

"You could have let him stay," replied Mitchell. "Sarah and Susan wouldn't have complained if we were gone a day or two. They're used to my plans getting changed without any warning."

The old man smiled and shook his head. "Couple of days, sure… not eight."

"Eight!"

"Eight. Jackman must have kept that bullet in a dirty sock for a couple of years, 'cause you been burnin' up with fever almost from the git-go. Besides, what you and me got to do ain't nothin' that Pratt kid needs to be involved in."

"And what do *we* have to do?"

"We got some trainin' to do while we *collect* a killer."

"I seen you *collect* a fellow one time. I'm not sure I want to be part of anything like that.

The old man snorted and shook his head.

"*You* ain't *collectin'* anyone 'til I'm done with this calling and you take over. 'Til then it's just participant observation for you."

"Partici—what?"

"You just tag along and see how things is done. Then maybe sixty, seventy years from now you'll be ready."

"Sixty or seventy years from now, I'll either be dead or a hundred years older than dirt."

The old man smiled. "Just about prime for this job, I'd say."

Mitchell rolled over on his uninjured side and tried to ignore the old man's crazy talk and the suggestion that he train as the old man's replacement. He had never given any credence to the old man's claim that he was the 'angel of death' and guided by a heavenly voice that no one else could hear. For the most part, he had been able to avoid thinking about the old goat's mental problems and simply accept Mort as a friend worth having.

Now, it seemed the old man was intent on dragging him deeper into some imaginary world where death was a scruffy old man riding a pigeon-toed horse named Milo.

"You're mighty quiet."

"Just pondering our situation."

"Don't worry none about that," said the old man. "Most all them fellows that was camped over by the pond high-tailed it out of here before the gunfire stopped. Them that survived anyways. The fellers that stayed ain't goin' nowheres."

"Jackman?"

The old man smiled and pointed toward the canvas covering the opening of the shelter.

"Stiff as a fence post somewhere over yonder."

"What about Kelson?"

"That feller sneaked out of there like a stinking coyote as soon as the shootin' started."

"We have to go after him," said Mitchell.

The old man brushed at the corner of his mouth, pushing stray whiskers back into place.

"Whenever you're ready to climb on that hard-headed critter of yours."

"Kelson may have gone back to town," Mitchell reasoned. "That's probably our best chance of finding him."

"Eight days ago," the old man corrected. "That Pratt kid has been back up here three times since then. Last time was this morning. He left a couple of hours before you woke up.

"According to the kid, Kelson has been in and out of town several times, but early this morning he had some angry words with his wife over at his store; then he rode out of town.

"The kid thinks Kelson headed for Center Creek. If that's true, we should be able to pick up Kelson's trail easy enough."

"If I can ride that far."

"Ain't all that far. I moved camp a couple of times whilst you as feverish. We're only about half a mile from the Center Creek trail."

Three hour's later, Mitchell shifted in the saddle to ease the constant ache in his shoulder. Mort claimed the wound had close up nicely and was healing cleanly, but the grulla's jouncing gait over uneven terrain left Mitchell feeling worn-out and bruised.

"I think he's headed for that old camp near that bald knoll," he said when the grulla thumped to a halt beside the pigeon-toed Milo.

"I figured as much," the old man responded. "Things always seem to come back to that camp."

"You really don't like that camp."

"No, I don't. It's an uneasy place."

They took the trail slowly, letting the horses take the slope at their own pace. Threading their way through small meadows thick with dry cheek grass and stunted sagebrush, they wound their way steadily toward higher ground and a mountainside densely packed with the gray and white of leafless aspen and the deep green of ponderosa pine.

From the mountaintop, a cool breeze rushed down through the pines, rocking the treetops fitfully and filling the air with the rushing sound of wind through pine boughs and the bone-like clatter of aspen—branch against branch.

Mitchell turned the grulla from the trail and reined the animal to a halt in the shade of a weathered old pine. Within the shade, the temperature dropped fifteen degrees in a matter of seconds.

"That feels mighty, nice," the old man muttered as he nudged the pigeon-toed Milo into the shade beside the grulla.

"Seems hot for October," reasoned Mitchell. "I thought we could cool off a bit."

The old man scrunched his face in a frown. "A few minutes shouldn't hurt nothing, but we oughta keep movin'."

An hour later, Mitchell tossed his bedroll at the base of a tall aspen and eased himself to the ground. Quietly, he leaned back against the broad trunk and surveyed the overgrown camp site.

The stillness of the mountains soothed his nerves, and a moment's rest from the saddle and the grulla's unfriendly gait was like a miracle easing the ache in his side. For a moment, he closed his eyes and let the sun bake him into a drowsy repose.

"Tell me about this journal," he said finally. He had a feeling the old man's story would turn into a whopper of stupendous proportions, but hoped for a splinter of truth amongst a forest of deadfall.

The old man frowned. "Where do I start?" he muttered.

"Start with that journal," Mitchell suggested, pointing to the dry pages encased in brittle leather.

The old man nodded. "A feller named Salazar wrote this one. He was the leader of an expedition that came up from Mexico lookin' for a lost treasure."

"Mexicans?"

"Nope. Weren't no Mexicans to speak of then, just the Spanish and what was left of the Aztec empire. Cortez and *his* boys pretty much decimated the population of Tenochtitlan and took control of the whole region. Once they had control, they went after every ounce of gold and silver they could lay hands on. They got tons of the stuff. The king's fifth was more than ninety ship loads sent back to Spain.

"But there was a rumor that before the fall of Tenochtitlan, Cuauhtémoc had secretly sent the bulk of the empire's treasure to Atzlan where it was hidden. That same rumor claimed there was a map locating the places where the treasure had been hidden. 'Course nobody had ever seen the map, and nobody knew where Atzlan was, so nobody ever done nothin' about it—until Salazar.

"Salazar come from Spain with a Captaincy and a small land grant about eighty years after Cortez sacked Tenochtitlan. Salazar took possession of a small hacienda and everything in it. Not long after that he found the map among his new possessions. In less than six months, he had permission from the governor to take twenty-five men, locate the first cache and return with everything they could transport.

"Salazar and his men rode north to Santa Fe, then northwest into these mountains. It was here that things began to go wrong and men began to die.

At first they just figured it was accidents an' such—a feller goes down to the river for water, slips on the wet rocks, falls and cracks his skull—another feller's horse suddenly gets stung by a bee and jumps off the trail an' into a pile of rocks a hundred feet below. Stuff like that. Salazar recorded everything, an' after the fourth man died he began to suspect somethin' was fishy. He wasn't the only one neither.

"His men was a superstitious lot, an' they had a couple of the Utes guidin' 'em north. Them Utes said something about some spirit or god, called the Shinob, protectin' the mountains, and' before long. Them Spanish fellers had it figured they was cursed, an' they had a demon straight from Hell killin' 'em one by one.

"It couldn't have been no worse after that—noises in the night, dead men in the morning. But Salazar kept watchin' an' thinkin'. He never believed in no demon.

"At first, he thought they'd been followed, thinkin' someone knew about the map an' intended to kill em' all an' take the treasure. But no matter what he tried, he could never discover anyone on their back trail. Finally, he realized it had to be one of his own men.

"He singled out the only man he could trust, Antonio de Guevara, and told him his suspicions. That night they camped here, and they laid a trap for Salazar's lieutenant, Rafael Mendoza.

"As it turned out, Salazar trusted the wrong man, and when morning came, every one of 'em was dead except Guevara."

Mitchell frowned and glanced about the camp.

"Guevara killed them all?"

The old man shrugged. "All but the first one... He actually slipped on some rocks whilst he was fetchin' water an' cracked his skull. After that, it was all Guevara."

Mitchell frowned in thought. "Something don't track with that last part," he objected. "If Salazar laid a trap for Mendoza and was killed, how does his journal say it was Guevara that killed everyone?"

"It don't."

"Oh brother…"

"I told you I collected the crazy bastard."

"That was two-hundred years ago!"

"I keep tellin' you, time don't work the way you think it does."

Mitchell looked at the ground and shook his head. "Crap."

For more than a mile, the tracks of Kelson's horse followed a meandering course through the pines on the mountainside above the old-Spanish camp and the small lake that lay hidden so well among the trees. At first, it seemed as though it would be a simple matter to follow the storekeeper, who seemed completely unaware of their presence and doubtless hadn't even the most rudimentary knowledge of how to cover his tracks. But the storekeeper's wandering course soon proved to be a tedious and often treacherous route.

Mitchell reined the grulla to a halt near the edge of a steep talus slope.

"Seems to me we've been here before," the old man complained.

"Appears so," Mitchell confirmed. "Looks like he picked up on someone's trail and he's trying to follow them."

"So this other feller is lost and Kelson is wanderin' around on his back trail?"

"I don't think this other fellow is lost," Mitchell admitted. "I think he's looking for something, and Kelson knows it."

"Lookin' for what? There ain't no gold mine down here in the thick of these pines."

"Didn't that journal say something about markers?"

"I suppose it did," muttered the old man.

"I have a feeling this other fellow knows about the markers, and he's looking for them," Mitchell confided.

"How would he know about the markers, when we have the journal?"

"There was a map," Mitchell replied." The Campbell girl had it, and someone stole it."

"You think Kelson has the map?"

"I think Kelson is following the fellow who took the map."

"We could wander around forever at this rate," the old man muttered unhappily.

Mitchell searched the talus for a possible trail. "I can't see any sign of a trail through that stuff," he grumbled.

"Everything looks the same," the old man concluded. "That stuff is loose as a goose,"

Mitchell nodded. "That's what worries me. Kelson might have crossed it, but he's a damn fool if he did. It wouldn't take much to get all that rock moving like water. A fellow could be buried before he could let out a squawk."

The words were barely spoken, when a large chunk of rock tumbled from the cliffs above and sped downward toward the alluvium composing the fan-shaped talus slope. With an explosive *crack*, the boulder slammed into the loose material at the head of the alluvial fan and buried nearly half of its bulk in the talus. Stunned, the two riders sat transfixed, staring at the base of the cliff, nearly two-hundred yards above them.

For a moment, all was still, as though the impact and the resultant shockwave had done nothing to destabilize the rocky fragments of the alluvial fan. Then with a deceptive slowness, the entire upper quarter of the fan began to shift.

"That ain't good!"

The old man's bellow echoed Mitchell's own thought's, as he yanked on the grulla's rein and fought to turn the animal on the narrow confines of the trail.

"It's spreadin' out!" Mort yelled.

Mitchell heeled the grulla and the animal leaped forward, colliding with the rear end of the pigeon-toed Milo. The grulla slammed to a stiff-legged halt, ears flattened and eyes rolling in terror at the clattering wave of stone rushing swiftly toward them. For a moment, the grulla refused to move, as though frozen in place.

"Don't lock up on me now!" Mitchell bellowed as the animal ignored a boot heel and stood fast.

Suddenly angered, Mitchell leaned forward and slapped the animal full in the face. The startled animal jerked its head away from the offending hand and leaped from the trail, bounding through the undergrowth between the pines like a terrified jackrabbit. Mitchell grabbed for the saddle horn, clinging to the pitching animal for dear life.

Twenty yards below the lowest edge of the talus, the animal finally began to calm and Mitchell reined the animal to a halt amid a thin stand of old, half-dead pines.

"Hell! I ain't seen ridin' like that in a coon's age." The old man howled. "One time I seen this feller strap a tiny little saddle on his dog and this little monkey feller was just a hangin' on for dear life. I about busted a gut... that dog a leapin' about like a deranged jackrabbit, and that monkey a flappin' in the breeze like long johns on a clothes line..."

"How about I set you on this deranged jackrabbit and light his tail on fire?" grouched Mitchell. "I suppose you'd look like long johns flappin' in the breeze."

"I wouldn't make it past the first jump," the old man admitted. "Never was much of a horseman."

Mitchell dismounted and took the grulla by the headstall. Gently, he rubbed the flat of his hand across the grulla's face. The animal tensed and laid back its ears.

"Easy, you knot-head," Mitchell crooned softly. "I only smacked you to wake you up." Gently, he stroked the animals' face, neck, and shoulder until the tension eased and the grulla's ears regained their normal position.

"He locked up on me," Mitchell told the old man. I had to slap him a good one to bring him out of it."

Mort nodded and climbed down from the saddle. "Heard of it," he admitted. "Never happened to me, but I heard tell of it. I knew this fellow in Colorado. He was out huntin' elk with two of his brothers. They was up in the high country, over to Bellyache Mountain, when this fellow spotted one big old bull on the mountainside below. That old bull spotted 'em an' took off like he seen the devil himself.

"The two brothers took off down the hill after that bull runnin' flat out. The fellow I knew kicked his horse into a gallop but stayed on the trail up above, hopin' his brothers would push that bull out in the open where he could get a shot.

"His horse was runnin' flat out when they rounded a bend an' ran head long into that old bull; with his antlers right up on either side of that horse's throat... scared the crap out of that horse. He locked up tight—stiff as a board from the shock of it.

"When that old bull untangled himself an' run off down the hill, that feller piled off his horse an' took off after the elk. When he come back an hour later, that horse was still standin' in the same spot, stiff as a board."

Mitchell looked back at the talus slope and let his gaze travel to the top of the cliff. "That rock had some help getting off that cliff," he concluded.

The old man frowned and glared at the cliff. "Kelson?" he asked.

"Could be. I saw someone just before that rock came tumbling over the edge. It might have been Kelson."

"Somebody oughta shoot that fellow," the old man grumbled.

"We better not," Mitchell advised. "I couldn't tell who it was, and if we shoot him, we might never know what happened to Stokes and Larkin. Besides, we might have missed that marker, if he hadn't rolled that rock."

"What marker?"

"Take a look at that dead pine."

The old man squinted against the glare of the late morning sunlight until he found the ancient tree and the design carved deeply into its bark.

"That's a marker?"

The old man edged his mount closer to the tree and traced a finger along the path of the deep gouges. "Reckon I seen a few trees carved like this. Can't say as I paid any attention to 'em though…. Just figured somebody liked carvin' on trees."

Mitchell nodded. "I've seen one… down in the foothills near the mouth of Daniels Canyon. I wondered then what it was, but it sort of slipped my mind until I saw this one. Then I suddenly realized Salazar might have left them as markers so he could find his way back."

The old man nodded. "Better than bread crumbs," he observed. "What do you think it means? Looks like a flower with a curly stem."

"I think it's a little map," Mitchell concluded.

"A map?"

"A map. The stem of that flower reminds me of a trail following the curves of the mountain. I don't know what the flower itself means—maybe the mine at the end of the trail. But I have the feeling we should ride around the curve of this ridge and up the canyon on the other side. That would seem to follow the shape of that flower stem."

The old man nodded and surveyed the surrounding terrain. "I reckon you could be right," he admitted. "Things have changed a mite, but I reckon the cave of the Serpent is somewhere hereabouts."

Mitchell frowned. "If you know where we're headed, why didn't you say so in the first place?"

"Now why would I do that? You're full growed, an' I ain't here to hold your hand an' pass you a sugar teat when you start feelin' picked on."

Mitchell scowled, his eyes narrowing down to a harsh squint. "I ain't askin' you to hold my hand, you ornery old fart. I'm askin' if you know where that mine is. 'Cause I figure that's where Kelson and this other fellow will end up if they found those markers."

The old man shrugged. "Been a while... an' things have changed, like I said... But I reckon if we go like you said we'll get to that cave just in time."

"Good."

Mitchell nudged the grulla onto a faded trail running eastward beyond the dying pine and its strangely carved flower. The grulla stepped out onto the nearly obliterated path, took three steps, threw back its head and collapsed, dragging Mitchell to the ground.

The sullen boom of a heavy caliber rifle reverberated down the mountain as Mitchell fought the grulla's dead weight and struggled to free the leg pinned between the saddle and the rocky ground. The leg came free as the thundering echo of the gun-fire faded and died in the distance.

Mitchell flashed a look toward the old man and the pigeon-toed horse, but Mort and Milo had disappeared as though they had never existed. No movement, no sound, nothing gave even the slightest hint of their whereabouts; the mountain seemed to have swallowed man and animal alike, leaving Mitchell to scramble for the cover of a nearby copse of half-dead pines with nothing more than a Navy Colt for protection. The grulla lay on its side pinning both rifle and saddle bags to the ground with its dead weight.

Near the animal's body, sparse grass swayed with the gusts of a fitful breeze. Dry leaves clattered among scattered aspen, skeletal pines hummed with the passage of the wind.

On the ground, where the wind commanded less power and the sun seemed more than able to bake anything caught within its uncaring gaze, Mitchell squirmed tightly against the hillside and waited for the next shot. The wait was only momentary.

Lead pounded the rocky soil near the trail ten feet below his position, flinging a spray of rocky fragments into the brush below the trail. Quickly, Mitchell scrambled to the grulla and yanked both Sharps and saddlebags free of the grulla's weight. The acquisition of rifle and ammunition took less than thirty seconds, and Mitchell had jammed himself tightly against the protective girth of the hillside before the third shot roared from the cliffs above.

"You ain't hit. Are you?" Mort's voice called invisibly from somewhere well below Mitchell's more open position.

"No. I ain't hit! But he's tryin' damn hard!"

"Is that critter of yours crippled or dead?"

"Deader than a doornail. The bullet hit him high in the neck—took him right in the spine."

"Figured as much. He dropped like a rock. Lucky it wasn't you."

"If the damn fool was going to miss, he should have missed altogether! I liked that horse!"

"Leastwise we still got old Milo; we won't have to walk fifteen miles to town."

Mitchell hugged the ground as another bullet slapped the dirt near the dead grulla. "You would think that feller would give up about now. He ain't got a chance of hittin' anything."

The old man poked his head from concealment behind the broad trunk of an old pine and waved a gnarled hand in Mitchell's general direction. "Why don't you make a run for it after the next shot? He ain't reloadin' all that quick and you got time to get out of there."

Mitchell waved a hand in agreement and sat back, waiting for Kelson to fire his next shot. Kelson was slow reloading the old Sharps that had filled the leather scabbard attached to his saddle, and Mitchell waited, feeling time pass as though the clock had been filled with molasses by some prankish child. Forty seconds – sixty seconds – two minutes… nothing.

"Think he gave up?" The old man called out from his hiding place behind the pine.

Mitchell leaned back against the hillside. "He might be waiting for me to poke my head up like some dumb turkey before he cuts loose."

Suddenly, the old man stepped from behind the pine into plain sight.

"Reckon he won't be shootin' no more!" he advised.

Mitchell rose cautiously and peered toward the cliff top. "Think he gave up?" He asked.

For a moment, the old man stood quietly, gazing toward the cliff tops. "I got a feelin' he won't ever kill another horse," he replied.

Mitchell strode to the dead grulla and fought the weight of the animal until he had stripped the body of its gear.

"Leave it under that tree," Mort advised. "We'll pick it up on our way back down the mountain."

"Shame to lose that animal," Mitchell grumbled unhappily.

"He was a good one," the old man agreed.

Mitchell pushed aside the undergrowth beneath one of the pines and cached the grulla's gear where it would be invisible from the trail. He pushed the concealing brush back into place.

For a moment, he paused as his eyes caught and held on something unusual among the undergrowth at the base of the marker tree—something hidden, invisible in the undergrowth—something unusual, yet familiar all the same.

I've seen that before.

The thought flashed through Mitchell's mind, dragging with it an uneasy feeling of déjà-vu. The feeling grew as he strode through the brush to the old pine and shoved aside the tangled undergrowth.

There at the base of the tree, sitting as though he had merely paused for a rest, was the skeletal remains of a man still dressed in the rotting wool of a heavy coat and pinned to the tree by a wooden bolt through his forehead.

The old man forced his way through the undergrowth and pushed an obscuring branch aside. His voice was grave when he spoke. "Looks like you found Aaron Stokes."

Mitchell paused, hooking the toe of his boot under a dead branch and flipping it into the brush on the lower side of the trail. "These boots ain't made for this," he grumbled, feeling the soreness in an ankle twisted once too often by the combination of riding heels and a rocky trail.

"I'd trade an' let you ride a bit," offered the old man, "but my knees ain't been the same since back in 'fifty-seven'. Reckon they wouldn't hold out more than a mile on a trail like this."

Mitchell grunted unhappily and shaded his eyes with one hand. The rockslide above the trail remained motionless beneath the shimmer of hot air rising from the sun-baked surface of the rock. "That slide makes me nervous," he told the old man.

"Looks stable enough," Mort replied. "Another hundred yards an' we'll be past the thing anyways."

The old man prodded the pigeon-toed Milo with his boot heels and was soon beyond any danger of sliding rock. Mitchell's pace was slower, but he soon caught up with the old man who waited among the pines where the trail started its curve to the south around the belly of the mountain.

"You don't have to stop every ten feet," Mitchell grumbled. "I can keep up."

The old man shrugged. "Maybe so," he said quietly, making surreptitious motions toward the pines on the slope rising to the east.

Mitchell stepped up beside the old man's left stirrup and studied the terrain ahead.

The trail followed the curve of the mountain, but the slope itself dropped steeply to the east, falling at a forty-five degree angle for several hundred yards, until it reached the stream at the bottom of the canyon. The opposite slope, like a mirror image of their own, rose steeply to the east under a thick blanket of pines.

"Thought I saw something movin' through the trees across the canyon," the old man offered.

"Kelson?"

"I doubt it. I reckon he ain't had enough time to drag his sorry self across that canyon."

Mitchell studied the pine covered slopes, estimating the difficulty of crossing over. "Some of Jackman's boys," he suggested thoughtfully.

"Nah. Them boys took out of here with their tails tucked. They ain't comin' back. I reckon this fellow is a Ute, maybe one of Black Hawk's boys what didn't care to make peace."

"Not just one though," Mitchell corrected.

"Hell no! I only seen the one, but you can bet your last dollar he ain't alone."

The old man shoved his rifle back into its boot and arched his back in a bone cracking stretch.

"I got no word on collectin' any Utes today. Maybe they're out huntin' deer. 'Course they might be renegades an' they heard *you* was up here. Could be lookin' for a little prestige by takin' your hair."

Once again, Mitchell scanned the opposite slope for movement. Nothing moved, and the vast stillness of the mountains suddenly felt overwhelming and threatening.

"Let's keep moving," he told the old man. "I don't want any trouble with Utes."

"You may get trouble anyway," the old man muttered in reply.

"Kelson's trail seems to be leading to the top of the cliffs," Mitchell observed. "We might go carefully, in case he's laying for us."

The old man shook his head. "I think these Utes are a bigger problem than Kelson," he grumbled. "It ain't gonna do us any good to ignore 'em."

Mitchell shrugged. "I ain't ignoring them; I ain't even seen one yet. Want me to shoot a couple of trees so you'll feel better?"

"Sarcastic pup!"

Mitchell grinned at the old man's irritation. "If the Utes start something, we'll do what we have to. Until then, let's keep after Kelson and hope the Utes are just passing through and have no interest in us."

"The Utes are interested in everything that goes on in these mountains," the old man grumbled.

Minutes later, the trail twisted sharply back to the north and a short scramble to a flat table and the cliff-tops where Kelson had lain in ambush.

"Go careful," Mitchell advised. "Kelson may be waiting."

"I keep tellin' you—Kelson ain't no problem."

"You know that?"

The old man shrugged. "Take a look in them rocks at the edge of the cliff."

Mitchell frowned, not caring to discover what the old man might be suggesting. Still, he followed the old man's pointing finger like a well trained dog—right to the edge of the cliff, where Kelson's body lay twisted among the rocks, his head seriously and irreparably damaged.

"Told you he wouldn't cause no trouble."

"You didn't tell me someone bashed his head in."

"Didn't know that part; just had a feelin' he was beyond causin' trouble."

Mitchell scowled at the body. "This doesn't make sense," he grumbled. "Who killed him? The Utes didn't do this."

The old man shrugged. "Kept him from shootin' at *us*. I suppose we oughta be grateful for that."

Quietly, Mitchell knelt beside the body and studied the rocky ground. "Too many rocks to show any tracks," he reported.

Grimly, he emptied the dead man's pockets of all their contents. When he was finished, he placed the salvaged loot on a large flat-topped rock and contemplated what lay before them.

"Not much for such a well-to-do feller," Mort concluded.

"Seems like more than enough," Mitchell responded as he thumbed through the dead man's billfold and the green-backs inside. "More than three thousand U.S. dollars here... all paper... no gold or silver coin... nothing local... not even a note on the Bishop's storehouse."

"That's unusual?"

Mitchell nodded. "Very unusual."

The old man shrugged. "I don't get it."

Mitchell dropped the billfold and its contents back on the pile and picked up Kelson's watch.

"Look," he said quietly. "This whole territory was part of Mexico twenty years ago. Folks came here so they could get away from a bunch of Americans who thought religious freedom didn't apply to Mormons.

"We set up the State of Desert, and before you knew it, we were grabbed up as a U.S. Territory. Since then we've had little contact and hardly any trade with anyone outside the territory. That means no goods or services going out of the territory and no resources or money coming in.

"We've been surviving on God's good will and our own hard work for twenty years. We even had to develop our own currency for exchange… some gold coin, but mostly notes backed by the Bishop's storehouse and whatever agricultural or industrial commodities we could develop for ourselves… like the woolen mill the Brethren plan to build down in Provo.

"The point is—it's unusual for a fellow, even a businessman to be packin' around that much U.S. money."

The old man stooped and snapped a twig from a clump of dry sagebrush. For a moment, he picked at his teeth with a sharp end of the twig. Finally, he flipped the twig over the edge of the cliff. "So where did Kelson get that money?"

Mitchell shrugged. "Had to be the railroad, I suppose."

"The railroad?"

"I'm thinking Kelson made some kind of deal, selling beef to the railroad. They're down on the Weber River right now blasting their way through Devil's Gate. They're always short on supplies, especially fresh beef."

"You think Kelson had a deal with them rustler fellows over on Lake Creek?"

"I think Kelson was mighty friendly with Ike Shaffer and Dave Langley. And Jackman was just the kind of fellow who could take the loose ends of a deal like that and tie them all together in a neat little package."

The old man studied the trees far below, where Aaron Stokes' remains lay hidden among the pines. "So you think Kelson killed Stokes and Larkin?" He asked thoughtfully.

Mitchell scowled unhappily and stared at the watch. "No, I don't," he replied, handing the watch to the old man.

"What am I supposed to do with this?"

"Look at it," Mitchell instructed.

"What am I lookin' at," the old man demanded.

Mitchell shook his head and lifted the watch by its braided leather fob. "This is a two dollar watch and that ain't a gold chain, is it?"

The old man shrugged. "Reckon not," he muttered.

"You think it likely that a fellow like Kelson would own a two dollar watch on a leather fob?"

"Nope."

"Me neither," Mitchell admitted. "Besides, I think I've seen this watch before. No blood on it then," he added, wiping a bright red streak from his fingers to a pant leg.

"Murphy's store," he said suddenly. "The Hunter kid had it when he paid for some candy. There was a chunk of quartz woven into the leather braid."

The old man peered at the leather braid. "Don't reckon I seen any of that," he replied. "I was busy pickin' out some new duds."

Mitchell frowned at the blood on the watch and glanced downward at Kelson's body. "Hunter had the watch," he said thoughtfully, "but how did Kelson end up with it?"

Impatiently, the old man leaned back against a tall rock and folded his arms.

"Maybe someone killed both of 'em and shoved the watch in Kelson's pocket... That fits better, I think. Someone trying to make it look like Kelson killed Hunter."

The old man shrugged and pushed away from the rock. "Got anyone in mind?" He asked.

For an instant, Mitchell glanced toward the steeply rising mountain beyond the cliffs, knowing instinctively that the killer was somewhere on the trail ahead. "The fellow who's been one step ahead of us all morning," he grumbled irritably.

Sarah shifted uncomfortably, dozing fitfully in a rocking chair tucked in one corner of the Campbell's small living room. The chair was hard, and though uncomfortable, it was not the source of her discomfort—rather, it was the booming reality of her dream and her inability to escape the thunder of gunfire and the *crack* of lead hammering the tall rocks where Mitchell and the old man crouched and returned fire.

Some distance away, three Utes lay hidden among the trees, firing repeatedly while two of their fellows crept cautiously toward the rocks. Franticly, Sarah cried out a warning.

Mitchell turned as though surprised, firing his pistol into the brush between two large rocks. A howl of pain answered the shots, and a single Ute staggered from the rocks, making his way toward the trees and calling to his companions.

Sarah woke with a start, feeling the hair on the back of her neck bristle with the eerie reality of the dream.

"You look as though you've seen a ghost," Susan observed from across the room. "Another nightmare?"

Sarah shivered uncomfortably. "They seem so real, vivid to the point I can hear gunshots and even smell the pines and the sagebrush."

"Conquistadores again?"

"No… not this time. This time it was Mort and Collin in the rocks on a cliff–top somewhere, and there were Ute renegades shooting at them from the trees while others crept up on Collin and Mort through the rocks and the brush."

"I called out to warn them, and Collin shot at one of them."

Susan frowned in thought. "You seem to have some strange and unsettling dreams of late," she said quietly.

Sarah sighed and left the rocking chair. She positioned herself near a window and peered toward the mountains far to the south. "There is something uncanny about these dreams," she replied. "It's as though they are connected and somehow trying to tell me something."

Susan moved to the window and stood beside her sister. "Something about Aztec warriors and conquistadors?"

"Perhaps… yet somehow it isn't really about all of them. It's like they're connected by a common thread—a thread that seems connected to us as well."

"Connected to us in what way?"

"I haven't a clue."

"You must have some feeling for the connection. You've had enough of these dreams. You've even got *me* seeing men in armor riding through the trees."

"I have a feeling, but it seems nonsensical."

"Nonsensical in a humorous way or in a way that's going to leave me chittering with fear?"

"I think the connection is Collin."

"What has Collin to do with Aztecs and Conquistadors?"

"What has anyone to do with them? They're three-hundred years dead and gone."

"I have no idea, but before I saw them on the cliff, I saw a narrow canyon with steep slopes covered in pines. There were a few cliffs and the whole area looked nearly impossible to traverse. But there was a staircase of stone leading to a huge serpent carved from obsidian. Somehow, I knew the belly of that serpent held death. I tried to look away, but I couldn't, even though I knew death was there and about to come out of the serpent's mouth."

For a moment, Sarah stood quietly, remembering the terror she had felt at the sight of the figure standing within the shadows of the serpent's open mouth."

Susan looked quizzically at her older sister. "Then you saw Mort." She said hopefully.

Sarah shook her head. "I saw Collin," she answered bleakly.

The old man leaned back against the hard face of his rocky shelter and holstered his pistol. "I expect they all took off," he grumbled.

Cautiously, Mitchell raised his head and scanned the trees beyond the boulder strewn cliff-top. "Appears so," Mitchell replied. "I can't imagine why. They had us pinned down and nowhere to go."

The old man chuckled. "That last fellow seemed mighty certain. He was hollerin' about witches all the way back into them trees. Seems he was hearin' voices."

Mitchell sighed shook his head. He eased himself down beside the old man and began reloading the cylinders of both pistols. "Must be something strange in the water out here," he muttered." Makes folks prone to hearing voices and seeing things."

The old man laughed. "You're a fine one to talk. You been seein'an' talkin' to me for more than ten years."

"That's different," Mitchell objected.

The old man grinned. "That's an original statement if I ever heard one." The old man stood and holstered his pistol. "Well..," he muttered, "the voice is says its' time we pass into the mouth of the serpent."

Thirty minutes later, the old man paused at the mouth of the tunnel and peered into the darkness. Twenty paces back, Mitchell looked upward and studied the rocky face of the cliff.

"*That* is amazing," he muttered quietly.

The old man looked up at the rocks and nodded. "Took a day or two," he admitted. "But Tlacmatzin and his bunch had Spanish picks and shovels, and when the fightin' was done, there was plenty of time and not much to keep a feller occupied."

"It's a snake's head," Mitchell concluded, as he examined the huge square nosed face and the stone fangs protruding downward into the black opening of its mouth.

"Itzcoatl," offered the old man. "Obsidian Serpent is what you folks would call him."

"Don't look like obsidian to me," Mitchell responded.

The old man snorted. "Obsidian Serpent is his name," he growled, "not what he's made of."

Mitchell strode quietly to the mouth of the mine shaft and peered past the serpent's fangs into the shadows beyond. "I don't like the look of this," he objected. "Those timbers are rotten. The whole thing looks ready to collapse."

The old man frowned and stepped between the stone fangs. "Looks fine to me," he argued, giving one of the timbers a solid kick. "This here is hard rock, an' them timbers seem solid enough to me."

Mitchell's gaze narrowed. "I ain't impressed by your opinion. I can see the rot in that wood from ten feet away."

"Maybe so, but this here mine ain't gonna collapse just 'cause we have to go inside."

"There ain't no reason for us to go chasing around inside that thing," countered Mitchell. "We can wait right here."

"You can only watch one entrance," the old man retorted.

"I ain't thrilled about crawling into a hole like that."

The old man shrugged. "How about I go first? You can follow when you finish things up here."

Mitchell turned and scanned the trail behind them. For nearly a quarter of a mile, the trail wandered up and down the rocky face of the mountain, crossing barren stretches of rock with barely a hint of vegetation near the trail, and in those places where sagebrush and other plants clung tenaciously to the mountain side, no human could possible find a foothold beyond the trail. Any trouble the old man expected could only be waiting beyond the curve of the mountain.

"I don't see anything," he objected, turning back to the dark opening of the serpent's mouth. But the old man was gone, and the mountain was silent beneath the brightness of the afternoon sun.

Mitchell turned away from the mouth of the serpent and made his way back along the trail. He was glad to be away from the mine and the oppressive feelings that issued from the depths of the earth, and a long walk in the brightness of day made him glad he had never worked in such a place. His thoughts were pleasantly engaged in relishing his good luck when a sharp bend in the trail brought him into a small depression in the mountainside. There, a small rivulet of icy melt-water cascaded from the rocks above, cutting into the mountainside and carving a small nearly flat alluvial shelf where the melt-water collected in a small icy pool.

Half a dozen Utes stood near the edge of the pool, watching from behind a tall, dark haired man with a drawn pistol. Nothing about the man was familiar—a man who called himself Coleman and was nothing more than a face seen for a moment days before. In every respect, the man was a complete stranger, yet a name whispered in Mitchell's head, refusing to be ignored.

"Max Harding," Mitchell observed stiffly.

Harding lifted the pistol and held it rock steady on Mitchell's chest. "Do I know you?"

Mitchell shrugged. "Reckon not," he replied. "Your name just came to mind."

The Utes shifted uneasily, whispering among themselves.

"I ain't used that name in twenty years," Harding snarled.

"Time don't work the way you think it does," Mitchell responded. "It was you who killed the Hunter boy wasn't it?"

"Killed the little bastard and fed him to the pigs."

"And Kelson?"

"He wasn't useful any more. He had no idea where to find the mine."

"So you bashed his head in?"

"Why waste a bullet?"

"I don't suppose it was you who killed Larkin and Stokes?"

"Heard of 'em, but someone else done it. I ain't been here but a month."

"So you come all the way out here just to look for a lost treasure? Seems a little chancy for a fellow who always wanted a sure thing."

"That gold is just a handy little sideline. I been paid good money to come out here and give *you* a lethal dose of lead poisoning."

"You've been paid to kill me?"

"You and every one of your kin."

Mitchell glanced quickly at the Utes standing silently among the sparse cluster of aspen near the edge of the pool.

"Don't worry about them," Harding advised. "They're here out of curiosity."

"Curiosity?"

"More of a trade really. I kill you; they let me haul out all the gold my horses can carry. They get your hair of course. They're curious to see it done though. They got some mighty strange ideas, even for heathens. I figure it's these damn Mormons tellin' all kinds of lies."

"Did they tell you I've come to collect you?" Mitchell asked.

"You ain't collectin' nothin' but lead."

Harding cocked the pistol in his hand, and Mitchell stared hard at the open bore of the gun, knowing that in an instant the flash of burning powder would signal his own death. Yet the flash did not come, and the whisper of a voice thundered across Mitchell's consciousness.

"Voice says your time is finished," he advised.

Mitchell let his hand sweep downward, snatching the Colt from its holster. He saw the widening of Harding's eyes and the sudden look of shock as Mitchell's bullet tore into his chest and shoved him backward a step. For a moment, Harding stood as though petrified. Then the light of awareness went out of his eyes; his knees buckled, and his body slammed face first into the rocky ground.

Mitchell turned on the Ute renegades. Not one of them had moved. None of them moved now, as though time crawled, and they waited for some unseen force to pass judgment.

"I didn't come for any of you," Mitchell said grimly. "And I don't want the gold."

The eldest of the Utes took a step forward. The look on his face was one of burning hatred. "We were all at the canyon of the ancient ones," he said quietly. "Thirty of us... hidden in the brush and the rocks. You should have died with the others. We wondered then if the Shinob had taken an interest in you. Now we see that your Mormon God protects you. We'll wait for a better time."

When the Utes were gone, Mitchell turned and made his way slowly along the trail—back toward the Obsidian Serpent and a task he wanted no part of. He knew now who had killed Larkin and Stokes—who had raided their camp and set fire to Murphy's store—he knew whom, but not why.

Larkin and Stokes had been killed long before Harding or Jackman, or any of their ilk had ever come to Heber Valley, and only one person could have followed Stokes and Larkin from Lake Creek the day of the picnic. The realization made Mitchell feel ill, and the mouth of the Obsidian Serpent loomed before him like a black gate leading into the depths of Hell.

CHAPTER 16

8 October

The torch threw a fitful yellow light that was swallowed almost before it reached the rough and blackened walls of the tunnel. The roof ranged low, forcing Mitchell to move slowly and half crouched to avoid banging his head on the ragged rock or the occasional timber supporting it.

The silence was deep and oppressive, and the crunch of loose gravel beneath the soles of his boots was sucked into the depths of the earth, leaving nothing familiar, nothing to secure a sense of reality or rightness in a world where all sensation had been reduced to an area no bigger than a closet. A closet with the weight of the world poised overhead like a locomotive waiting to crush a tiny ant beneath its wheels.

The experience was strange, oppressive and even terrifying in a way that made Mitchell want to escape and never return.

"More of a cave than a mine." Mort's voice came out of the darkness, startling Mitchell and setting his heart pounding at his throat.

"Damn you, Mort! You done that on purpose!"

"*Did*... I *did* it on purpose. Don't waste your down home dialect on me."

"You scared the crap out of me."

The old man smiled in the flickering light or the torch. "Nothin' left but your clothes," he muttered under his breath.

He re-lit his own torch from the one in Mitchell's hand. "Everything seems darker because of the smoke," he offered.

"What smoke?"

"On the walls. This was a narrow little passage leading to other parts of a larger group of caverns. It was too narrow, and we had no explosives. We heated the walls with fire and threw water on the hot rock. The rock fractured and we were able to break some of it loose and widen the passage. That's why it's so rough. We didn't have proper tools for the job."

Mitchell frowned. "Who's we?" he asked, dreading the answer.

The old man turned and led the way deeper into the cave. "Eagles… a few Jaguars… mostly Wolves."

"Animals," Mitchell grumbled as he trailed along in the wake of the old man's torchlight.

Forty paces later, the tunnel branched to the right. The old man ignored the branch and continued along the main passage.

"One of us should check that side cut," Mitchell suggested.

"Later," the old man called back. "We can see to that later. There's something I want you to see first."

With that the old man's torch seemed to sink into the ground until nothing remained but a dim yellow glow.

"Mort?"

The old man made no answer, and suddenly cautious, Mitchell moved slowly toward the dim glow that had been the old man's torch.

"Mort?"

"Watch your step Danite! It's a thirty food drop down that shaft!"

Mitchell stopped at the the old man's warning and peered downward to where the old man stood in the greater light of two torches now wedged into crevices on either side of the shaft.

"I ain't no Danite, and you know it, you old goat. How'd you get down there without breaking a leg?"

"Used that ladder. It's old, but it's sturdy enough."

"You're nuts," Mitchell protested. "That ain't nothin' but a tree trunk with notches cut in it."

"Chicken ladder," the old man responded. "You ain't afraid are you?"

"Damn right! A fellow could break his neck on that thing!"

"Aw, come on. We're almost there."

Unhappily, Mitchell mounted the ladder and began the descent. The old tree bowed and cracked ominously with his weight. His boots threatened to slip from the shallow notches with every step, but eventually he reached solid ground. "What's so important?" he demanded.

The old man barked out a derisive grunt. "You wouldn't want to come all this way and not see Motecuhzoma's treasure. That would be a shame. Besides, you want to capture a vicious killer, don't you?"

"I'm losing interest with every step," Mitchell protested. "I ain't fond of caves, and I have a feeling you're pushing me toward something I'm not going to enjoy."

The old man stopped and turned back, raising his torch until he could see Mitchell's face clearly. "I reckon you won't enjoy it none, but it can't be avoided now."

"That's not reassuring," Mitchell complained.

"Sorry. This is one you just have to make the best of. I can't fix it for you." The old man turned, crouched low, and disappeared.

For a moment, Mitchell stood hesitantly at the waist high opening where the passage ended in a solid face of rock. Then with an unhappy sigh, he stooped low and followed the old man. The sight that greeted him beyond the opening was the strangest he had ever witnessed.

He stood at the edge of a steep incline leading downward to the floor of an egg-shaped cavern, a cavern more than a hundred feet high and two-hundred feet long—a cavern so large that the small grove of petrified trees, standing at the cavern's farthest edge, seemed dwarfed, though their leafless branches topped more than thirty feet above the cavern floor.

Mitchell stared at the trees and the branches that glittered in the torchlight as though covered by a sparkling winter frost. "Good Lord…," he sighed quietly.

"Quite a sight, ain't it?"

Mitchell shook his head in disbelief. "How in heaven's name did they come to be in here?"

The old man shrugged. "Some kind of earth movement, I suppose."

"What in the world makes them glitter like that?"

"Silver. The cavern must have filled with water now and then. The water could have washed out silver somewhere up on the mountain. Flakes and particles must have caught in every nook and cranny in the bark. Looks like a winter frost, don't it?"

"Is that the treasure you wanted me to see?"

"Naw. That's just below us."

"And the girl?"

"Just below."

Mitchell raised his torch and peered over the ledge into a glowing array of gold and silver artifacts. And there, like a little girl lost, Jean Kelson sat on the cavern floor, amid the treasure of a forgotten empire, rocking back and forth, sobbing in misery.

Mitchell picked his way down the path to the cavern floor. He glanced toward the glittering artifacts heaped upon the rocky floor, artifacts that could easily be worth more than he could imagine, and made his way to the girl now sitting within the meager light cast by the lantern at her side. Quietly, he knelt beside her and touched a hand gently to her shoulder.

"Jean," he said softly.

The girl stared blankly and continued rocking.

"Tell me about it," Mitchell prompted. "It might help if you talk about it."

"I don't know," the girl moaned. "It's like a bad dream. She pushes at me all the time. They're both bad, but she's not the worst. She's horrible.... The things she wants to do are awful, but she's not the worst."

Mitchell frowned. "Who is *she*?" He asked gently.

"Martha. At least that's what she calls herself, but I don't think it's her real name. She lies to me whenever it suits her."

The girl's rocking eased a bit as she leaned toward Mitchell as though seeking comfort.

"Martha pushes at you?" Mitchell suggested.

The girl shuddered and leaned into Mitchell's shoulder. "Yes," she murmured.

"Why does Martha push at you?"

"She wants us to go away... They talk behind my back, and then they want me to do things."

"Things you don't want to do?"

"Sometimes."

"Martha wants you to do these things?"

"And Ann. Ann tells Martha, and the two of them push at me and lie, so I never know what they really want, except I know they want me to do bad things."

"What kind of things"

The girl looked up, and the sobs began again. "They wanted me to follow Aaron and Nathan and kill them when they found their gold mine."

"And you told them you wouldn't do it."

"I told them they were wicked, and it was wrong to even think like that. They just laughed at me and told me they would take the gold whether I helped them or not."

"Did they kill those boys?"

"I don't know. I think they must have."

"Where are they now?" Mitchell asked, wondering if the two women were hiding among the silver encrusted trees at the far end of the cavern. In the dimness, they could be anywhere.

The girl moaned as though in anguish. "We're right here," she hissed suddenly, shoving away from Mitchell's shoulder with a strength unusual for such a slightly built woman.

"Stupid girl! We told her not to talk to you!" she growled. "But she thought you liked her...thought you wanted another wife...."

Mitchell leaped to his feet, backing away as the girl lashed out with the obsidian blade she had concealed within her skirts.

"What!"

"We told her you weren't interested! But she wouldn't listen. Now everything is fouled up!"

Mitchell took another step backward, adding distance between himself and a stone blade that was sharper than any razor. "Jean!"

"She's hiding," hissed the girl. "I'm Ann"

"Ann?"

The girl thrust the black blade in front of her, pointing it toward Mitchell's heart. "You think you're so smart. We've been watching you the whole time. You would never have found us if Jean hadn't been so stupid. Now I'm going to have to kill you too."

Mitchell raised his hands in an effort to curb the girl's anxiety. "Be careful with that thing," he said quietly. "Why don't you put it down and we'll talk."

Mitchell dodged as the girl lunged forward. The obsidian blade slashed through his sleeve, leaving a thin trail of blood along his forearm.

"You better leave her to me," Mort's voice called out from above. "This one is dangerous."

The girl stopped in her tracks and peered at the ledge above, where Mort's skinny frame stood partially hidden among shadows unlit by the flickering torchlight.

"Who's there?" she hissed angrily.

"Just a friend, Missy."

"I have no friends. Come out where I can see you."

The old man eased himself from the shadows and moved slowly down the incline of the ledge. "You do have friends," he countered softly.

The girl stepped backward as the old man moved steadily toward her. "What kind of friends are you referring to?" The girl hissed. "The kind who are all attentive until they've got you pregnant, then abandon you as though you didn't exist... or maybe you're thinking of the ones who help spread gossip about their friends without a thought of whether it was true or not... the ones who were so close that they never came to visit our house even once. Or maybe you're thinking of the ones who wouldn't even consider sharing a little of that!" she snapped, pointing toward the glittering pile of artifacts.

The old man shrugged. It was a gesture that passed nearly unseen in the shadows of the cavern.

"When I followed them up the mountain, Aaron just laughed when I told him I wanted a share of the gold. He didn't think it was so funny after I stuck him with a couple of bolts from that crossbow. I got the journal from his saddlebags. It took a lot more to get Nathan to admit there was a map, but he wouldn't tell me where he had hidden it. Then I found out he had given it to that little witch of a Campbell girl."

The old man took a step farther down the stone ramp.

"Stay where you are!"

The old man stopped, but the girl was already moving. The obsidian blade sped through the air like a black bullet, shattering against the rock face of the cavern wall. Before the old man could move, she snatched up the lantern and bolted toward the glittering silver trees.

Mitchell lunged and grabbed for the girl, but the girl dodged and sped through the maze of silver trunks like a rabbit with a hound on its heels. In less than twenty paces, she had left him far behind, and her lantern was soon only a glowing spot of light blinking on and off as she passed on the far side of the silver forest.

"Gettin' old, ain't ya."

"Dang near twenty years older than that little catamount," Mitchell growled. "I didn't see you draggin' your sorry butt after her."

"No need. She's headed for a tunnel that connects back the way we come. We'll meet up with her back near the main entrance. I think the other way out must have caved in some time back. She's got nowhere else to go."

Mitchell frowned and knelt beside a silver encrusted tree. The ground beneath the bare limbs glittered with a carpet of silver leaves. Mitchell collected three of the palm sized leaves, wondering how the precious metal had impregnated and finally replaced the organic matter of each leaf.

"Place like this could be the eighth wonder of the world," Mort said quietly.

Mitchell nodded and fished around in a pocket, retrieving three ten dollar gold Bees. Deliberately, he dropped the gold coins to where the leaves had lain for countless centuries.

The old man shrugged. "Fair trade, I suppose. Them coins are gonna be rare as hen's teeth some day."

Mitchell shrugged and placed the leaves in his shirt pocket. "Thought maybe Sarah and Susan might like to have them. Something like this might never be seen again, if this mountain shifts and everything comes crashing down."

"So, what now?" Mitchell demanded, knowing that the girl might even now be waiting, plotting the best means for disposing of two old men. "I like that girl, and if you're here to collect her, I want no part of it—especially if she's gone mad."

Mitchell frowned unhappily. He had no designs on the woman. He simply liked her as a person, and the whole situation made him gut-sick. Yet something had to be done. The girl had already killed two men and looked to be a danger to others if she were left to run free.

The old man shrugged and re-lit the torch Mitchell had extinguished in his rush to catch the fleeing girl. "I reckon we ought to go careful from here on."

He hooked a thumb toward the mound of Aztec gold. "Plenty of souvenirs amongst that lot," he suggested.

"Mitchell frowned at the hoard and shook his head. "I've got no use for any of it," he replied grimly. "That stuff will cause nothing but trouble if folks find out about it."

"Caused a damn sight of trouble long before it ever came here," the old man muttered. "Thousands of folks died when Cortez laid siege to Tenochtitlan. All because of this stuff and the power it could buy...plagues and starvation... the city was nothing but a graveyard when it finally fell."

"Blood money," Mitchell responded. "I want no part of that."

The old man shrugged. "We best split up or we'll never find her in here," he concluded. "I'll go back the way we came. You go after her. Maybe we can put the squeeze on her, before she can get out."

Mitchell peered into the gloom. "You think she's hiding in there?"

The old man shook his head. "I think Ann or Martha is waiting in there," he corrected. "Neither one of them will want us to leave here."

Ten minutes later, Mitchell paused for a rest. He felt as though he had wandered under half the mountain, and his torch was showing signs of burning out—a sure sign that it was time to be out of this place, and back in the light of day.

Darkness gathered closer about the dying light of the torch, and Mitchell's pace dwindled to a crawl that left him wishing he had never seen the Obsidian Serpent or the silver trees trapped deep in its belly, trees now lost far behind, along a tunnel littered with fallen chunks of rock from the smallest gravel to massive blocks that nearly choked the tunnel completely. More than a dozen times, he stumbled, nearly cracking his skull on jagged walls until finally the torch flickered and died. Blackness engulfed him instantly.

For a moment, Mitchell froze in panic. His natural reaction to the sudden blackness was to stare blindly ahead, as though in time his eyes would adjust and light would somehow penetrate solid rock. Finally, he reached out, pressing a hand to the roughness of a wall, where damp rock created a tiny sense of stability in an environment suddenly turned dangerously alien.

Cautiously, he stepped forward, testing the ground with each step. "You're in a mess now," he muttered, dragging his hand along the wall, in search of the support beam he had seen just before the light had gone out.

Might have missed it.

The thought came with visions of rotted wood ready to disintegrate at the slightest touch. The light of the torch had been feeble towards the end, and had not illuminated any great distance along the passage, but he had seen the support and knew that this was not a place to be stumbling around—a place where any disturbance to the rotted timber could bring the mountain down in an instant.

That thought still plagued him when something soft and warm bumped him from behind. Startled, Mitchell began to turn. There was no time for anything more. The girl shoved away with surprising strength and struck.

Suddenly, lights flashed amid the blackness, and Mitchell's head roared with pain. He staggered back, but the girl gripped his shirt and struck again. Pain flared as the rock hammered his collarbone, glancing upward to pound his jaw. Instinctively, Mitchell grabbed at the girl, clutching a handful of dress and flinging her hard. She gasped as she struck the wall.

Wood groaned and shattered. Mitchell stumbled backward and fell as the clattering roar of falling rock thundered, filling the passage with a choking fog of dust. The mountain groaned in protest as it shifted and settled, dropping millions of tons to conform to its new shape, yet leaving only the slightest depression on the mountainside high above.

In the blackness, Mitchell lay stunned. He felt as though his entire body had been shaken to the core. Minutes passed before he finally reached out, blindly searching for the tunnel wall. When he found it, he crawled to the hard stability it offered and sat with his back to the stone, listening as the groaning of the earth echoed through the passageway. Within moments, deadly silence claimed the ruins of the passage.

Carefully, he assessed the damage he had taken in the conflict—a bloodied skull, a sore collarbone, a bruised jaw—all taken in the tussle with the girl, yet nothing else. With tons of rock crushing downward like a gigantic avalanche of stone, he had taken neither a cut nor even a bruise.

"Bloody miracle," he muttered, wondering if the girl too had somehow survived and even now lay dazed in the blackness nearby.

"Jean!" The call echoed through the tunnel, but evoked no answer.

Mitchell sat quietly in the blackness, considering his options—options that seemed extremely limited. That the tunnel had collapsed was obvious. But the extent of the damage was impossible to ascertain, given the fact that the blackness within the tunnel was absolute. It was a miracle he had survived, but in all likelihood, it would not be for long. Only Mort knew where he had gone, and there was little chance that the old man would be able to move the tons of rock that certainly blocked Mitchell's escape.

Minutes stretched into what seemed like hours, and Mitchell began to fidget from the inactivity. The silence grew oppressive, and when the faint odor of kerosene became noticeable, he could no longer control his impatience. Resolutely, he stood and began a blind exploration of his prison.

The roughness of the tunnel wall was just as solid as it had ever been in the light, and when he came to the rubble blocking one end of the passage, he was certain rescue could never come from that direction—the massive blocks of stone from the collapsed roof would never be moved by human muscle alone.

Resigned, he turned away form the collapse and shuffled to the second wall of the passage. Before his outstretched hand could make contact with the wall, something clattered away from his shuffling boots. Intrigued, he knelt and searched the floor until he found the wooden shaft of his burned out and discarded torch. The instant his fingers touched the wooden shaft, he remembered the smell of kerosene—the kerosene from Jean Kelson's lamp. Suddenly, he wanted that lamp, and judging by the smell, it was close.

When he found it, the lamp was nothing more than a flattened piece of metal and shattered glass, and the kerosene itself had formed a small puddle on the hard surface of the tunnel floor.

With the lamp destroyed, his choices were few. He needed light. Nothing could be done without it. Even now, he had no real knowledge of his situation and though it seemed bad enough, a little light might satisfy the spark of hope that had ignited when he heard the echoing of his voice along the passageway—echoing that told him the passageway might still be passable. Quietly, he removed his shirt and shredded it into a dozen ragged strips. When he was finished, he pressed the wadded cloth into the pool of kerosene and began the task of making a new torch.

Minutes later, flint sparked against steel, and the makeshift torch burst into flame. Only then did he see the total blockage at one end of the tunnel, and at the other, the rubble free passage leading downward into the bowels of the earth—back to the cavern of silver trees.

Thirty minutes later, covered with scrapes and bruises, Mitchell climbed wearily to the top of the chicken ladder. His makeshift torch flickered fitfully as he strode toward the entrance of the cave, then finally, it died. In the gloom, less than a dozen paces away, Mort's torch glowed dimly within the main tunnel. The old man had stopped, blocking the path toward the faint glow of sunlight a hundred paces farther along the tunnel.

"What now?" Mitchell grumbled.

"Now we go home."

CHAPTER 17

8 October

Mitchell leaned back in the camp chair and propped his feet on a rough-cut log. He stared glumly at the mountains, knowing he had been the cause of the Kelson girl's death. That thought had made him miserable since Mort had convinced him of the impossibility of clearing a path to the girl before her injuries finished what the earth had begun.

"It's no use boy," the old man had muttered as they stood at the foot of the rubble blocking the passage. "Both ends are blocked, and she's caught in a tiny pocket. Her leg's broke, and she's near gone now. Besides, I'm here to collect her, an' there ain't no getting' around that."

"You're mighty quiet," Turner protested suddenly, breaking Mitchell's thoughts. "Now ain't the time to go all quiet. Tell me just what makes you so sure the Kelson girl killed four full grown men," he demanded. "I have trouble believing it. And the sheriff ain't gonna be easy to convince either. Why would she kill one, let alone four?"

"Only two," Mitchell answered. "Larkin and Stokes. It all started long before any of them were killed—at least a year, maybe more. The Kelson's were never a happy family. Sister Kelson finally admitted that and told Sarah what had been going on. Ed Kelson had a wandering eye and he was the kind of man who could make people quite unhappy if he wanted.

"He made Sister Kelson miserable from the day they married, and it carried over to include Jean, when she came along. The girl and her mother were a comfort to one another, but it wasn't enough. Outwardly Jean was happy and friendly, but inwardly she was a mess. She trusted no one and had few friends. When Kelson uprooted both women and brought them here, both women hated it, but there wasn't much they could do about it. They had no other resources.

"But something interesting began to happen. People liked the two women, and Jean fell in love with the Stokes boy. Before long, they were engaged. But things began to go bad again, and Jean realized she was pregnant. When Kelson found out, he threatened to kill the father, and he beat the girl senseless when she refused to tell who it was. Kelson was enraged and went back to Salt Lake the same day.

"Jean lost the baby a few days later. She was very ill for a while, but her mother took good care of her and nursed her back to health. But it wasn't long before her mother conceived the notion of telling everyone the girl had gone to visit relatives in Denver. A month later Stokes brought a letter to the house, breaking off their engagement."

"And no one knew? Turner asked.

"No one visited much, and when they did. Jean just kept out of sight. That lasted about six months, and when someone finally saw the girl, it was easy to say she had just returned from her trip."

Turner frowned unhappily. "What made her kill those fellows?"

Mitchell shrugged. "Mort says Jean had been ill for a long time, but no one had noticed. I didn't understand half of what he said, but it amounted to a brain problem. She was seeing strange balls of light and extremely vivid colors. She started hearing voices she couldn't block out, and now and then she would just freeze up on a thought and get stuck.

"Mort had a name for the disease, but I can't recall what it was. Whatever it was, it caused the girl extreme distress and she blamed the whole of her troubles on her father and Aaron Stokes. When she learned that Larkin and Stokes were searching for an old mine, she knew it was her chance to get away and start a new life.

"The day of the picnic, she got angry at something Larkin said and she left the group. Everyone thought she rode home in a huff, but she stopped at home just long enough to gather up that crossbow and follow Stokes and Larkin. She confronted the pair of them at that old Spanish camp and told them she wanted a share of what they found. Stokes laughed and told her to go home. They rode away and left her humiliated and at the end of her rope. Her mind just broke.

"She took out the cross bow and shot Larkin's horse. Larkin went head over heels into the brush and lay there dazed. Her second shot took Stokes through the shoulder. He fell and lost his horse. When he ran, Jean followed. She caught up with him at the base of the rock slide and put two more quarrels into him. When she went back for Larkin, he was gone. He had taken Stokes' horse and gone back down the mountain.

"Larkin came off the mountain dazed and confused. He wasn't sure what had happened to Stokes. He wasn't even sure if Jean had been trying to kill him. She caught up to him near the foundation of his house and shot him in the leg before he had a chance to move. He tried to appeal to her, but she was no longer in her right mind. She stepped to where he lay sprawled on the ground and cracked him in the face with the butt of the crossbow. After that, it was easy to drag him to the privy and dump him into the hole.

"She knew about lime and its reaction with water from something she overheard at her father's store, and Larkin had two bags of the stuff for mixing mortar. Even then, he told her little, only that there was a map and a journal. But he never told her where they were hidden."

"How could she be so callous?" Susan whispered.

Mitchell shrugged. "Normally, I don't think she was. When she rode away from Larkin's place, she didn't remember a thing she had done. But she knew there was a map and a journal hidden somewhere. So she enlisted Bradley Hunter in the search.

"Hunter was to search the canyons for any signs of a mine, while Jean watched for any evidence of the map or the journal. Everything was quiet for awhile. No one knew what had happened to Larkin and Stokes, and Hunter and the girl were free to search without interference.

"But things changed suddenly when we showed up, and Jean, in her tangled state of mind, had made a mistake. She had given Larkin's pocket watch to Bradley Hunter. The watch itself was of no importance. It was a cheap, two dollar thing, and there are hundreds of them scattered around the territory. But it was the watch fob that drew attention. It was a simple thing of plaited leather woven about a piece of quartzite laced with gold.

"The day we arrived in town, Hunter came into Murphy's store. He bought some candy, and when he paid, he emptied his pocket on the counter. Everyone in the store saw that piece of quartzite."

Susan nodded. "And Jean was there. She must have started that fire to divert attention from the watch."

"Partly," Mitchell agreed. "She also wanted time to search the Sheriff's office for the map or the journal. She found nothing but the skull and smashed it to pieces."

"She must have gone to the Campbell house as soon as she left the sheriff's office," Sarah suggested. "It would have been easy for her to cross Main Street in all the confusion and reach the Campbell place just as I went into the yard. She could have seen the pattern and thought it was the map she had been looking for."

Mitchell nodded in agreement. "When she discovered her mistake, she ransacked Lynne's room and found the map. After that, she simply dressed in her father's coat and hat, and took his horse whenever she went searching for the cave.

"It was Kelson himself who really took note of the watch fob. He enlisted Feldman's help, but Feldman was suspicious of Kelson and did little to help, so Kelson went to Jackman and Harding. That proved to be a bad move."

Silently, Mitchell peered into the evening shadows to where the horses were hobbled and grazing quietly. Milo was gone. The pigeon–toed animal had been there only moments before, and now without a sound, like wind in the tops of the trees, he was gone.

The last rays of a red-orange sun flowed across the peaks of the Timpanogos, and Mitchell knew without a doubt that the Obsidian Serpent had claimed Milo for his own.

Mitchell sat quietly, listening and peering into the darkness that hid the mountains to the south, remembering the blackness beyond the gaping mouth of the serpent. In his mind's eye, the flickering light of the old man's torch cast a feeble glow until suddenly, like the snuffed flame of a tiny candle, it ceased to exist.

Vaguely, like a fading echo only half perceived, he heard the plaintive cry of a woman's voice. A moment later, the deeper, calming tones of the old man's voice rolled up from the darkness. "It's okay, Missy. You don't need to worry. I've come to take you home."

Glumly, Mitchell turned his back on the mountain and the canyon of the Obsidian Serpent. But a half-smile tugged at the corners of his mouth as he realized that nowhere did the scriptures report that Death rode a pigeon-toed horse.

Author's Note

This story and its characters are fictional. It is a mingling of three genres, historical, mystery, and western. The historical facts are as accurate as I could make them and still allow enough flexibility for a very limited interaction between historical individuals and fictional characters.

Although there is no evidence that either Aztecs or Spanish conquistadores were present in the Wasatch Mountains at the time of Cortez's siege of Tenochtitlan, there is some evidence that the Spanish mined for gold and silver in the mountains of Utah long before Escalante ventured into the region.

However, the cavern of silver trees actually existed. It was discovered when a mining operation in central Utah opened a large cavern containing numerous silver encrusted trees. The trees were harvested for their silver, and a wonder of the world was lost forever.

Susan and Sarah Flitton were real Mormon pioneers, although neither was ever involved in plural marriage or any gunfight that I am aware of. They were, however, part of the inspiration for this story, and I have taken the liberty of using their names for two of my main characters.

Susan Flitton was my 2nd great grandmother, and Sarah was her sister. Susan lived into her nineties, and in 1949, the State of Utah awarded Susan a bronze medal for being the oldest living Utah pioneer.

Many of the scenes in this story unfold in settings that have changed greatly in the last one-hundred and fifty years. Heber City is now a popular and scenic place to live.

Any Latter-day Saint doctrines mentioned in this work are expressed in the context of a fictional character's interpretation, and may not represent *true* LDS thought on the subject.

Mort is a fictional character whom I have yet to meet.

About the Author

J.T. Fleming is a *Magna Cum Laude* graduate of Weber State University with a B.S. in English as well as a B.S. in Anthropology. Mr. Fleming works as a technical writer for an international manufacturing company and has published numerous stories as a community news correspondent with the Standard-Examiner in Ogden, Utah.

Mr. Fleming has written two books in the Collin Mitchell series: *Tracks of a Pigeon-toed Horse* & *The Obsidian Serpent.* The third book in the series, *Mouriel,* is soon to be released.

Born and raised in Utah, Mr. Fleming is a member of the LDS church and has hunted deer, elk, and gold in the mountains and deserts of Utah and Colorado. With his wife and family, he lives west of the Wasatch Mountains, near the Great Salt Lake.